THE CASE OF THE WHALE WATCHING WEDDING PLANNER

BUTTERCUP BEND MYSTERIES
BOOK FOUR

DEBBIE DE LOUISE

Copyright © 2024 Debbie De Louise

Layout design and Copyright © 2024 by Next Chapter

Published 2024 by Next Chapter

Edited by Elizabeth N. Love

Cover art by Lordan June Pinote

This book is a work of fiction. Names, characters, places, and incidents are the product of the author's imagination or are used fictitiously. Any resemblance to actual events, locales, or persons, living or dead, is purely coincidental.

All rights reserved. No part of this book may be reproduced or transmitted in any form or by any means, electronic or mechanical, including photocopying, recording, or by any information storage and retrieval system, without the author's permission.

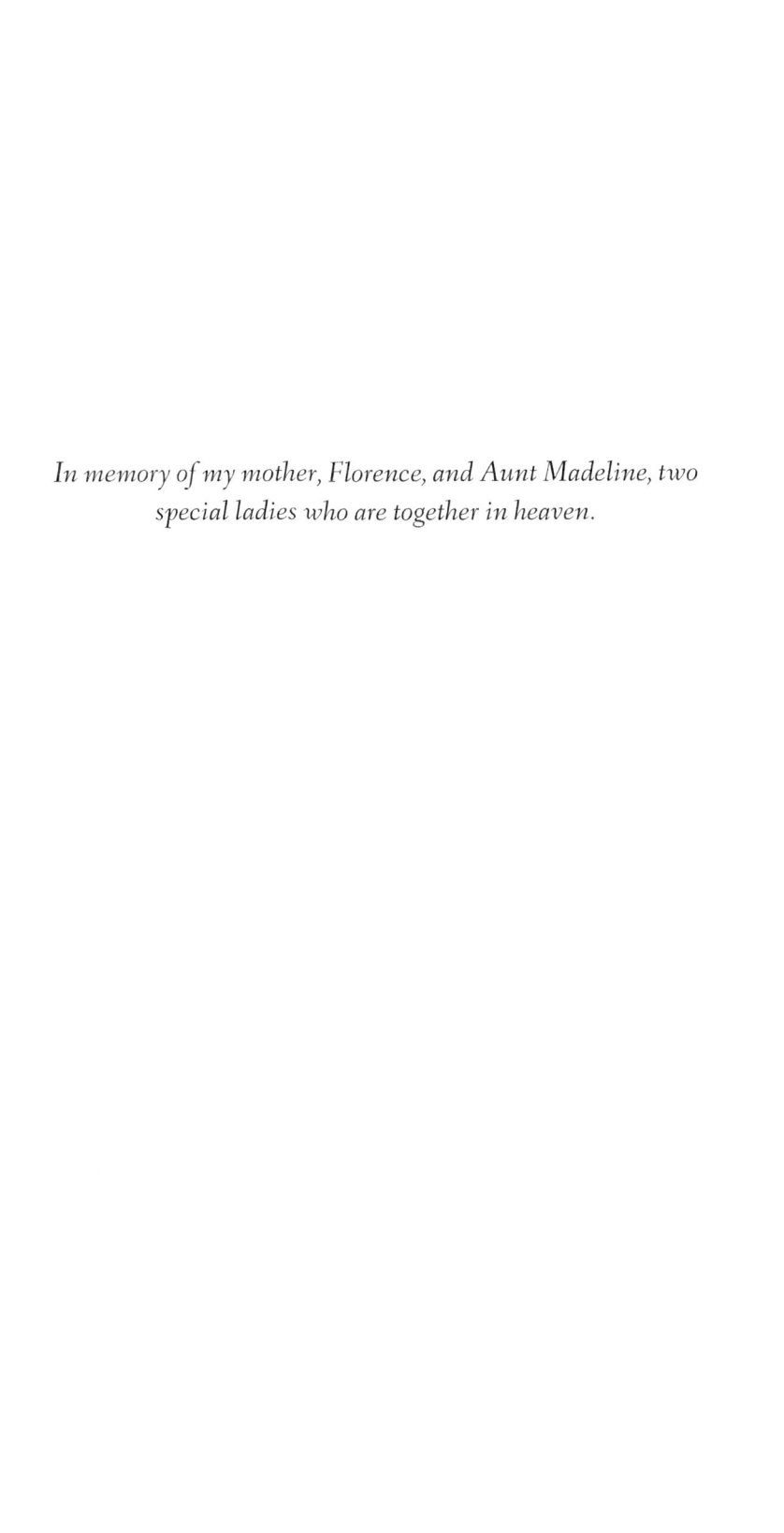

In memory of my mother, Florence, and Aunt Madeline, two special ladies who are together in heaven.

CHAPTER ONE

Cathy sat across from her friends, Nancy and Mildred. They were in her grandmother's kitchen discussing wedding plans. It had been six months since Cathy accepted Steve's marriage proposal after she returned from Oaks Landing Farm where she'd help solve the murder of Mildred's co-worker, a retired librarian. Following Cathy's announcement, Nancy, who'd been at the farm with Cathy, visited her boyfriend Brian. She'd expected him to be angry with her for not telling the truth about why she went to Oaks Landing. Instead, Brian presented her with a ring. He said he missed her so much that he realized it was time to ask her to be his wife.

As Nancy sipped tea that Florence brought along with home-baked muffins for the girls to share, she said, "It's funny how things work out, Cat. Both of us engaged! Can you believe it?" She flashed her ring. The diamond was about the size of the one that Steve gave Cathy. Both were small, as neither man earned much money in their occupations as a gardener and an assistant deputy. Nonetheless, their value was high in feelings.

"I know, Nance. What's even stranger is that Mildred is engaged, too." She glanced over at the librarian who'd convinced Cathy to go to Oaks Landing to help solve her colleague's murder. During her time at the farm, Mildred met a widower, and they hit it off. When she returned, Henry put up his house for sale and planned to join Mildred in Buttercup Bend.

Mildred said, "I was surprised that Henry proposed, but he's a gentleman and doesn't believe in cohabitating before we tie the knot." She winked. Mildred, although she'd been married briefly and had a grown daughter, was known as a spinster in Buttercup Bend. Like Henry's spouse, her spouse was dead. Nancy rented the basement apartment that Mildred's daughter, who lived in another state with her husband, used to occupy.

"I asked Cathy to invite us here to talk about our wedding plans," Nancy said, picking up a muffin from the platter and placing it on her dish. She paused, waiting for them to look toward her. Then she continued. "Cathy, you've been dragging your heels setting a date, and you, Mildred, haven't mentioned your plans at all. I want something memorable but haven't a clue on how to go about it. It takes time to arrange a decent wedding, so I thought we needed to get together and make some decisions."

"I'm eager to marry, Nancy, but everyone is giving me different ideas of where to do it. Gran wants it here in her house. My brother says we should have it in a hall. Steve wants it in a garden."

"It's your wedding, Cathy," Mildred said. "You decide where you want it. As for me and Henry, we're at an age where we can elope. Henry won't move here until we're married."

Nancy ate a piece of muffin and wiped her mouth with a napkin. "I think this may help." She reached into her purse and withdrew a business card. Placing it in the center of the table, she said, "This lady was recommended to me by Pauline. She did a feature on her once for the *Buttercup Bugle*."

Cathy glanced at the card. "Georgia Hampton, Wedding Planner, Georgia and Ginny's Wedding Services." The address was on Long Island. "Are you crazy, Nancy? She probably charges a fortune, and she's too far away."

"Pauline said she'll give us a discount for the referral."

"Us?" Mildred had finished her tea and pushed the cup aside. "I don't need a wedding planner."

"Ah, but you will if we have a triple ceremony."

"Now I know you're crazy," Cathy said. "Why would the three of us marry on the same day?"

"Why not?" Nancy smiled. "We can all chip in on the cost. It'll be a blast. We have an appointment with Georgia tomorrow. I suggest you both start packing."

CHAPTER TWO

Cathy wasn't thrilled that Nancy made an appointment with the wedding planner without consulting her or Mildred. When she told her grandmother, Florence said, "Seeing a wedding planner isn't a bad idea, but I'm not pleased that Nancy is hoping to plan a triple wedding with you and Mildred. It might take away from a day that should be special for you, not two other brides."

"I'm not sure how I feel about that either, Gran, but what should I do about seeing the wedding planner?"

Florence sighed. "Because Nancy already scheduled that, why don't you go? I'll take care of the kittens and also Hobo if Nancy needs me to watch him. Since you'll be on Long Island, you can stop by to meet my sister. In fact, why don't you stay there overnight? I'll call Madeline and arrange that."

Cathy had forgotten that her great aunt Madeline still lived on Long Island. She knew that Florence kept in touch with her older sister, but Cathy hadn't seen her since she came to her parents' funeral five years ago and before that only as a child when she visited her grandmother.

"That'll be nice if she doesn't mind. But does she have room for the three of us?"

"I'm sure she does. Her husband died before you moved in with me, so she's in her house all alone."

Cathy wasn't sure Nancy and Mildred would go along with the idea, but she looked forward to catching up with her great-aunt. "Okay, but I need to tell Steve I'll be away. We're having dinner together tonight."

"Of course, dear. I'll call Madeline and let you know what she says."

Steve took Cathy to a new Italian restaurant in Buttercup Bend. When she told him about her wedding planning appointment, he said, "A wedding planner might be helpful. As the groom, I don't have much say in the details. If it were up to me, I'd ask Pastor Green to marry us in a garden somewhere. As far as our getting married with our friends, I won't argue with that if it's what you want, but Nancy can't force you to sign any contracts."

Cathy looked down at her plate of lasagna that she'd barely eaten. "That's what you think. Nancy can be very convincing when she wants to be."

He chuckled.

"It's not funny. She's gotten me into a lot of serious predicaments in the past."

"She also showed you your sleuthing side."

Cathy sighed. "It's true that I would've never considered becoming a detective until Nancy had me investigating Maggie Broom's murder. But I don't owe her anything for that."

"She is your best friend." He raised a blond eyebrow.

She sighed again. "You're right. I'm going, and I'll keep an open mind. I'll try, anyway."

He smiled. "That's my girl. Now eat your lasagna."

After she had dinner with Steve and he dropped her home, Gran told her that everything was arranged with her sister. Cathy called Nancy to ask if she wouldn't mind staying a night on Long Island at her great-aunt Madeline's house and told her she could bring Hobo over the next day for Florence to watch while they were away. Nancy loved the idea. She hadn't yet made any hotel reservations and said she'd thought about asking Brody to watch Hobo but was worried that his adopted cat Stripey would have a harder time with him than Harry and Hermione since Stripey was old and set in his ways. Besides, Hobo had stayed with Florence when Nancy had gone to Oaks Landing, and Cathy's cats had gotten along well with him.

When they finished talking, Nancy promised Cathy she'd tell Mildred that they'd be staying overnight at Cathy's great-aunt's house after their wedding planning appointment.

Nancy brought Hobo over in his carrier the next morning. Mildred was still at home finishing her packing, which Cathy thought was unusual because the librarian normally prepared early for everything. Cathy kissed Florence goodbye, grabbed her overnight bag, and drove with Nancy to Mildred's house to pick her up. When Nancy opened the door, Mildred answered. Her cheeks were flushed, and she smiled widely. "Good morning, ladies. I have something to show you. Please come in."

"What's up, Mildred? You look excited."

Mildred led them into the living room. Cathy was used to meeting Nancy in the downstairs apartment so wasn't familiar with the main level of Mildred's home. She found it suited the librarian with wall-to-wall bookshelves and comfortable-looking seating. There were photos of her daughter and her family in frames on the walls and side tables. There was also a photo of a man with a younger Mildred. Cathy assumed that was her dead husband.

"Come here." Mildred brought Cathy's attention back. She walked over to a desk that faced the window. It held a desktop PC. "Nancy, you haven't seen this yet either. While you were bringing Hobo over to Cathy's house, I did some research." She tapped the space bar, and Cathy saw what was on the screen. It was a Google search for Georgia and Ginny's Wedding Planning Services.

Cathy skimmed the page that included photos of two women, the Hampton sisters who were partners in the company, and their bios. Georgia had dark curly hair and wore purple-framed glasses. She looked to be in her mid-thirties. Ginny, listed as "Virginia," had long blonde hair and wore a bright pink and white polka-dotted scarf. She appeared to be a few years younger. She reminded Cathy of Stacy, the vet who'd moved from Oaks Landing to work with Michael at his animal hospital. She still felt guilty at turning down his proposal and hoped he would develop a relationship with Stacy. When she first thought they might be involved, she was jealous. But now that she and Steve were engaged, she wanted Michael to share their happiness.

"Don't you notice something strange about these ladies?" Mildred asked.

Cathy and Nancy stepped closer to view the page. The wedding planner's bios said that they'd been in business for five years and had organized over fifty weddings. Georgia had a degree in hospitality. Ginny had previous experience working in event planning. "I don't notice anything odd, Mildred," Cathy said.

Nancy nodded. "Neither do I."

"For one thing," Mildred said, "I think it's strange that both of them are in their thirties and unmarried, even though they work in wedding planning. Also, read Georgia's hobbies."

Cathy hadn't paid attention to the pastimes the Hampton sisters enjoyed. Rereading the bios, she saw that Ginny liked to cook and dance. When she viewed what was listed for Georgia, she understood what Mildred meant. Georgia had a part-time gig hosting whale-watching tours. "I see, Mildred, but I don't think it's an issue that Georgia has an unusual side job."

"Am I missing something?" Nancy asked, moving closer to the computer screen. "What unusual job are you talking about?"

"Georgia watches whales," Mildred said.

"She leads Whale-Watching Tours," Cathy corrected.

"Cool! Maybe we can go on one. It might make a fun honeymoon," Nancy said.

"I don't think Brian would agree." Cathy turned to Mildred. "Would you go on a whale watching honeymoon with Henry?"

The sixty-year-old librarian smiled. "I'd be up for it."

"What?" Cathy was shocked. "Am I the nerd here? Mildred, I thought you found it weird about Georgia leading whale-watching tours."

"I did, but that doesn't mean I wouldn't be interested in it, and Henry is as hip as I am."

"Well, you can count me out. I don't think Steve would want to watch whales on his honeymoon."

Nancy grinned. "All he'd want to do is look at flowers."

"Flowers are beautiful, and there are many gardens all over the country, all over the world, too."

Nancy glanced at her watch. "Enough talk about whales and gardens. I don't want us to be late for our appointment, and there might be a lot of traffic heading down there."

Cathy knew Nancy wasn't usually prompt, but she seemed eager to meet with the wedding planner, something Cathy wasn't in a rush to do.

Mildred shut down her computer, took her purse off a nearby chair, and then went down the hall to get her suitcase. When she returned, she said, "All right. Let's go see Georgia, the whale lady."

CHAPTER THREE

They threw their overnight cases into Nancy's car, and she drove. Mildred sat next to her. Cathy took the back seat in consideration of Mildred's bad knees. Cathy had given Nancy the address of Madeline Mayfair's house on Long Island. Madeline lived in Minnick, a town close to the wedding planner's office in Fogport.

Georgia and Ginny's Wedding Planning Services was in a building located in a small mall that included various stores. A bridal shop was conveniently located adjacent to it.

"Oooh, we have to look in there after our appointment," Nancy said when they arrived, pointing in the direction of the window displaying a lacy white gown with pearls and a tight-fitting bodice.

"I'm not planning to wear anything like that, even if I could," Mildred said. "I was thinking of an off-white dress. It's my second marriage."

"Well, you can help me and Cathy pick out something nice. You have great taste, Mildred."

"Thank you, but you two should choose your own gowns."

Cathy wasn't ready to start picking out a wedding gown. "I don't think we should do any looking until we've booked a date, and we should shop closer to where we live."

"I agree we should shop near Buttercup Bend, but it's not a good idea to wait, Cat. It could take a long time to find what we want and then there are fittings. We also have to choose the gowns for the maid of honor and the clothes for the rest of the bridal party. They might have a section for tuxedo rentals, too. Wait!" Nancy stopped in the middle of the street, and Cathy was worried a car would speed by and hit her. "Haven't you been browsing wedding catalogs and clipping out stuff you like, as I have?"

"We can talk about this later, Nancy. Our objective right now is to speak with Georgia Hampton."

Mildred was already at the glass door of the wedding planner's office. "Are you two coming or not?"

Cathy was relieved that the librarian had shut up Nancy. Mildred held the door open for them.

As they entered, Cathy felt as though she'd stepped into a romantic fantasy. The office was decorated in pastel colors with roses of all shades in crystal vases everywhere. She sniffed the fragrant air and followed Nancy to the front desk where a woman about their age sat answering a phone and typing information into a computer. She looked up as they approached.

Finishing her call, she smiled at them "Sorry to keep you waiting. It's June, the busiest time here, although October is now a close second for weddings. I'm Stephanie, the office manager. How can I help you?"

"We have an appointment with Georgia Hampton," Nancy said.

Stephanie tapped a few keys on the computer and glanced at the screen. Cathy figured she was checking an online calendar.

"What were your names again?"

"The appointment is under Meyers. That's me. Nancy Meyers. I was referred by Pauline Harding from the *Buttercup Bugle*."

"I see." Stephanie was still looking at her screen. "Was the appointment just for you or for your sister and mother, too?"

Mildred's face reddened, but Nancy corrected Stephanie. "It was for the three of us. These are my friends, Cathy Carter and Mildred Hastings. We're planning our weddings."

Stephanie took her eyes off the computer. "Georgia only books one wedding at a time. You'll need individual appointments."

"You don't understand," Nancy said. "We're planning a triple wedding. We all want to get married together."

Cathy wasn't yet on board with that idea, and she knew Mildred wasn't either. But she figured that white lie might get them in the door. She was wrong because Stephanie, after glancing back at her computer, said, "That's fine, but I don't see any appointment on Georgia's calendar for you, Ms. Meyers, or any of your friends."

"I made it two days ago."

"I'm the only one who books appointments here, and I didn't speak with you."

"Someone answered the phone when I called and said she'd take the message and book us."

Stephanie looked annoyed. She sighed. "That might be Ginny. She answers the phones when I'm at lunch and often forgets to give me the messages and add bookings to the calendar. I've complained to Georgia about that many times."

"That's not our fault. Is there any way Georgia can fit us in today?"

Stephanie shook her head at Nancy. "I'm afraid not. Georgia's leading a Whale-Watching Tour this afternoon. She already left."

"What about Ginny? She's a wedding planner, too, right?"

"Yes, Ms. Meyers, but she isn't here either. She's out with a client showing a venue. I can book you all for next week."

Cathy watched as Nancy placed her hands on her hips and took a step forward. "We can't wait a week. We traveled from upstate for this appointment. What type of business is this that you can put off three potential clients?"

"I'm sorry," Stephanie repeated. "It's a busy time for us. That's the best I can do. Neither Georgia nor Ginny has any openings until next week. May I put you down for 1 p.m. on Monday?"

"You may not. We'll take our business to another wedding planner. C'mon, ladies. We're out of here." As Nancy turned, Stephanie called her back. "Please reconsider. Georgia organized my own wedding. It was lovely. She does a wonderful job, and you'll find her prices quite reasonable. With your referral, you'll also get a discount. A week isn't that long to wait. I assume you all recently became engaged."

"It's been six months," Nancy pointed out. "I'm sick of waiting."

Cathy placed a hand on her arm. "I can wait, and so can you. Let's go, Nancy."

With a huff, Nancy turned around and let Cathy lead her to the door. Mildred followed behind.

Cathy was relieved that Nancy seemed to have forgotten her interest in going to the bridal shop. But when they were seated in her car, Nancy didn't start the engine right away. Instead, she pulled out her cell phone and began tapping it.

"What are you doing?" Cathy asked.

She continued typing. "I'm trying to find out where the whale-watching tours are given."

From the back of the car, Mildred asked, "Why?"

"So I can find Georgia and complain about her company's poor service."

Cathy sighed. "What good will that do? We should just look for another wedding planner, one closer to us. I'm not even happy you want us to use a wedding planner."

Mildred agreed. "I already said I'm not interested. I only joined you because you were so insistent. Why don't you take us home? Cathy can call her great-aunt and tell her we've changed our plans."

Nancy ignored her. "Ah! I found it 'Captain Sharp's Fleet and Whale-Watching Tours.' This has to be the one. It's close to here."

"Are you listening to us?" Cathy asked. "We don't want to go, and you shouldn't either."

"Too bad. Unless you want to hitch a ride home or pay for a rideshare, you're coming with me."

Mildred said, "Then I guess we're stuck going along with your fruitless venture, Nancy."

Cathy kept her mouth shut. She knew there was no sense arguing with her stubborn friend.

CHAPTER FOUR

Following the GPS on her phone, Nancy pulled up to a dock where boats were moored. There was a white, blue-lettered banner hung over a weathered wooden building a few yards away that read, "Captain Sharp's Fleet and Whale-Watching Tours."

"I think we can ask for Georgia in there," Nancy said, glancing toward the building.

"I'm not getting out." Cathy kept her seatbelt clipped.

"Neither am I," Mildred said. "This was your idea, Nancy, and we didn't want to go along with it."

"Fine! I'll be right back." Nancy got out of the car and stepped onto the dock to make her way to the building. But as she did, her shoe heel caught on a plank, and she took a tumble.

"Are you all right, Miss?" a voice asked. Cathy saw a young man approach from the other side of the parking lot. He had light brown hair styled in a crew cut and a navy t-shirt with a graphic of a whale on it.

The man rushed to Nancy and gave her his hand. "Let me

help you up. That board needs to be fixed. I'll tell Captain Sharp."

Nancy leaned on him as she stood up and adjusted her shoe. She smiled. "Thank you, sir. I was about to go into the building and ask for Georgia Hampton. I understand she works here and gives whale-watching tours."

"That's right. Georgia is setting up for one right now." He glanced toward the boats. "She's cleaning *Lady Star*. She prefers that boat. I give tours, too, but I use the *Lucky Maiden*. Are you registered for Georgia's tour?"

Nancy shook her head. "No. I need to speak to her about another matter. I'm Nancy Meyers, by the way." She extended her hand. The man shook it.

Glancing at the ring on her left hand, he said, "Nice to meet you, Nancy. I'm Tommy Mueller. I guess you want to see Georgia about a wedding."

"I do. I mean, yes." She laughed.

Tommy turned and glanced at Cathy who had gotten out of the car when she'd seen Nancy trip. "Are you with Nancy?" he asked.

"Yes. I'm her friend, Cathy Carter. Thank you for helping her."

"Does the old lady need a hand?" He glanced at Mildred who still sat in the passenger seat. At that comment, she jumped from the car. "I do not, young man. I may have weak knees, but I'm as spry as I was at your age."

Tommy grinned. "I don't doubt it, ma'am. Are you ladies all looking for Georgia or just accompanying Nancy?"

"Both," Cathy said.

At his puzzled expression, Nancy added, "We went to the wedding planning office for an appointment we had today and was told Georgia was leading a whale-watching tour. There was a misunderstanding, and I'd like to speak with her about it."

"Of course. I can take you to her. The tour doesn't start for an hour. She likes to prepare in advance."

"We'd appreciate that." Nancy spoke for the three of them.

"Then follow me, ladies, but please be careful on the dock."

The dock was longer than Cathy had observed when they'd arrived. It wrapped around the water for what seemed like a mile. She realized she wasn't in great shape when she had trouble keeping up with Tommy. Nancy, on the other hand, was right at his side, while poor Mildred hung several feet behind all of them.

As they turned a corner, a young woman came running toward them, her long blonde hair billowing in the wind. She wore cut-off jeans and a tank top with the same whale logo as the one on Tommy's shirt. When she saw them, she yelled, "TOMMEEEE! I've been looking for you."

A blush rose on Tommy's cheeks as he stopped short, and the girl embraced him in a bear hug. "I just got in, Angel. I met these ladies who are looking for Georgia, so I was taking them over to her boat." He turned around. "This is our deckhand, Angela Price. She prefers to be called Angel."

Nancy said, "Hi, Angel. I'm Nancy, and these are my friends, Cathy and Mildred." Cathy noticed she didn't bother including their last names.

Angel nodded. "Are you signing up for a tour or getting married?"

"They're getting married. That's the reason they want to speak with Georgia," Tommy explained.

"Hmm. Good luck. She's in a mood today."

"What do you mean?" Nancy asked.

Angel bobbed her blonde head. "Georgia's very temperamental. I saw her speaking with Captain Shark. I mean, Sharp. I nicknamed him 'shark' because he can be like one sometimes. They were arguing in the office about something. Then she grabbed the keys to the boat and stalked off. That was about a half hour ago. I've been jogging on the dock since then, but I stopped for a latte in the coffee shop. I thought you might be working on the *Lucky Maiden*, Tommy, so I looked for you over there." She glanced at her watch. "Shark won't be happy you're late. Have you checked in yet?"

"No. I had a late night, and my alarm didn't go off this morning. I was headed for the office when I saw Nancy fall on a loose board. I'm sure the captain will understand. If she got hurt, she could've sued us."

Nancy didn't deny that. Instead, she said, "We're not in a rush, but we'd like to speak to Georgia before her tour starts."

"Sure. Her boat's right over there." Tommy pointed to a light blue boat a few feet away. Its red lettering read *Lady Star*. Gold stars were painted around its name.

"I think I'll pass," Angel said. "I'll meet you in the office, Tommy, and let Shark know you're here and what happened. Don't take too long." With that, she jogged off in the direction of the wooden building.

"That's strange," Tommy said as he led them toward the boat. "Georgia usually works on the top deck. Angel's supposed to help us clean out the boats, but Georgia insists on doing it herself before her tours."

"Could she have stepped away?" Nancy asked. "I hope we didn't miss her."

"We would've seen. I'll help you ladies on and then call down to the bottom deck to see if she's there."

"How long has Georgia been doing this?" Cathy asked as he gave each of them a hand onto the boat.

"She's been with our team for two years now. She started as a deckhand like Angel, but then Sharp taught her how to give tours. He's still doing them, too, but she's built up a following." He smiled. "Some of the women come because they know she's a wedding planner and hope to get free advice."

As they boarded the boat, Tommy called out, "Georgia, are you here? I've brought some people who want to talk with you. Georgia?"

When there was no answer from below, Tommy said, "She sometimes uses earplugs to listen to music when she's cleaning so might not hear us. I'll go check."

He opened the hatch, which was a square door cut into the boat, and descended the stairs. Nancy started to follow him. "Nancy, wait up here," Cathy said. "You don't want to trip again, do you?"

"I don't want her getting away."

"She might not even be down there."

Nancy ignored her.

Cathy sighed, but she followed them.

She remembered what she told Steve about Nancy leading her into dangerous situations. "Wait for us up there, Mildred," she called back, but the librarian was already behind them placing two feet on each step and hugging the wall. The stairway was narrow and dark.

At the bottom, Tommy switched on a light. Cathy wondered why the light switch hadn't been placed at the top.

"Georgia," he called again. "Are you down here?"

As Cathy's eyes adjusted to the brightened area, she saw a body on the ground and a trail of blood around it. At first, she thought the woman had hit her head on one of the low beams she'd avoided when she'd stepped below deck. But then Nancy began to scream. "Oh, my God! Look at her head. She's been shot."

CHAPTER FIVE

Tommy rushed over to the body. "Georgia!" he exclaimed. He took her limp wrist and felt for a pulse. Then he put his head to her chest and began to administer CPR. "Call 911," he said. "She's not breathing, but she's still warm."

Cathy took out her cell phone and entered the emergency number. When the dispatcher answered, she told them that someone had been shot aboard a boat docked at Captain Sharp's Fleet and Whale-Watching Tour Company and to send help right away.

Nancy, who'd stopped screaming, seemed frozen. Cathy was surprised because Nancy was usually the calm one in emergencies. Mildred was also quiet, but Cathy could tell by the sound of her quick breathing that she was also scared.

The paramedics arrived quickly and pronounced Georgia dead. The police followed them. The officer in charge, his badge read, "Dooley," asked them to go up on deck. When they did, Cathy saw that a crowd had gathered on the dock. She realized these were the people signed up for Georgia's tour.

"What's going on?" the man at the head of the line asked.

Tommy said, "Sorry, sir. There's been an accident. We'll refund your ticket." He turned to Officer Dooley. "Can I take them to the office? I need to get their names and phone numbers."

"You're not going anywhere." He addressed his partner, "Get those people out of here. Have them contact the office tomorrow."

The younger police officer said, "Shouldn't they be questioned and checked for the gun?"

"You have a point, Palmer. Go to it. I'll take care of these folks."

A murmur rose through the crowd as Officer Palmer jumped to the dock. A heavyset woman wearing red Bermuda shorts and a white top with a beach scene, said, "I don't know what's going on, but you can't touch me. I'll sue you."

"I won't frisk you, but I have to check your bag."

"I only have sunscreen and my wallet in there. This is an invasion of privacy."

"If you were flying, they'd have you go through TSA. Now hand over the bag."

Cathy was amazed the nerdy-looking policeman could be so aggressive. Officer Dooley watched with a crooked smile. "That's the end of the sideshow, people. Those folks may not need to be frisked, but you four have to be. I want your names and IDs first and what you were doing on this boat when you found the body."

Tommy said, "I'm Thomas Mueller. I work here. You can check with my boss."

"And who is that? Where is he?"

"He's in the office. His name is Captain Shark. I mean Sharp."

"I'll head there next." He turned to Cathy. "Do you work here, too?"

"No. I'm Cathy Carter. I'm here with my friends, Nancy Meyers and Mildred Hastings." She looked over at them. "We wanted to speak to, uh, the deceased about a wedding."

Dooley raised his gray eyebrows. "A wedding? I thought this was a whale-watching tour."

"It is," Nancy said. "But Ms. Hampton, the, uh, deceased, was also a wedding planner. We had an appointment with her, but her receptionist had no record of it. I wanted to let her know about that misunderstanding."

Nancy was coming out of her shock. Mildred, however, looked as though she was about to faint. It was obvious she'd never seen a dead body before. The murder that she investigated with Cathy at Oaks Landing Farm had occurred before they'd arrived.

After Palmer released the tour customers and Dooley was satisfied that Cathy and her friends weren't armed, he asked Tommy to take him to see Captain Sharp.

"Can we go?" Mildred asked. Cathy still thought she looked shaken.

"Yes, but I'll need your contact information in case we have further questions."

Tommy said, "That really isn't necessary, Officer. I can vouch that they're innocent. They only came to talk to Georgia about a wedding. She was already dead when I brought them down."

Dooley narrowed his eyes. "How can you be sure they weren't here earlier and shot Ms. Hampton? Maybe they made the wedding story up, or maybe they were unhappy with a wedding she arranged."

Nancy said, "Are you calling us liars? And if that were true, how come you didn't find the gun on any of us?"

Dooley looked over the side of the boat and pointed to the water. "Because you could've dropped it in there. We'll have divers check that."

"One more thing." He looked at Tommy. "I'll need to notify Ms. Hampton's next of kin. Would you have that information?"

"She has a sister," Tommy said. "They're partners in the wedding business. Sharp has her contact, but you could always call her office."

"We were just there," Cathy said. "We were told Ginny was out with a client."

"I'll need her cell then," Dooley said. "I hate to break news like this over the phone, but that's how everyone communicates nowadays." He walked to the edge of the boat and said to Tommy, "Take me to Captain Sharp. He needs to be told that one of his employees has been murdered and answer a few questions."

As Dooley and Tommy walked away, Palmer helped the rest of them off the boat. "Dooley needs your phone numbers," he said, "then you're free to go." He took out a pad to write down their information.

"I think you should know that Cathy and I are detectives," Nancy said. "We're with the Hunt, Meyers, and Carter Agency in Buttercup Bend. We might be of help to you."

"Why didn't you say anything about that before when you were questioned?"

"I was in shock. Although Cathy and I have solved a few cases, seeing a dead body up close like that still upsets me."

Mildred said, "I'm not a detective. I'm a librarian, but I could help with research if necessary."

Cathy didn't offer her assistance. She felt this was more of a police matter than one that called for detectives. She also thought Nancy should've waited to speak with Howard before promising their services.

When they were in Nancy's car driving away, Cathy said, "Nancy, why did you mention that we were detectives?"

"Why not? I think Howard would love us to pursue this case."

Mildred said, "Don't you have to be hired first to conduct an investigation?"

"Mildred's got a point, and the police aren't going to hire us." Cathy knew how resistant the Oaks Landing police had been when they'd been investigating Doris Grady's murder at the llama farm. She knew there wouldn't be much difference with the Fogport officers.

Nancy made the turn onto Cathy's great-aunt's street. "I have a plan. I'll contact the sister. She might be interested in our assistance."

"What makes you think that, and are you checking with Howard about that first?"

"No, Cathy. I don't have to check with Howard about every case I wish to follow, and I think Ginny will want our help when I explain how incompetent the police can be."

As they pulled up to Madeline's house, Mildred said, "What if Ginny killed her sister? You don't even know for sure that she was with a client."

"We can verify that." Nancy parked the car and looked back at Cathy. "Don't say a word to your great-aunt about this or your grandmother when you call her. It'll be tough enough to keep it from Pauline, who'll want to cover the murder in the *Buttercup Bugle*. Even though it's not local news, she's always looking for filler."

"You know how I feel about lying, Nancy."

"It's not lying. It's just keeping certain information to yourself."

Cathy got out of the car. "Whatever you say. At least we're done with wedding planners."

"Not necessarily. I'm planning to book Ginny for us. It'll be like killing two birds with one stone."

"As long as we're not those birds," Mildred said.

CHAPTER SIX

Cathy felt odd ringing her great-aunt's bell. She didn't know what to expect. But when the door opened, she faced a lady similar in appearance to Florence. Madeline was about her sister's height with short, curly silver hair. She wore a paisley-printed housedress. Her gray eyes sparkled as she smiled at Cathy. "Hello, there. You must be Catherine. You look just like Florence when she was your age. Please come in and bring your friends."

Cathy vaguely remembered Madeline. Her parents' funeral had been a blur. But meeting her now, she felt welcomed by a family member and not a stranger.

As they all entered the small ranch, Cathy smelled the scent of chocolate chip cookies. "I just finished baking," Madeline said leading them into the living room. "I'll bring out the cookies. You must be hungry from your trip. I can put on tea or coffee if you'd like."

Cathy said, "Please don't bother, Mrs. Mayfair."

Madeline's smile widened. "The name's Madeline, Aunt Maddie to you. Please don't use the 'great.'"

Nancy stepped forward. "It's nice to meet you. Thank you for allowing us to stay here tonight. I'm Nancy Meyers, Cathy's friend from Buttercup Bend. Shall I call you Maddie, too?"

"Of course." Madeline glanced at Mildred. "You must be the librarian. I always wanted to be one, but I was a secretary until I retired ten years ago. My husband was a professor at the university. He died too young. Although we'd traveled a lot before that, there were many other places I would've enjoyed going with him." She sighed.

"Sorry to hear that," Mildred said. "Life is too short. I lost my husband, too, and my fiancé lost his wife." She paused and then said, "I'm Mildred. You can call me Millie if you'd like. That's what Henry calls me."

"Millie and Maddie," Madeline said smiling. "I like that. Let me get the cookies."

As she walked toward the kitchen, Nancy said, "She's sweet. Just like your grandmother."

"Yes. I'm sorry I never got to know her."

"Now you will, and I have a feeling we'll be here longer than we anticipated. We have a crime to solve, after all."

"I don't know about you two," Mildred said, "but I'm leaving tomorrow, even if I have to pay for a taxi or ride share."

"That won't be necessary," Cathy said, staring down Nancy. "We're going back to Buttercup Bend in the morning and forgetting all about wedding planners and whale-watching tours."

Nancy didn't have time to reply because Maddie was back with the tray of cookies, a white china teapot adorned with roses, matching cups, saucers, and an assortment of tea bags. "Here you go," she said, setting the tray down on a table in front of the couch. "Have a seat and help yourselves."

"Thank you," Cathy said. She poured some hot water into a

cup and added a bag of Earl Grey. "We appreciate you putting us up with such short notice."

Nancy grabbed a cookie and took a seat next to Cathy on the couch. Mildred sat on the other end. "Yes, Maddie. That's kind of you. Is Florence your only sister? Do you see one another often?"

Maddie shook her head, and a silver curl slipped over her eyebrow. "It's just the two of us. Our parents are gone many years now. We don't see one another as often as we should, but we talk on a regular basis. Florence has sent me photos of you, Catherine." She turned to her great-niece. "And Douglas, Becky, and their baby, too." She took the chair next to the couch and addressed Nancy, "I heard you and Catherine are detectives. That must be exciting."

"It is," Nancy said. "We've solved three murders so far, and there's another we hope to investigate right here on Long Island."

Cathy gave Nancy a warning look, but she ignored it.

"Really?" Maddie's gray eyes twinkled again. "Can you investigate murders in other places?"

"We can and we have," Nancy said. "Our last investigation was undercover at a llama farm. Mildred helped us with that."

Cathy nearly choked on her tea. She said, "Mildred and I were the ones who went undercover, Nancy. You joined us later."

"Only because you kept it from me."

Maddie waved her hand. Cathy noticed it was misshapen and considered that her great-aunt suffered from arthritis like her grandmother whose spine was affected by the disease. "It's no matter," she said, trying to diffuse the situation. "I'm sure you ladies all work well together. I also know you're engaged to fine young men and that's why you're here to see the Hampton wedding planners."

"Well," Nancy said, "that's true. Unfortunately, one of them was murdered."

Maddie gasped. "Oh, my. That's awful."

"It's Georgia Hampton," Cathy said. "We found her body on the boat where she works part-time giving whale-watching tours." Cathy figured the cat was already out of the bag, so she should fill in Maddie.

"That's the case Cathy and Nancy are planning to investigate," Mildred said. "I don't think Cathy really wants to, and I'm only here for the wedding planning. It's not my first walk down the aisle, but I'm going along with them because they're my friends."

Nancy said, "Thank you, Mildred, but if we're hired to investigate Georgia's murder, we'd like your research skills to help us."

Cathy placed her empty teacup on the table. "I don't think that'll be necessary since we're leaving tomorrow."

"Please, ladies," Maddie said, "there's no rush. You can stay as long as you like. In fact, I'd love to have you. It gives me a chance to get to know my great niece better."

"Even if we wanted to, we only have clothes for tonight," Cathy pointed out.

Maddie smiled. "Not a problem. My granddaughter, Christine, your second cousin, lives a block away. You and Nancy look about her size. I'm sure she wouldn't mind your borrowing some clothes. As for Millie," she turned toward Mildred, "I think she would fit into a few of my outfits."

"Then it's settled," Nancy said, munching another cookie. "We'll stay until we can get another wedding planner appointment and are hired to work on Georgia's case."

"If we're staying, I should let Gran know," Cathy said.

Maddie agreed. "Yes, please give Florence a call, and you other ladies might want to contact your fiancés, so they won't worry. I'll call Christine and ask her to bring the clothes over."

Maddie left the room to make the call. As Cathy took out her cell to contact her grandmother, Nancy and Mildred looked on. Cathy paused. "Aren't you both making calls, too, as Maddie suggested?"

"I don't need to call Brian. He doesn't keep tabs on me," Nancy said.

"Neither does Henry," Mildred added.

Cathy sighed and pressed the button for Florence's contact. The phone was picked up on the second ring.

"Catherine, is everything okay? How did your appointment with the wedding planner go? I didn't expect you to call yet. Are you at Madeline's house already?"

Cathy hesitated. She didn't know how much to tell her grandmother, but she knew Florence would notice the change in her voice if she lied.

"We're here, but we didn't see Ms. Hampton. There was a misunderstanding with the appointment."

"That's odd. Did you manage to get another appointment?"

"Not exactly."

"Catherine!" Florence's tone convinced Cathy to tell her the rest.

"We went to the dock where Georgia gave whale-watching tours when she wasn't planning weddings. Mildred and I didn't want to, but Nancy was driving. When we got there, we met one of the tour guides. He took us to Georgia's boat, and we, uh, we found her dead. She was shot."

"Oh, no! Not again. Catherine, how do you keep finding bodies?"

"Gran, I'm a detective."

"I keep forgetting. Are you coming home then?"

Cathy looked across at Nancy. "Maddie said we could stay

longer if we wanted to. Nancy thinks we can still get a wedding planning appointment, and she also believes we'll be hired to work on this case. The police are already looking into the murder, so I don't know if that will happen."

"Knowing Nancy, I'm sure she'll find a way to get you hired."

"Will you tell Howard?"

"Only if it comes up. I'm glad you're spending more time with my sister. I wish I'd asked her to visit us after you moved in with me."

"It's hard when family doesn't live nearby, Gran. That's why it's nice having Doug and Becky next door. By the way, how are Harry, Hermione, and Hobo? Do you mind watching them another day or two?"

"Of course not, dear. Harry and Hermione are so much fun. I love taking care of those two. They sleep in your room when you're not here. I know they miss you, but I spoil them, so they don't notice much. Hobo gets along with them fine."

Cathy recalled how the cats ran to her when she returned from the farm six months ago and looked like they'd grown while she was away. No doubt her grandmother had given them special treats and let them play with their favorite toys.

"Thanks, Gran. Be back soon." As Cathy ended the call, she doubted those words.

CHAPTER SEVEN

They spent the rest of the afternoon chatting. At one point, Maddie brought out a photo album. Cathy enjoyed seeing pictures of her and Florence as children. Nancy pointed out the similarity between Florence's high school graduation photo and how Cathy looked now. "I told you," Maddie said, "my sister looks very much like her granddaughter."

As they flipped through the album, Maddie told stories from the past. "Florence was always the adventurous one, even though I'm two years older. She used to scare me with ghost tales. I remember one Halloween when she pulled a prank on me with spiders. I'll never forget that." She grinned.

Cathy couldn't quite see Florence doing the things Maddie mentioned, but she figured it was natural to feel that way about her grandmother, since she hadn't known her as a young girl.

"What about my mother?" she asked. "Did you know her?"

Maddie's eyes clouded over. "I did. In fact, I watched you once for her when you were a baby. Florence was away on vacation with Bill then."

"You were at the funeral." It wasn't a question.

"It was a difficult time." Maddie closed the album. "I'm not surprised you don't remember me well. You were just out of the hospital."

"Gran speaks of you sometimes, and Doug, too, but those are their memories. I'm glad I'm meeting you now."

Maddie smiled. "So am I." She stood up. "I'll put this away, but you're free to look at it whenever you want. Christine is coming soon to bring the clothes. She offered to bring dinner, as well, and I'll show you your rooms later."

"You're very kind, Maddie," Nancy said.

"I wish I'd had a sister," Mildred added.

Christine showed up at a quarter to five. She had the same honey-brown hair as Cathy but wore it cut shorter and appeared a few years older. In her hands, she held a covered casserole dish that she handed to Maddie as she came in. "It's a chicken casserole. I hope everyone likes it. I made a second one for Ben and the kids, but I'd like to eat with you to meet my cousin and her friends."

"That would be wonderful." Maddie turned around and introduced her to Cathy, Nancy, and Mildred.

Cathy had a wonderful time the rest of the evening chatting with Maddie and Christine. Nancy and Mildred also seemed to be having a good time. Christine left at nine, saying she would drop by again the next day with more clothes if they needed them. Cathy said she was sure they wouldn't be staying that long, but Nancy made a face at that comment.

After Christine was gone, Maddie said, "It's been quite a nice day getting to know you all, but I'm sure you'd like to get some rest. I have two guest rooms upstairs. One has two cots. If

Cathy and Nancy don't mind sharing that, Mildred can take the other."

Nancy said, "That's perfect. We often share a room at Florence's when I stay over."

"Let me take you up then." They followed her up the wide stairway. Cathy noticed Mildred was having a challenging time on the stairs, so she turned back to her and said, "Take your time, Mildred."

The first guest room Maddie brought them to was the single one. She'd already placed some of her clothes and Mildred's overnight case near the bed. The room was wallpapered in a cream color with blue stars. The bedspread was sky blue, and there were cream pillows on it. The bed was a double that faced a window.

"This is lovely," Mildred said entering the room behind them. "Thank you so much, Maddie."

Maddie smiled. "My pleasure, Millie. Have a good sleep." She turned back to Cathy and Nancy. "Your room is right across the hall."

They followed her to the other guest room. It was painted a rose color with white trim. The pillows had roses on them, as did the blankets on the twin cots. Maddie had left Christine's clothes on top of the oak bureau for them to choose. Their suitcases were next to the beds.

"I hope you find everything comfortable. If you need anything, my room is right down the hall."

"Thanks so much," Cathy said.

"No need to thank me. You're family, Catherine, and Nancy and Mildred are my guests."

After she left, bidding them goodnight, Nancy chose the cot by the door, which Cathy found odd because, when they stayed together, she usually preferred the side of the room by the window in case she needed air during the night.

"Nance, how come you want that bed? It's not near the window."

"It seems bigger."

"They're the same size."

Nancy ignored that comment and walked to her overnight case, took out a nightgown, and said, "I'm pooped, Cathy. I'm going to use the bathroom and get ready for bed."

Nancy was a night owl compared to Cathy who always got up early with the cats and to help Florence with the pet rescue center. She figured the drive and the drama of finding the wedding planner dead had exhausted her friend. "Okay. I'll use it next. I'm calling Steve to let him know I might be staying here another day or so. I'm sure Gran has already filled him in, but I want him to hear it from me."

"That's cool, I guess." Nancy closed the bathroom door. Cathy heard the water running a few minutes later.

After Cathy called Steve who'd seemed happy to hear from her, although Florence had notified him that Cathy was staying with her sister a little longer than planned, she prepared for bed. Nancy was already curled up in the cot. Cathy didn't hear snoring, as she usually did when she slept with Nancy, but when she told her she was going to use the bathroom, there was no reply, so she assumed her friend was fast asleep.

After a quick shower and change into her nightgown, Cathy slipped into her own cot. It took a few minutes for her to fall asleep as her mind kept replaying finding Georgia murdered and then meeting her great-aunt and second cousin. It had been a day of ups and downs for sure.

CHAPTER EIGHT

The next morning, Cathy woke to sunlight filtering through the window next to her cot. For a moment, she thought she felt Harry and Hermione on the bed waking her up for their breakfast, but then she remembered she was at Maddie's house in the guest room she was sharing with Nancy.

She stretched, put on the slippers she'd taken from her overnight bag, and walked over to Nancy's cot. She was still sleeping with the covers over her head, but then Cathy realized the blanket wasn't moving. She put her hand out to touch the mound and felt the soft pillows underneath. Nancy wasn't there.

Her first thought was that her friend, having gone to bed early, had ventured downstairs ahead of her. However, on an impulse, she went to the window and looked out at the street. From this side of the house, Nancy's car would've been visible. It wasn't. Nancy had taken it somewhere.

Cathy felt anger bubbling up in her. It made sense now. Nancy chose the bed closest to the door for an easy escape.

She'd left an outfit from her suitcase on her nightstand instead of placing it in a drawer. She wondered how she got past Maddie and how long ago she'd left. It was already nine a.m. Cathy hadn't expected to sleep so late, but the cot had been comfortable and the house quiet.

As she went to the bureau to choose clothes for the day, a knock sounded at her door. She thought it was Nancy, but when she answered it, Mildred stood there in a pair of slightly long blue slacks and a tight plaid shirt she'd obviously borrowed from Maddie.

"Hi, Mildred."

"Cathy, Nancy's left us. I couldn't sleep well and, about a half hour ago, I heard footsteps down the hall. I peeked out of my room and saw her. She was dressed and heading downstairs. Then I heard the front door close and her car start a few minutes later. Do you know where she went?"

Cathy shook her head. "She didn't say anything to me. I woke up, and there were pillows under her blanket. I noticed her car was missing. Maybe she spoke with Maddie. We should go downstairs and see."

Mildred nodded. "Do you want to get dressed first?"

"Yes. I won't take long. I'll meet you down there in fifteen minutes."

After Mildred walked out, Cathy took a quick shower and changed. By the time she got downstairs, Maddie and Mildred were at the kitchen table talking and eating breakfast. Maddie stood up when she saw Cathy. "I'll get another bowl for you. It's only instant oatmeal. I don't do much cooking anymore. You can help yourself to coffee. Mugs are by the pot."

"Thank you." Cathy got her coffee and the bowl of oatmeal Maddie passed to her and sat across from Mildred. When Maddie joined them, she asked, "Did Mildred tell you about Nancy? Did you see her leave the house?"

Maddie smiled. "Yes, Catherine. I can understand the two of you being upset, but Nancy wanted to surprise you. She told me she's setting up a meeting with Virginia Hampton."

Cathy dropped her spoon in her bowl. "What? That poor woman just lost her sister. I'm sure she's taking time off from her wedding planning business, and I thought we were going to check somewhere closer to Buttercup Bend."

"That's not what Nancy said. She's pretty set on using the Hampton's wedding planning services."

Mildred looked at Maddie. "That's because she wants to investigate Georgia's murder. I'm not a part of Howard's detective agency like she and Cathy are, so I'd rather not be involved in her plans."

"I can understand that," Cathy said, "I'm hesitant myself, but you were very helpful at the llama farm."

"I can see how a librarian's skills would be useful in a criminal investigation," Maddie said. "Even if you don't go along with Nancy, Cathy, I'm glad to have you visit with me. Christine is over often, but I miss Florence. Having guests including my great niece means a lot to me."

An hour later, after Cathy had helped clean up the breakfast dishes and Mildred was reading the paper where she pointed out the news story about Georgia Hampton's murder, Nancy came in, her face flushed, her eyes bright. "Ladies, I have news."

"It better be good after you disappeared on us," Cathy said.

"Sorry about that, but it's very good. Ginny hired us, but you haven't heard the best part."

"I'm sure you'll tell us," Mildred said, putting down the newspaper.

"We're booked on a whale-watching tour with Tommy."

"What? How does that help us solve Georgia's murder?"

"It'll give us a chance to question him about his co-workers, Cathy, and also meet his boss, Captain Shark."

"It's Sharp, Nancy."

"I like "shark" better. It'll also be fun. I'm including Steve and Brian." She looked at Mildred. "You can invite Henry, too. I made a reservation for the six of us. Tommy's giving us a private tour."

"Have you told Brian and Steve?" Cathy didn't think they'd be able to take time off from their jobs to come to Long Island for a whale tour.

"I called Brian. He asked Leroy for a few days off."

"What about Steve? Am I supposed to break the news to him, and when are we going?"

"You can tell Steve. The tour is the day after tomorrow. I didn't want to wait so long before the trail gets cold."

"So, I assume you have something planned for tomorrow?"

"Of course. I told you that I managed to get us a wedding planning appointment with Ginny, so you and Mildred can meet her. I want your impressions of the sister. She also promised to share Georgia's files for the last few months along with any complaints by clients who may not have been pleased with her service."

"I guess you're killing two birds again."

Nancy laughed. "That I am, Cat. Multitasking is such fun."

Cathy hated handling two tasks at once. "Isn't Ginny in mourning? She should at least be handling her sister's funeral."

"She'll take care of that. She seems competent to me. I believe Georgia's being cremated, but the police are holding on to the body for now while the murder is under investigation. Ginny said they're having a memorial service on Friday. We should plan on attending."

Cathy was hoping to be back in Buttercup Bend before then. "Ginny's still working? Not taking time off?"

"She's rescheduled her appointments and Georgia's. She's only speaking with us as a courtesy."

"What does Howard make of all this?"

Nancy was quiet.

"You've told him, haven't you?"

"Don't worry, Cat. I'll fill him in soon. I promise."

Cathy recalled how Nancy hadn't told Howard about the murder case at the llama farm. She didn't like to keep cases from their boss at the detective agency who also happened to be her grandmother's boyfriend, but Nancy had her own agenda.

CHAPTER NINE

Cathy was still mad at Nancy, and Mildred didn't seem pleased with her either. She took Cathy aside later that day while Nancy had gone to the bathroom, and said, "I'll go along with the wedding planning, but I'm not asking Henry to go whale watching. I need to get back to the library."

"They'll survive without you, Mildred, but I'm not sold on the whale watching myself. I'm delaying calling Steve even though Nancy keeps reminding me to do that."

Maddie, overhearing their conversation, said, "It sounds like you're both hesitant about the plans Nancy's made. May I suggest that you don't discount them? I'm not being selfish because I want you to stay here as long as possible, although I do. I just think you should enjoy yourselves. Wedding planning can be fun, and a whale-watching tour is quite an adventure."

"I know what you mean, Maddie, but it's the idea that Nancy wants us to investigate the murder that bothers me."

Maddie smiled. "But you're a detective, Cathy, and Millie has helped you before."

"Cases take a long time to investigate," Mildred pointed out. "Cathy and Nancy should find ones closer to Buttercup Bend."

"Oaks Landing wasn't near Buttercup Bend," Cathy said. "You were the one who got us involved with that."

Before Mildred could reply, Nancy was back. "Talking about me?" she asked with a grin.

Cathy surprised herself by saying, "Yes. While we're not thrilled that you set up the wedding planner appointment and whale-watching tour, we'll go." She winked at Maddie. Mildred kept her mouth shut. Cathy figured she realized she was outnumbered again.

Christine dropped by around five o'clock with more clothes but, this time, Maddie had cooked dinner with Cathy and Nancy's help. Neither woman had much cooking experience, but they managed. Mildred, being warned about too many cooks in the kitchen, set the table.

The rest of the evening passed pleasantly, and Cathy found she was looking forward to more time with her great-aunt and second cousin. Mildred even seemed happy with the company, and Nancy kept the conversation going with her usual inquiring but interesting questions.

In bed that night, Cathy said to Nancy who'd switched back to the cot by the window, "I was mad at you for making plans without consulting me and Mildred. I'm going along with the wedding planning meeting tomorrow. It gives me more time to spend with Maddie and Christine, but I'm not sure about the whale watching trip. I haven't even spoken to Steve yet."

"That's okay. I think you'll feel better after we speak with Ginny. If so, Brian is driving down tomorrow night. He's staying at a hotel not far from here. I'm sure he'll be happy to give Steve a ride and Henry, too, if Mildred asks him."

Cathy wasn't pleased with this news. If Nancy convinced Brian to join them, it was possible he told Steve. Just as she had that thought, her cell rang. Steve's name came up on the display.

"Speak of my fiancé; he's calling now."

Nancy smiled. "Great! I'll get ready for bed and give you privacy to talk." She walked into the bathroom.

"Hi, Honey," Cathy spoke into her cell.

"Hi, Cat. I hope you're doing okay. I had a call from Brian about a whale-watching tour Nancy booked over there. He asked if I would drive him down tomorrow night to join you guys because his car is having some problems. I think he's calling Henry, too."

"Nancy booked that tour, but I'm not sure I want to go. However, I'd love for you to come here. I miss you."

"It's only been a day, but I miss you, too." Steve paused. "I already told Brian I'd ride with me, but I'm also not sold on the whale-watching tour. I'm not fond of boats because I'm prone to seasickness. I'll pick up something from the drugstore just in case because I know Nancy will insist on all of us going."

"You're right, Steve. Maddie thinks it will be an adventure for us, but I think she's saying that because she wants us to investigate the murder."

"Murder? What murder?"

Cathy was sorry she slipped. "We never got to see the wedding planner because they couldn't find our appointment. Her receptionist said she was on a whale-watching tour. Nancy found the location. We went there and, long story short, we found Georgia Hampton's body on her boat. The police are investigating, but Nancy spoke with the wedding planner's sister, Ginny, this morning and arranged an appointment with her tomorrow to discuss our wedding."

"Wow!" Steve said. "That puts this in a whole other light. Does Brian know about this?"

"I don't know what Nancy told him, but he's taken off work to come here."

"I can get a few days off, too. Although it's my busy season, a bunch of my clients are on vacation."

"Are you sure you want to join us?"

"Even more now that I think you could be in danger."

Nancy was glad when Cathy told her that Steve and Henry were coming down with Brian the next night.

"Perfect!" She smiled. "You guys are going to have a ball on the whale tour."

Cathy doubted that but didn't reply. Instead, she got ready for bed and then turned out the lights.

CHAPTER TEN

The next day, after a quick breakfast with Maddie, Cathy and Mildred got into Nancy's car to head to the wedding planner's office.

As Nancy drove to Fogport, Cathy asked Mildred, "Have you heard from Henry? Steve called me and said he's riding here with Brian tonight. He wasn't thrilled about the idea of the whale-watching tour, but he'll be joining us."

"Yes, Henry called and said the same thing. I'm glad they're coming, but I still don't think we should get involved in investigating Georgia Hampton's murder."

As Nancy pulled up to the wedding planner's office, she said, "I don't understand you two. You were so helpful at the farm, and you hadn't even found a body then."

"That was different," Cathy pointed out. "Danielle asked me and Mildred to look into her mother's suspicious death. You followed us there later."

"Well, now I'm asking you to look into Georgia's murder. Her sister was happy to hire us."

"You mean hire you and Cathy," Mildred said. "I'm not part of your agency."

"You should be. You'd make a great detective."

"I'm not interested. The only reason I'm going along with this is because I have a few days off from the library. I could be spending it with Henry."

"You will be," Nancy said. "You'll be whale watching with him tomorrow. Besides, once we speak with Ginny, we should have a good idea about our wedding. I know you wanted to keep it simple, Mildred, but you deserve to have something nice. The three of us do."

Cathy said, "I'm keeping an open mind, but I think it'll be hard to arrange a wedding for three brides. We all have different tastes and ideas about what we want."

"Don't worry, Cat. It'll work out, and we might just solve a murder at the same time."

There was a "closed" sign in the window of Georgia and Ginny's Wedding Services, and the place looked dark.

"Are you sure Ginny's here?" Cathy asked as Nancy parked the car. "There aren't any lights on."

"She's here," Nancy said, pointing to a red sports car in the space next to them. "She told me to call when I arrived. She doesn't want anyone to know she's working today." Nancy took out her cell phone and tapped it. It was on speaker because Cathy heard it ring. Then she heard a woman's voice say, "I'll be right there, Miss Meyers."

"It's Nancy. We agreed to be on first-name terms."

"Sorry. That's right, Nancy. Come in."

Nancy ended the call, turned to them, and said, "Let's go."

Cathy and Mildred joined her at the door. A tall blonde woman in her early thirties stood there. She wore a gray and white striped scarf over a white sweater and gray slacks. Switching on a low light, she ushered them in.

"I apologize about the sign and the lights, but I don't want anyone to know we're open. I'm leaving right after our meeting. I have to make the arrangements for my sister."

Cathy noticed Ginny's eyes were red. Her mascara had smudged, and the dark blouse she wore over slacks seemed to be on backwards, but she didn't feel it was right to say anything about it. The woman was obviously grieving.

The office manager, Stephanie, wasn't at the front desk. Ginny walked around it. "Please come to my office. We can talk there." They followed her down a hall where she opened the second door. Cathy noticed the first door was closed and bore a sign that read, "Georgia Hampton, Wedding Consultant."

"Please excuse the mess," Ginny said, as she took the chair behind her desk that was cluttered with papers. She indicated the three chairs situated around it.

"No worries," Nancy said. "It looks like business is booming."

"It is this time of the year. The worst time for..." She paused and glanced down. Then she took a breath and exhaled. Lifting her head and looking toward Nancy who'd taken the chair closest to the desk, she said, "I didn't tell you everything yesterday. I was, well, the police had already spoken with me. I was in shock."

"That's understandable. We were shocked, too, when we discovered your sister." Nancy turned to Cathy and Mildred. "These are the friends I mentioned, Cathy Carter and Mildred Hastings. Cathy's with our agency. Mildred's a librarian, but she was helpful on a previous case. As I mentioned, the three of us are planning a triple wedding."

"That can be tricky, but we can discuss it."

"Let's talk about Georgia first. You mentioned we could see her files."

"I'm afraid that's not possible. I know I promised you, but the police returned after you left and requested them. However, there's something I didn't mention to them that I think would interest you."

Nancy's eyes widened. "Anything you can share might benefit our investigation."

"I told you that my sister was well-liked. She had more clients than I did, but we split the profits equally. There was one client recently who wasn't pleased with her service."

Cathy watched as Nancy leaned forward. "Go on. Please tell us about that."

"The young woman wanted a fall wedding. We usually don't involve the grooms in a large part of the planning, but in this case, her parents didn't approve of the match. Instead, her husband, a wealthy man who'd recently immigrated from India, was picking up the tab for the whole affair. His extended family and friends were planning to fly in to attend."

"Are you saying that Georgia worked with the groom?" Cathy was curious, despite her reluctance to be involved in the matter.

"That's correct." Ginny picked up a pen on the desk and absently began fiddling with it. "Georgia developed an attraction to Shankar. It was reciprocated because he broke off his engagement."

"Oh, no," Mildred said, "I bet his girlfriend was devastated."

Ginny nodded. "She was quite angry. Georgia's relationship with Shankar didn't last long, but the damage was done. His fiancée posted terrible reviews online about our wedding service and Georgia."

"We'd like her name and contact information," Nancy said. "She definitely would have a grudge toward your sister."

"I can provide that. I looked her up. I figured you'd ask." Ginny scribbled on a pad, tore out the sheet, and handed it across the desk to Nancy.

Cathy asked, "What about Shankar? Did he return to India? Did he meet and marry someone else here?"

"I believe he was ashamed to go home, and he'd already landed a nice position at the hospital. He was a doctor in India, you see. We gave him his money back, of course."

"How come you didn't share this with the police?"

"I wasn't thinking at the time. I told you I was in shock. It came back to me later. I could call the officer on the case. His name is Dooley."

"No," Nancy said. "Let us check it out first. He's probably working on other leads. Is there anyone else you can think of who might have had something against Georgia?"

Ginny shook her head. "Not really, but I'll let you know if I think of anybody else. I only met a few people Ginny worked with at Captain Sharp's once, so I didn't know them well."

"What made your sister decide to give whale-watching tours?" Cathy asked.

"She started two years ago after she arranged a wedding. As a thank you, in addition to the cost of her services, the groom offered her a free ticket on a whale-watching tour. She loved it, noticed there was an opening for a part-time boat hand, and applied for the job. A few months later, she was trained to give tours."

That was the story Tommy shared. "Did you ever take a tour?" Nancy asked.

"No. I get seasick."

Cathy had another question. "Who was the man who gave her the complimentary whale-watching tour ticket?"

"Why, that was Captain Sharp himself," Ginny said. "His wedding was, excuse the pun, a splash."

Cathy could tell Nancy found that interesting, as did she, but she had another question to ask. She worded it carefully. "How did you and Georgia get along? Did the police ask where you were yesterday?"

Ginny met her gaze. "Yes, Cathy. The police wanted to know about my appointment with the clients I was meeting. Unfortunately, they cancelled at the last minute. I waited for them at the venue and then left with my apologies to the owners."

Nancy picked up on this. "Did you come right back here?" Cathy knew the office manager would then be able to corroborate this, but Ginny shook her head. "I'm afraid not. I didn't have another appointment for an hour, so I took a break."

"Did the police have a problem with that? Did you go anywhere that someone would've been able to back up your story?" Mildred's question addressed Cathy's thoughts and, likely Nancy's, too.

"The police didn't seem satisfied with my answer. I had taken a drive and then a walk." She glanced toward Cathy. "As far as my relationship with my sister, it was a good one for the most part. I don't know if any of you have siblings, but there's always a bit of tension, especially if you're in business together."

Cathy thought of her brother and how close they were and that they hardly disagreed about anything including how to run their pet business. Their parents' death had brought them even closer.

Nancy said, "I've been wondering about something else. I hope you don't mind my asking but, since you're in the wedding business, how come you're still single?"

Cathy saw Ginny hesitate and glance down at her bare ring

finger. "I was engaged once a long time ago. I was in my twenties. It didn't work out."

Cathy was surprised that Nancy pressed the issue. "How come?"

"Georgia started to see him, but that didn't last either. I realized I was better off without him."

"That seems to be a pattern," Mildred pointed out. "Your sister took men away from other women and then left them."

Ginny cast her an angry look. "I'm done answering questions. Let's move on to your wedding, please."

"That wasn't a question," Mildred said, but Nancy jumped in. "Yes. Let's drop this for now."

Ginny cleared her throat and shuffled the papers on her desk. "Okay then. Let's start with your time frame. How much time do you have before the special day?"

"As soon as possible," Nancy said. "We've already been engaged six months. The only reason we're starting now is that I was waiting for Cathy and Mildred to get their acts together. I thought working with you would give them that push."

Mildred said, "I'd also like to get started soon. Henry was hoping to find a new place for us to live together once we get married, but I think he'll move into my house until we find one." She turned to Nancy. "You can stay downstairs until then. If you and Brian are interested in the house once we find another place, I'll make you a good deal."

"I appreciate that, Mildred." Nancy looked at Cathy. "What about you, Cat? Are you and Steve staying with your grandmother? I know you want to live near your pet rescue center."

Cathy had considered that. "I think we'll stay with Gran initially, but I'm not in a rush to get married. Steve and I have talked about finding our own house, and Gran suggested we have one built on the land near our second rescue center. That will take nearly a year."

Before Nancy could object to a delay in their arrangements, Ginny said, "A year isn't that long. Wedding venues fill up fast. We might be able to manage a wedding next June for the three of you."

"We don't need a venue," Nancy said. "Cathy has plenty of space in Rainbow Gardens, and her fiancé is a gardener. He'll take care of the flowers."

"Are you kidding, Nance?" Cathy couldn't believe that her friend, who kept saying she wanted a fancy wedding, would consider her pet cemetery as a location. "I know Steve would like that idea, but I don't. Gran wants us to use the house but that would limit the number of guests we could invite."

"Henry and I won't be inviting many people," Mildred said. "Unfortunately, at our age, most of our relatives and friends are dead."

"But your co-workers at the library would want to come," Nancy pointed out.

Ginny said, "Look, you ladies need to discuss this among yourselves. For now, I'll check into venues. I know you're not from around here, so I'll see if I can find something closer to Buttercup Bend. We might get lucky if a wedding is cancelled or rescheduled before next summer. Give me a week, and I'll get back to you. If a venue opens up, you can visit the place and make a deposit. Then we'll start talking wedding gowns, tuxedos, flowers, cakes, and all the other necessities." She stood up. "Now let me go, so I can take care of my sister's memorial."

The three rose from their chairs. Cathy said, "Thank you for seeing us. I know it's a difficult time for you."

Nancy said, "You have my cell. Call me when you find something. We're staying nearby at Cathy's great-aunt's house until the weekend, and we'd also like to attend the memorial. Please text me the details."

"I will. Thank you." Ginny walked to the door and opened it.

"I'll also be in touch with you about the investigation," Nancy added, as she stepped into the hall.

Mildred, the last one out, said, "My sympathies on your loss. I didn't know your sister, but I'm sure it was a shock. I hope Cathy and Nancy can catch the killer."

"So do I," Ginny said. Cathy wondered why the statement sounded false off her lips.

CHAPTER ELEVEN

"Okay, ladies," Nancy said once they were back in her car. "We're off to see the jilted bride." She passed Cathy the address for Tina Farrell. It was on the way back to Maddie's house.

"Are you sure we should do this today?"

"Why not, Cathy? The sooner we rule people out, the quicker we'll catch Georgia's killer. Attending the Memorial will also help. I wasn't all that convinced of Ginny's innocence, especially when she has no alibi for where she was at the time of her sister's murder."

Cathy agreed, but she kept silent as Nancy started the engine. Mildred said, "I'll go along now, but I hope you don't lead us anywhere else. I'm meeting Henry for dinner tonight when he gets in from Buttercup Bend."

"I also want to see Steve when he arrives," Cathy added.

Nancy said, "Don't worry. There'll be plenty of time for all of us to meet our boyfriends for some hoochie coochie. We'll also be seeing them tomorrow on our whale-watching tour."

"Why do you have such a dirty mind?" Cathy asked.

Nancy, who'd held out for Brian until he proposed but not a second longer, said, "Excuse me if I'm not a prude, like you."

"My personal life is private." Cathy hadn't shared with her friend her first physical experience with Steve because she knew how it would be spread all over Buttercup Bend like the news she covered for Pauline, the editor of the town's paper.

Mildred said, "At my age, hoochie coochie trumps solving murders anytime." Cathy had the impression that, despite that comment, Mildred was as interested in the case as she and Nancy were.

Cathy, still hurt from Nancy's remark about her being a prude, retaliated by asking, "So have you spoken with Howard about this yet?"

"What makes you think I haven't?"

"Answer the question, Nance."

"I'm planning to call him once we get back from seeing Miss Farrell."

"I don't understand," Mildred said. "I thought Howard was your boss. Don't you have to run all the cases by him when people hire you?"

"Each of us are detectives. Even though Howard's name is first in our agency's title, it doesn't mean he's in charge. In fact, I've solved more cases than he has."

"I don't know if that's true, Nancy, but he still deserves to know." Cathy watched Nancy turn onto Tina Farrell's street. The GPS directed her to a green house on the left.

"Thank goodness we're here," Nancy said. "I'm sick of arguing with you, Cat. I'll tell him in good time, or you can if you want. Right now, let's see this woman and what she has to say about where she was at the time of the murder."

The three got out of the car and approached the house. Like Nancy, Ms. Farrell rented a downstairs apartment. There was a separate entrance. Nancy tapped on a white door down three steps with the name "Farrell" next to it.

When there was no answer right away, Cathy said, "Try the buzzer."

Nancy pressed the button, and a voice came through an intercom. "Shankar, if that's you, I'm calling the police."

Mildred said, "That's weird. You better let her know we're not her ex."

Nancy spoke into the intercom, "It's not Shankar. We're with the Hunt, Meyers, and Carter Detective Agency."

There was silence followed a minute later by footsteps at the door. A young woman in her mid-twenties opened it. Her curly red hair was a shade darker than Nancy's. Her hazel eyes surveyed them. "Are you here about my restraining order?"

Nancy said, "No. We're here about Georgia Hampton's murder."

Cathy watched a shadow cross the woman's face as she swore softly. "If Georgia was killed, she deserved it, but she did me a service by stealing that creep Shankar away from me. Ever since she broke up with him, he's been begging to get back together. He sends me stuff. He stalks me. I had to file a restraining order. I have another boyfriend now. I want nothing to do with him. My mother thinks I'm crazy to give up the money, but I want someone who'll make me happy and not cheat on me."

"We're sorry to hear that," Nancy said. "May we come in? We have some questions to ask you about Ms. Hampton."

"I have nothing to say about her."

"It will only take a minute."

Tina paused, considering Nancy's request, and then opened the door to admit them. "Come in but be quiet. Raff is still sleeping. Your buzzer didn't wake him. He'd sleep through a hurricane."

As Nancy stepped into the foyer, she asked, "Is Raff your boyfriend?"

"You're sharp for a detective." Tina laughed. It was meant to be sarcastic. "His full name is Raphael Wright. He's an artist."

Cathy noticed a few paintings on the stairway wall. They featured seascapes, lighthouses, beaches, and sailboats. "Did he paint those? They're very good."

"There are more downstairs, but let's talk here. I'm sorry we'll have to stand. You said it would be quick."

Nancy nodded. "Yes. We just want to know where you were yesterday around 10:30 a.m.?"

Tina's green eyes narrowed. "Why are you asking me this and not the police? Aren't they handling the case?"

"Ginny didn't share your story with them. She forgot," Cathy explained. "She also hired us to find her sister's murderer."

"Oh, she did, did she? That's cool considering they never got along."

"She told us that they had their differences, but nothing that siblings don't experience."

Tina glanced at Nancy. "From what I could tell, they hated one another. I'm surprised they opened a business together, but then their dislike may have started when Georgia stole Ginny's fiancé. Did she tell you about that?"

"Yes," Nancy replied, "but she said she was better off. She felt like you do."

"Hmm. I doubt that." Tina gazed at one of her boyfriend's paintings, the one of a beach scene with dark clouds gathering on the horizon. It was the only one that Cathy thought looked menacing. The others were placid pastels.

"Getting back to where you were yesterday," Nancy probed.

"She was with me," said a voice from downstairs. They all looked toward the stairway to see a bearded man in a robe on the lower step.

"Raff. I'm sorry we woke you. These are detectives investigating Georgia Hampton's murder."

"Georgia?" He wiped a hand across his brow, sending a lock of dark hair away from his eyes. "Georgia's dead?"

Tina smiled. "Isn't that great news? I wish Shankar was, too, but karma doesn't always comply."

"Did you know Georgia?" Nancy asked.

Raff tightened the belt around his robe. He ignored Nancy's question and addressed Tina. "Why don't you invite the detectives down, and we can talk to them over coffee?"

"They said they only had a few questions, Raff. Let's go back to bed instead."

"It's nearly ten, Tina. I want to paint. I hate sleeping late."

Cathy didn't think Tina was talking about sleeping, and she caught the fact that Raff had something he wanted to say about Georgia, but Nancy turned around. "It's okay. We're sorry we intruded. If you think of anything that might help us, please call or text me." She handed Tina the business card to their detective agency.

As she took it, Raff asked, "How did Georgia die?"

"She was shot," Nancy said. "On her boat at the whaling tour center. We're going there tomorrow to speak to her boss and co-workers."

"Does Shankar know?"

Raff's question took Cathy by surprise. "Why do you ask?"

Tina answered for her boyfriend. "Shankar was as hung up on Georgia as he was on me."

Nancy said, "Ginny didn't say anything about that to us. Was he stalking her, too?"

Tina nodded. "When I went to the police to file the

restraining order, Georgia was there reporting Shankar. It was quite embarrassing."

"Did she also file a restraining order?" Nancy wanted to know. So did Cathy. Tina shook her head. "No. She said she just wanted to report his behavior, but it helped me get one."

Mildred, who'd been looking at the paintings on the stairway, said, "Do you know where we can find Shankar?"

Cathy was surprised she suggested this because she'd made it clear to Nancy she wanted to go back to Maddie's house to get ready for Henry's arrival.

"You can find him at the hospital. I'm not sure he'll speak with you. If that's all you want with me, let me see you out." Tina turned and walked to the door. As they followed, Cathy glanced back downstairs and noticed Raff was no longer there.

CHAPTER TWELVE

Back in Nancy's car, Cathy said to Mildred, "I thought you were eager to get back to Maddie's house to prepare for meeting Henry tonight."

Mildred checked her watch. "There's enough time for that."

"Great! You can come with us to speak with Shankar," Nancy said. "Doesn't he sound like a creep?"

"He's a doctor," Cathy reminded her.

"I wouldn't want to be his patient."

Chester Hospital was ten minutes away from Fogport. Nancy parked in the visitor's lot. "We're here. C'mon, ladies. Disembark."

Cathy followed Mildred out of the car. They walked toward the white building as an ambulance sped up to the emergency entrance. "I hate hospitals." Nancy made a face. Cathy secretly agreed. She recalled the time she spent in one recovering from the accident that had claimed the lives of her parents.

Mildred said, "I'm not a fan either, but they do serve a purpose."

Stepping into the waiting area, Cathy saw people sitting and others standing. A few were gathered by the information desk. They all wore nervous expressions, waiting for news of a loved one.

When the line at the desk cleared, Nancy asked the woman there if Dr. Shah was on duty.

"Yes, he is. Do you have an appointment with him today?" She glanced over at Cathy and Mildred.

"No, uh. We just need a word with him. Does he have a break coming up?"

The woman glanced at her computer. "He has a pretty tight schedule today. You should call his office and make an appointment."

Nancy took out another business card and passed it to her. "We're detectives. I think he'll see us without an appointment."

The woman's face changed as she read the card. "Of course. Give me a minute. I'll speak with his nurse. I'm sure he can fit you in. He's between surgeries now."

As the woman left the desk, Nancy turned to Cathy. "I love the way our business cards open doors."

"I wonder what type of surgeon Dr. Shah is," Mildred said.

Her question hung in the air as a tall blond man in green scrubs approached them a few minutes later.

"I'm told you ladies are looking for me."

Cathy was surprised. She didn't expect Shankar to look like Steve. She pictured a dark-haired, dark-skinned man.

Nancy stepped forward. "Yes. My name is Nancy Meyers. I'm one of the detectives at the Hunt, Meyers, and Carter Detective Agency." She turned to Cathy. "This is my associate, Cathy Carter. Then she glanced at Mildred. "Ms. Hastings is a friend."

"Nice to meet you all. Care to join me in the lounge?"

Cathy couldn't help staring. The man seemed charming and not a stalker, but maybe that was part of his persona.

Catching her eyeing him, Shankar said, "Many people are taken aback by my appearance. My mother is Swedish. My father died when I was young, and she remarried a gentleman from India. He adopted me and gave me his name. I changed my first name, too. We lived in India for many years."

Nancy said, "That's interesting, and, yes, we'll be happy to join you in the lounge."

They followed Shankar down the hall to a room with swivel chairs, a couch, TV, dim lighting, and a coffee bar. As he opened the door for them, he said, "This is our staff lounge, but we also bring guests in here when necessary." Cathy figured that would be for breaking bad news gently. The place had a soothing effect with low piano music playing and furnishings in gray and pink with cream walls. It was a contrast to the hospital's sickly green corridors.

"Please have a seat. We're in luck that we can be private. This room gets crowded."

Nancy headed for the couch. The three of them sat on it. Shankar remained standing. "I really don't have much time, but I'm going to grab a quick coffee. Would any of you like anything?"

It was close to lunchtime, and Cathy's stomach was beginning to growl, but she was afraid to ask for food. Nancy, on the other hand, said, "I see they have sandwiches. We haven't had lunch yet."

He smiled. "Then please come up and choose what you want. It's on me."

Cathy couldn't believe how wrong her initial impression of him had been based on what she'd been told by Tina, but she had to keep an open mind. She followed Nancy to the counter.

Mildred said she only wanted coffee. She was saving up for dinner with Henry.

After choosing their sandwiches, Cathy and Nancy returned to the couch. Shankar handed Mildred her coffee that he'd prepared the way she asked and then sat across from them sipping his own.

"So, what can I do for you, detectives? I mean, detectives and friend." He looked them over through his blue eyes. Cathy felt him size her up. He was a wolf in sheep's clothing.

Nancy bit into her ham and cheese sandwich and swallowed. Wiping her mouth with a napkin, she said, "Are you aware that Georgia Hampton was murdered yesterday?"

Shankar lowered his gaze to the beige carpet. When he looked up, his expression was neutral. "I'm afraid not."

Cathy wondered if his reaction was one that he commonly used when hearing of a death. As a doctor, it would serve him well. She said, "You dated her once, after you broke up with Tina Farrell."

He gulped down a swig of coffee. "You're correct. I made a big mistake. I thought I was in love with Tina, but when I worked with Georgia planning the wedding..." He waved his large hands in the air. Cathy again wondered what surgeries he performed. "Well," he continued, "I fell in love with her, but she broke it off."

"Do you know why?" Mildred asked. Cathy realized she wanted to be included in this questioning.

He looked toward Mildred as he answered. "I believe she found someone else."

"What about Tina?" Nancy asked. "We spoke with her, and she said you've been stalking her. She even has a restraining order against you."

Cathy caught a bit of anger that flashed through Shankar's

blue eyes darkening them. "That's true. I've tried to reconcile with her. She took it the wrong way."

"That's odd," Cathy said, "because Tina also told us that Georgia had gone to the police about you pursuing her."

Shankar shrugged and gave a short laugh. "I wouldn't listen to anything Tina says. She's still not over my leaving her for Georgia."

"It seemed to us that she was," Nancy said putting aside her empty plastic sandwich container. "When we visited, her boyfriend was there."

Shankar quirked an eyebrow. "That doesn't mean anything. He was her rebound to get back at me." He drank the rest of his coffee quick and stood up. "Thank you for coming by, ladies, but I must get back to work now. Good luck with your murder investigation."

Nancy said, "Thank you for seeing us and for lunch."

When they were back in Nancy's car, she said, "That was a productive meeting. We learned that Georgia left Shankar for another man. We need to ask Ginny about that."

"Do you believe him?" Cathy asked. "He also denied stalking Tina and Georgia."

"I'm not making any decisions until I know more." Nancy looked toward Cathy next to her in the front seat. "I guess we should go back to Maddie's place to get ready for tonight."

Cathy was thinking of what Shankar told them. Something seemed wrong. It was then that Nancy's cell phone buzzed. "Excuse me, ladies. Let me answer this." She answered the call. "Nancy Meyers." It seemed she didn't recognize the caller.

"Oh! Really? That's great." Nancy smiled. "Let me put this on speaker, Ginny. Cathy and Mildred are with me."

Cathy heard the wedding planner's voice from the other

side of the cell phone. "I'll repeat what I said. You're in luck that there was a cancellation in September for a wedding at Waterside Gardens. Are any of you familiar with that venue?"

When no one replied, Nancy said, "No. Is it near Buttercup Bend?"

"Unfortunately, it's here on Long Island, but it's lovely. It features a lake, gazebo, beautiful gardens, and a restaurant where I can book the reception. But I'll need a deposit tomorrow. I can give you the address for you to meet me there to look over the place. Bring your fiancés if you want."

"Uh," Nancy paused. "Can we do it later in the week? We have an appointment tomorrow." Cathy knew she was thinking of the whale-watching tour with Tommy.

"Sorry, Nancy. We have a wait list for this venue."

Nancy sighed. "All right. Can we come early or tomorrow night?" Cathy recalled that the whale-watching tour started at noon and ran for four hours.

"The only availability I have during that timeframe is 9 a.m."

"That'll work. Thank you, Ginny. But can we arrange everything in three months?"

"If you like the place, I can make that happen. See you tomorrow. I'll text the address and directions to you."

CHAPTER THIRTEEN

As Nancy started the car, Cathy said, "I don't like the idea of visiting this venue Ginny found for us tomorrow. It'll be too far for our wedding guests to attend."

"I don't think so." Nancy clicked her phone into place in her dashboard's holder and began tapping in Maddie's address. "Everyone will enjoy a weekend on Long Island. I'm sure Maddie will host your grandmother at her house along with us. They'll be able to catch up with one another. As for the other guests, there are a lot of nice hotels on Long Island. We could get a group rate for them."

Mildred said, "I think Cathy's right. We should look closer to home."

Nancy started her car. "Before you both make up your mind to nix this place, I already agreed to meet Ginny there tomorrow. The guys will be here tonight, so it's perfect timing. Let's see what they think." Neither Cathy nor Mildred replied. They knew it was senseless to argue with Nancy, and she had a point about seeking the men's opinions.

. . .

When Nancy told Maddie about their plans to visit Waterside Gardens, she said, "How wonderful! I used to go there with my husband. Even before that, my parents used to take me and Florence there."

Cathy was shocked. "Gran has been there? How long has the place been open?"

"It's changed owners a few times, but the gardens opened in the early 1900s. They didn't always have weddings there. I'm not sure when they started that, but it's a beautiful place. You'll love it."

"It sounds nice, but it's a drive from Buttercup Bend."

"I already told you, Cat, that everyone can make it a weekend. A lot of people don't like driving home from weddings because they drink or are too tired, so I think this will work out well."

Maddie smiled. "I agree with Nancy. Once you make your decision, if you choose that as your wedding venue, I'll be happy to have Florence stay here with the three of you. It's been a long time since we've seen one another."

Nancy turned to Cathy and winked. "See? I told you."

Later that day, Cathy's cell phone buzzed. She'd received a text from Steve. "The guys are here," she told Nancy and Mildred. They were sitting outside on Maddie's porch sipping fresh-squeezed lemonade her great-aunt had served them.

"Cool!" Nancy said. "Find out what hotel they're at. We can go over and meet them."

Maddie, stepping outside with a tray of cookies, said, "Have them come here. They can eat dinner with us. I'd love to meet them."

"Are you sure?"

"Of course, Catherine. I was thinking of barbecuing tonight. I have plenty of burgers and hot dogs."

Nancy smiled. "That sounds great. Brian loves to barbecue. He'll be happy to help you."

"Henry barbecues also," Mildred added. Cathy didn't offer Steve's help because she wasn't sure how experienced he was around a grill. She texted him back Maddie's suggestion, and his answer was quick.

"They're all up for it, Maddie. Thank you."

"My pleasure."

The men arrived together in Steve's car. Cathy made the introductions, and Maddie invited them out on the patio where the burgers, hot dogs, buns, and condiments had been placed on a picnic table.

"It's nice back here," Steve commented, glancing around at the deck chairs, a tree swing that swayed gently in the late afternoon breeze, and two rockers. Nancy had helped Maddie bring folding chairs to accompany them all, and Cathy had helped her string up the outdoor lights.

"Thank you," Maddie said. "When the kids were small, we had a lot of barbecues. They invited their friends. Those parties lasted quite late."

"How many children do you have?" Cathy asked.

"Two, a son and a daughter. Christine is my daughter's child. Her parents moved out of state, but she chose to stay here. My son never married but has a nice job in California."

"That's interesting," Nancy said, "but I'm starving. We can chat later. Let's get the barbecue going. Guys, can you give Maddie a hand?"

Brian, at Nancy's side, took a short bow and said, "Chef

Fitzcullins at your service. I've never burned a burger or charred a hot dog."

Henry joined him at the barbecue. "I also have expertise grilling. My late wife wasn't much of a cook." He winked at Mildred.

Cathy was surprised when Steve joined them. "My specialty is flipping. It's all in the wrist. Have a seat and continue chatting with the ladies, Ms. Mayfair, while us guys take care of the dinner you were kind enough to invite us to join you at."

Maddie smiled. "Thank you all, and please call me Maddie."

After the men finished barbecuing, Cathy had to revise her opinion about too many cooks in the kitchen. Steve, Brian, and Henry worked well together and didn't get in each other's way. The result was plates of delicious and well-cooked meats. Christine also dropped by, not to bring more clothes this time, but a scrumptious apple pie she'd baked with her kids that Maddie added scoops of vanilla ice cream to that melted on the warm pie. Everyone dug in, and there wasn't a piece left.

As they sat on the patio digesting their food, Nancy mentioned the appointment at Waterside Gardens. The men seemed interested. "I know of that place," Steve said. "I visited once when I first became a gardener. It gave me a lot of inspiration." This was a fact Cathy hadn't known.

"It is somewhat far," Henry said. "But, as Nancy pointed out, our guests will probably enjoy a weekend on Long Island."

Brian was the only one who wasn't happy with the idea. "It's not the distance so much, but the cost. I know we're all splitting the wedding expenses, but putting people up in a hotel could be expensive."

"Not necessarily," Maddie said, "You should be able to get a group rate, and your guests wouldn't expect you to pay their way. I'm also happy to host the ladies and my sister right here."

Cathy realized they hadn't discussed the guest list or the members of the wedding party. "If we choose Waterside Gardens tomorrow, we have a lot of planning to do in a short amount of time."

"Three months isn't short, Cat. Remember, it's the three of us doing the planning, so that should make it faster."

"I don't think so," Mildred said. "We all have different ideas of what we want and who we'd like to invite."

"That won't be an issue," Nancy pointed out. "We're close friends and have similar friends. Brian and I have been discussing the guests and the wedding party. My father will come up from Florida to give me away. Brian wants Leroy to be his best man." She glanced at Cathy, "Since I would've wanted you to be my maid of honor and I think you would've wanted me, I suggest that we skip the maids of honors and bridesmaids. However, it would be cute to have a flower girl."

Henry said, "I'd like Dylan from Oaks Landing to be my best man, so we could have Sheri come with her parents. She'd make a sweet flower girl for the three of us."

Cathy said, "I know Danielle is due to have the baby soon. Will she be able to travel at that time?"

"If not, Sheri can come with her father," Nancy said. "But it'll be great to see Danielle and the new baby, too."

"I've been wondering about them and also about Lulu if she had her baby yet." Lulu was the llama at the farm where Cathy, Nancy, and Mildred helped solve a murder in January. When they left, they learned the llama was pregnant as well as the woman whose mother's murder they'd been investigating.

"Me, too," Nancy said. She turned to Mildred. "Do you know who you'd like to give you away?"

"I was thinking of my son-in-law if he and my daughter are able to attend."

"I'd love to meet them," Henry said.

Maddie smiled. "It sounds like you have a lot of your planning already organized. Now you just need to make up your minds about where you're having the wedding."

After discussing the wedding plans, the topic turned to the whale-watching tour. Steve said he was prepared with an anti-nausea pill he'd take before departure. Brian and Henry both said they had sea legs so wouldn't need anything. Cathy wondered if she should ask Steve for a pill because she often had issues with her stomach. Despite her earlier comment about being adventurous, Mildred said she'd stick to the middle of the boat where the motion was felt less, and Nancy laughed. "I'll be up front with Brian and Henry. Maybe I'll ask Tommy if I can ride shotgun with him."

"Famous last words," Brian teased her.

Henry said, "If Millie is staying inside, I'll keep her company."

Maddie said, "None of you should be too proud to take something. There's been hurricane warnings up the coast, so the seas may be rocky."

"I'll bring enough for everyone," Steve promised.

Cathy said, "While I'm nervous about being on that boat, what worries me more is that Nancy will be interrogating Tommy about the murder. That's why she wants to ride shotgun with him."

"Murder?" Henry raised a gray eyebrow. "Millie didn't tell me anything about a murder."

Brian said, "Neither did Nancy say anything to me."

"Looks like Cathy's the only one who confides in her

fiancé," Steve pointed out. "I wasn't thrilled when she mentioned it, but it gave me even more reason to drive down here and accompany her on the whale-watching tour." His words made Cathy feel relieved she'd told him.

"I'm sorry I didn't mention the murder," Nancy told Brian, but it was said offhandedly.

Brian shrugged. "Not the first time you've kept me out of the loop, hon, but I'll forgive you if you promise to be careful."

As Nancy nodded, Henry turned to Mildred. "I thought we said honesty was the most important thing in our relationship, but I'll also forgive you, Millie, if you make the same promise."

Mildred said, "Thank you, dear. I will."

When the evening ended, the men gave their ladies kisses and thanked Maddie and Christine. Maddie said they could come for breakfast the next morning before going to meet the wedding planner at Waterside Gardens, but they declined. "The hotel we're staying at includes free breakfast," Brian said. "I know it won't compare to yours, but we're fine meeting Cathy, Nancy, and Mildred at the gardens."

Cathy almost choked, thinking of the oatmeal Maddie served each morning. She almost wished she could meet them at the hotel and dine with them, but Nancy said, "That's fine. I gave you the address. Please be on time. We don't want to keep Ginny waiting, and we have a tight day with the whale tour afterwards."

That night, in bed, Cathy asked Nancy, "What do you hope to accomplish tomorrow?"

"What do you mean, Cat? Ginny's showing us a wedding

venue, and we need to decide if we want to put down a deposit to book it."

"That's not what I'm talking about. I'm referring to the whale-watching tour."

Nancy turned around in her bed to face the window, gathering the blanket around her. "What I want to accomplish is seeing whales. I think that's what people do on whale-watching tours."

Cathy sighed. "I'm talking about the murder investigation."

"Oh, that! I'll observe, throw in a few questions, and feel out the employees."

"Are you going to tell them that we're detectives?"

"Tommy already knows, and he seems cool with that."

"What about Captain Sharp?"

Nancy reached over and turned out the light next to her bed. "Don't worry, Cat. I know how to deal with men. Goodnight. We need our rest for tomorrow."

CHAPTER FOURTEEN

The next day Cathy swallowed down another bowl of oatmeal only to satisfy Maddie. At home with Gran, they usually ate different morning meals. Florence often cooked eggs in a variety of ways or Cathy's favorite French toast with strawberries, syrup, and whipped cream. Nancy didn't seem to mind because Cathy knew she often skipped breakfast altogether because she tended to sleep late, and Mildred was too kind to complain.

Maddie wished them good luck on their appointments and waved goodbye from the door as Cathy got into the back seat of Nancy's car. Mildred sat up front as in their previous arrangements.

"Are you both ready?" Nancy asked.

Cathy fastened her seat belt. "Sure am. It's a beautiful day to tour a garden."

Waterside Gardens was a ten-minute ride from Minnick. As they pulled into the parking lot, Cathy saw Steve's pickup truck.

"Steve's here," she said.

"That means Brian and Henry are, too." Nancy parked in the spot next to them as the three men got out of the car.

"Beat you, ladies," Steve grinned. He was wearing a white T-shirt and jeans. Brian was dressed more formally in a brown suit. Henry was wearing clothes that could fit either a casual or semi-formal meeting. As the women joined them, Nancy ran up to Brian and gave him a quick kiss on the lips. "I hope you're changing for the whale tour."

Brian nodded. "Yeah, Nance. I have a change of clothes in Steve's car. What about you and Cathy? Those dresses look nice but not appropriate for boating on the high seas."

"We also brought a change of clothes." Christine had given Cathy and Nancy some casual items to wear as well as nice dresses. Mildred was dressed simply in a navy and white blouse over white capris. "I'm fine with this." She looked around. "And Henry looks like he'll fit in with the boat tour, too." Henry was dressed as casually as Steve in a green polo shirt and brown trousers with sneakers. Glancing down at them, he said, "I figured we'd be doing a lot of walking in the gardens, and these are also safe for the boat's deck."

Brian looked at his own shoes. "I should've thought of that."

Cathy was glad she'd worn flats, and Nancy, who had a closet full of shoes of various heights, had chosen low pumps.

"Where are we meeting Ginny?" Mildred asked.

Nancy glanced toward a building in the distance. "She told me we can check in at the office."

The park's office was a brick building bordered by flowers. Steve admired them. "Looks like they have a great landscaper. Those marigolds are huge."

"We haven't seen the rest of the gardens," Nancy said, entering after Brian held the door open for her.

When Cathy stepped in, she saw Ginny immediately. The blonde was standing with a clipboard, looking official in a plum suit. A purple and pink flowered scarf accented the outfit. "Good morning, everyone," she said, glancing around. "Thank you for coming today. I know you have a tight schedule."

Nancy said, "Nothing's more important than planning our wedding."

Ginny smiled. "Glad to hear it. The gardens aren't open yet, but I managed to secure a private tour. Our guide will be here shortly. In the meantime, I have a few questions." She looked at her clipboard. "As I mentioned, if you're happy with this venue, I need a deposit to hold it. There's a separate fee for a minister unless you're providing your own. I'll also need the menu suggestions and if any of your guests are allergic to anything."

Cathy said, "We haven't even sent out invitations, and we won't need a minister. I'm planning to ask our pastor to preside."

Ginny turned to her. "That's fine." She tore off a sheet of paper. "You can take this and return it by the end of the week with all the details."

Nancy grabbed the paper. "I'll handle that and also the deposit. My friends can pay me back."

"What are we talking here?" Steve asked. "How much is the deposit?"

Ginny cleared her throat. Cathy was amazed that she appeared so in control after having lost her sister recently. It was a change from when they'd seen her the day before. "Although we aren't sure what the final price will be depending on your selections, the venue deposit is ten percent of the rental fee."

"And that is?" Brian prompted.

"Three thousand dollars."

Steve made a low whistle.

Henry said, "It costs $30,000 to have our wedding here?"

Nancy said, "That's reasonable. It'll be $1,000 for each couple for the deposit and then $9,000 more per couple for the balance."

Ginny nodded. "For this location, it's quite a steal, and it also includes the reception costs but not any of the extras you might want." She glanced toward the door where a man was standing signaling to them. He was tall with a dark beard and glasses. "Oh, there's Mr. Gannon now. Let's join him outside."

When they were gathered in front of the building, Ginny introduced their tour guide. "This is Mr. Roger Gannon. He's the manager here at the gardens."

Mr. Gannon said, "It's a pleasure to meet you all. I have to admit that, although we've had many weddings here, yours will be the first triple wedding. We had a double wedding last summer. It was beautiful. I think you'll find our grounds lovely and romantic." He turned around. "Our first stop will be the gazebo. That's where you'll make your nuptials. A minister is provided if you wish. Please note that chairs will be set up in front of the gazebo."

Ginny said, "They're using their own pastor, Roger, but thanks for mentioning that option."

He smiled and began walking. Ginny fell into step next to him, holding her clipboard, while the others followed behind.

Cathy was impressed with the greenery around them. The air was scented with roses as the group passed under a rose arbor that led toward the gazebo set on a hill.

"Glad I wore my flats," Nancy whispered to Brian who whispered back, "I hope there's no goose poo around here."

Nancy shushed him.

When they arrived at the gazebo, Cathy saw that it overlooked a lake in which swans and ducks swam. "This is beautiful," she said.

"Tell them about the legend," Ginny urged Gannon.

Their guide smiled. "Oh, yes. I mustn't forget to share that piece of trivia. The legend is that the couples who wed in the gazebo will be blessed with many years of happiness."

"Has that come true?" Cathy asked.

Gannon looked at her through his glasses. "I'm honored to say that the divorce rate of our couples is low. We've had over a hundred marriages performed here, and the longest-wed couple just celebrated their twenty-fifth anniversary."

"Interesting," Henry said. "You keep statistics?"

"Oh, yes. We have everything computerized. We also invite couples back to reaffirm their vows in an annual ceremony."

Cathy suspected the legend was a promotional gimmick, but the anniversary ceremony sounded nice.

"Will you need a photographer?" Gannon asked. "We can recommend a few who have worked here and done phenomenal jobs."

"We hadn't thought of that yet," Nancy said. "Cathy takes great photos for our local paper, but she can't be expected to photograph her own wedding."

Ginny laughed lightly. "Of course not. Let's check out the view from the gazebo, shall we?"

The group walked over to the dome-shaped structure which was lined with a circular bench and open at the front. "That's where your pastor will stand," she said, pointing to the area that overlooked the lake. "The guest's seats will be set up on the hill."

"Is there enough room for all of us?" Mildred asked.

"Yes, but I suggest that each couple take a turn. After you're all pronounced man and wife, you'll meet up with your bridal parties for photos and then head to the reception area which Mr. Gannon will show you next."

Gannon, prompted, began walking around the gazebo. Everyone followed. Cathy saw a building across in the distance. They skirted the lake and then came upon it. Gannon stopped. "This is Waterside Terrace, our premiere restaurant. For private parties, we use the Lake Room which overlooks the lake from the other side. Your cocktail hour will be set up in the Rose Room. If weather permits, we pull back the tenting, so your guests can mingle outdoors."

"That sounds great," Nancy said. Cathy watched her eyes light up as she gazed around at the flowerbeds bordering the restaurant and the climbing vines of ivy that clung to it. Steve let out another low whistle.

"There's a koi pond in back of the restaurant," Ginny said. "It's a wonderful spot for photos in addition to the ones you'll take by the gazebo."

Gannon smiled. "Let me show you the Rose Room first and then we can view the pond and, lastly, the Lake Room. We have musicians for hire, too, if you'd like a band."

Another detail they hadn't considered. Henry said, "I think live music is best, but Millie and I would prefer Big Band tunes or Sinatra songs."

Mildred tapped his arm. "Speak for yourself, dear. I like a good boogie or rock number myself."

"Our musicians can play a variety of music," Gannon said, leading them around the restaurant to a tented area. He stepped through an opening and signaled for them to follow.

As soon as Cathy did, she whiffed the scent of roses again and viewed round tables covered in white cloths set in a perimeter. Each table held a bud vase with a red, white, or yellow rose and a candle in a silver holder. On the other side of the room, a long table, also covered in white and garlanded with roses, contained shiny wine glasses. Behind it, stood a bar. There was one wall with a door that she assumed led into the main restaurant.

Steve asked, "Do you have roses in here all year?"

"We do. Our florist provides them or imports them for us."

Cathy added flowers to her mental list of items to consider for the wedding.

"This is where your guests will meet you after the photo sessions," Gannon continued. "Our waiters will circulate around the room and serve cocktails and hors-d'oeuvres."

"You'll select the choices for those on the sheet I gave you," Ginny said, glancing at Nancy.

After a few minutes, as they strolled around the room taking everything in, Gannon walked to the other side and pushed aside part of the tent, revealing the view of the pond, and beckoned them to join him.

True to his word, a bunch of orange koi darted through the water that also featured lily pods abloom with pink, white, and blue water lilies.

"Oooh," Nancy said admiring them. She walked to the edge of the pond and gazed down into the water.

Steve stood a few feet away. "This gives me landscaping ideas. Cathy, you might like a koi pond at Rainbow Gardens."

Cathy shrugged. "Are they difficult to maintain?"

"I'll research that. If we don't do it near Florence's house, we can do it near the new place."

Before Cathy could comment, Gannon said, "I can give you the card of the person who installed this." He checked his watch. "The gardens open soon, so let's go back inside to see the Lake Room."

. . .

The room where their reception would take place featured floor-to-ceiling windows that looked out upon the lake and a large dance floor. Tables with white cloths similar to the Rose Room skirted the area. A bar stood in the corner, larger than the one outside, and there was a platform where the musicians could play. A microphone was set up by a podium.

"You'll have an MC," Gannon explained. "It gives order to the reception. There'll be the first dance, the cake cutting, etc."

Since Cathy's father had perished in the automobile accident, her brother Doug, besides giving her away, would be dancing the father/daughter dance with her. Mildred would be dancing with her son-in-law. Cathy had never met Nancy's father, but she was looking forward to meeting him and her mother when they came up from Florida. Nancy's sister would be coming, too.

Henry asked, "Do you supply the cake?"

"Yes. We order it from the bakery we use," Gannon said. "You select the filling and frosting. The cake topper might be an issue with the three of you marrying. We could have separate cakes for each of you, but that would incur additional cost. Alternately, instead of our usual round cake, we could do a sheet cake where there should be room for each of your toppers."

"That sounds confusing," Cathy said, trying to picture it.

"I wouldn't worry about it," Nancy said. She looked toward Brian. "I already have our topper. I had it custom-made. I could share that info with you and Mildred."

"This is too much fuss," Mildred said. "I wanted something simple. I'm still considering eloping."

Henry said, "You'll do no such thing, dear. We need to celebrate with your friends, and many of mine are coming from Oaks Landing."

Ginny turned the discussion back to the deposit. "Since the

gardens are opening shortly, I need your decision about booking this venue and the deposit."

Nancy took her checkbook from her purse. "I'll make out the check right now. Do I write it to the gardens or your wedding service?"

"You can make it out to Waterside Gardens, but please return the sheet I gave you by Friday, and I'll handle the other arrangements."

Cathy asked, "How can we know how many people will attend by then?"

"You only need an estimate," Gannon explained. "You can confirm the number a week before the wedding."

As Nancy handed her check to the manager, she said, "Then we better get moving on the invitations and other details. Thank you for the tour. We're excited about having our wedding here."

CHAPTER FIFTEEN

Since they had a few hours before the whale tour, Cathy and Nancy took their change of clothes from Nancy's car and brought them into the restaurant's ladies' room to change. Henry invited Mildred to go out to a late breakfast with him. Steve and Brian said they'd drop them off on their way back to the hotel and then pick them up before driving back to the dock. Nancy gave Steve the address.

Cathy and Nancy were the only ones in Waterside Terrace's restroom. As Cathy changed in a stall, Nancy spoke to her from outside. "I always judge a place by its bathroom, and this one earns five stars from me. When you get out, check the marble sinks. Most importantly, they have beautiful hand towels. Granted they're paper, but not that ugly brown that a lot of places use now. These are white with imprinted flowers. Fancy. There's a liquid soap dispenser but also bar soaps in different shapes. One is a cat. It's adorable. You've got to see it."

"I'll be right there." Cathy finished dressing in cutoff jeans and a blue and white striped T-shirt along with Christine's white flats that fit her perfectly and then joined Nancy at the sink where she was fixing her makeup.

"Why are you putting on so much makeup for a whale tour?"

"I want to look my best. Brian's here, and a little flirting might also be necessary to obtain certain information from Tommy."

"You're too much, Nance."

"I know. Now check out these soaps. Aren't they cute?" She picked up the white, cat-shaped one and showed it to Cathy. "It smells nice, too. Sniff!"

Cathy laughed and pushed Nancy's hand aside gently. "It's pretty, but I'm not sniffing soap. Put it back." She walked over to the soap dispenser, pushed it, and lathered up her hands. Then she took a paper towel from a silver basket and dried them. "I agree everything here is nice, but that's because the place is so expensive."

Nancy shrugged. "That's true." She put the cat soap back in the dish with the others. "There's something I want to run by you, Cat."

"If it's more about the murder, I'd rather not hear it."

"No. It's about our wedding. I have a feeling Brian and Steve are plotting something."

"What?"

"I'm not sure, but I don't think Brian is on board with a lot of my suggestions about the wedding. It's the bride's day, so I can't see why he would mind unless it's the expense."

"There are a lot of decisions we need to make, and it isn't easy pleasing six people."

"Three brides."

Cathy laughed. "I stand corrected. We're not going to make everyone happy. Waterside is a beautiful place for the wedding and reception. I'm just curious why Ginny isn't as broken up about her sister as she seemed to be yesterday. Even if they didn't get along well, she's acting like nothing happened. I find that cold."

"She might be covering up her feelings. A lot of people, when they're grieving, throw themselves into work."

"I guess, but it doesn't sit well with me. Someone killed Georgia. It's likely a relative, and Ginny was the closest one."

Nancy nodded. "We need to investigate further. I have a suggestion. We're supposed to meet everyone at the dock at 11:30 for the noon tour." She glanced at her watch. "It's 10:30 now. What if we get there by eleven and talk to people beforehand?"

Cathy considered the idea. "We could do that. I really want to meet this Captain Sharp."

"Me, too. Let's get going. Mildred and Henry are very prompt and might be there already with Brian and Steve."

Cathy smiled. "Steve's the one driving, and he's like you. He's prompt for gardening appointments but never on time for social gatherings. It frustrates me."

"You could've had Michael," Nancy teased.

"Stop it! I don't regret my decision for a minute, and he's going out with Stacey now. I couldn't be happier."

Nancy grabbed her car keys, and Cathy followed her back to her car. "You get the front seat this time."

Cathy got in and fastened her seat belt.

The dock was as she remembered it except for a police car parked by the gate. Blue lettering against the white read, "Fogport P.D." As Nancy drove toward the building that housed the tour office, the car pulled away.

"I wonder if they were talking with Sharp," Nancy said.

"If that's the case, we better not interrupt."

"Why not? We're here for a whale tour."

Cathy rolled her eyes. "Nance, you know as well as I do, that we're investigating Georgia's murder."

"We don't have to tell anyone that."

"They'll figure it out on their own, especially since you told them we're detectives."

"Maybe not, if they're anything like Sheriff Miller."

Cathy didn't share Nancy's view of Leroy. She knew Nancy wanted to believe he was incompetent because of her faith in Howard. But Cathy shrugged off a reply as she followed her friend toward the office. A seagull swooped by, and the cloudy skies suddenly brightened. A light wind ruffled her hair.

When they got within a few feet of the door, she heard voices. Cathy recognized Tommy's but not the man who was speaking to him.

"I agree with Officer Dooley. We have to cancel all whale tours until this mess is cleared up."

"Do you really think that's necessary, Captain?"

"Yes, Mueller, I do. You had no right to book a tour with those detectives. The only reason they're interested is to snoop into our affairs."

Cathy placed a hand on Nancy's arm and whispered, "We better not go in now."

"I think we should. We have to defend ourselves. We're paying for the tour, and they can't cancel it on us at the last minute."

Before Cathy could stop her, Nancy walked up to the door and tapped briskly.

Tommy answered. When he saw them, he said, "You're early, and, uh, there's a problem with the boat. We have to cancel the tour. I was about to call you."

Nancy pushed ahead of him. "The boat is fine. We heard you talking. I want to speak with your captain."

Tommy stepped back, and Cathy followed Nancy inside. A stout man wearing a white cap stared at them. He sat behind a desk and was holding a coffee mug with the Fogport Café written across it. There was a half-eaten sandwich on a paper plate across from him. Cathy also noticed a painting on the wall behind his desk that featured sailboats on a stormy sea. The sea was as dark as his eyes.

"Are you Captain Sharp?" Nancy asked.

The man placed his coffee cup next to his sandwich, tipped his cap, and brushed a hand across his dark beard. "That's me, ma'am. Who may I ask are you? The dock is closed today. We had an, uh, incident this week."

"I'm Nancy Meyers and this is Cathy Carter. We have an appointment for a whale tour this afternoon with Mr. Mueller."

Recognition appeared in the captain's black eyes. He touched his beard again. Cathy thought it was an unconscious movement. "The detectives? Oh. Mr. Mueller made a mistake when he booked the tour. The police are keeping our business closed until further notice. We'll refund your money, of course."

"We're not here as detectives," Nancy said. She'd adopted her warrior pose with hands on her hips. "Our fiancés are joining us on the tour along with another couple who are friends of ours. They'll be here shortly."

"I don't care when they're here," Sharp said. "You can call them or wait until they arrive, but there won't be any tour today."

Tommy stepped forward. "Captain, I don't mind taking them out. I already checked the boat."

"Mr. Mueller, the police have requested that the tours be

cancelled. I don't plan to break the law. If you insist, you won't have a job when we reopen."

Suddenly, someone walked through the door. Cathy, who was still standing in front of it, jumped. When she turned around, she came face-to-face with Raphael Wright.

"Excuse me," he said, "I was told there's a whale tour this afternoon."

Tommy said, "Sorry, Raff, but it's been cancelled."

Raphael walked over to the captain. "Is that true, Dan?"

Sharp's expression changed. Cathy saw him swallow. His eyes cast downward. "I didn't realize you were called, Raff. I'll permit the tour since you're here."

Cathy was confused. How did the captain know the artist, and why was he here for their private tour?

Nancy said, "Good! I'd hate to publish anything derogatory about your business in the *Buttercup Bugle*. I'm sure it's taken enough of a hit by the murder."

After Nancy made her comment, no one spoke until she turned around, looked at Raff, and asked the question uppermost in Cathy's mind, "What are you doing here?"

"You know one another?" Tommy asked.

Raff smiled. "Yes. Ms. Carter and Ms. Meyers were at my house yesterday. It's nice to see them again." He directed his blue eyes at Nancy. "I'm joining your tour for two reasons. First, there's usually a naturalist on board for whale tours. Second, I enjoy sketching the whales and other sea creatures we spot."

"What is a naturalist?" Cathy asked.

"Ever heard of Charles Darwin?"

Cathy had studied the scientist in an anthropology class. As she nodded, she thought about Georgia's tour. "You say you go on every tour. Were you going on Georgia's?"

He shook his head. "No. Georgia uses another naturalist on her tours."

Cathy could understand why, given the fact that Raff was involved with Tina, who'd been hurt by Georgia.

"Which naturalist was going on Georgia's tour? We didn't see anyone when we boarded the boat with Mr. Mueller," Nancy pointed out.

Captain Sharp answered her question. "The police asked me about that. Georgia made her own arrangements with naturalists. We have a list, and the police are contacting everyone on it."

"I'd like to see that list," Nancy said.

The captain hesitated. "I don't think that's necessary."

Before Nancy could argue with him, Raff cut in. "Excuse me, but there's no harm in sharing information, Dan."

Cathy again wondered about the relationship between the two men. The captain walked to the desk in the corner, opened a drawer, and withdrew a sheet of paper. "You can take a photo of this with your phone," he told Nancy.

She did as he suggested. "Thank you."

He nodded and then, finishing his sandwich, threw it and the paper plate in the nearby trash can and picked up his coffee cup. Making a face, he said, as he gulped down the drink, "This is cold already."

It was then that Cathy heard voices and turned to see Steve, Brian, Henry, and Mildred standing at the door.

"The rest of our group is here," she said, going to let them in.

"Don't bother," Tommy said. "We'll meet them outside. I need to tell you all a few things before we begin the tour."

. . .

After everyone had exchanged introductions, Tommy led them to his boat, the *Lucky Maiden*. Angel was there. She waved to them. "I swabbed the deck, Tommy," she said. "It's all set for you."

Tommy smiled. "Thanks, Angel. I cleaned it earlier, but it's nice of you to give it another go-over. I wasn't sure you were coming today. The captain almost nixed the tour because of the cops, but Raff came to our rescue." She jumped off the boat and gave him a quick kiss. "I had some work to tie up around here and when you told me you were taking people out, I thought I'd help. Have fun. I hope you see lots of whales. I'll catch you later."

As Angel walked away, Cathy couldn't help but stare at the boat next to Tommy's that was covered in yellow crime-scene tape. Georgia's boat, the *Lady Star*.

"I have to go over some safety precautions before we board," Tommy explained, "and also offer the proviso that we may not see any whales on this trip."

Nancy took a pair of binoculars from her purse and slung them over her neck. "It doesn't matter to me. I think it's fun just being on the high seas."

Steve mimicked a yawn. "As long as my pills prevent me from getting seasick and I'm not too bored."

Raff, who stood next to Tommy, said, "Don't worry. I can't promise you you'll be comfortable, but you won't be bored. I'll fill you in on whales and other sea life throughout our journey."

Nancy, unexpectedly, blurted out, "I'm sure you will, but I'd like to know your connection to the captain. You certainly have him wrapped around your finger. Is he a friend? A relative?"

Raff smiled. "Dan is my brother-in-law. I introduced him to my older sister, Eloise, a few years ago. I guess he feels beholden to me."

"That depends on how happy his marriage is," Nancy said with a smile.

Raff smiled back. "You have a point there, Miss Meyers."

Tommy said, "Come aboard, everyone. Sit or stand wherever you want. I'll announce any whales or other sea animals we spot."

As they boarded the boat, Nancy walked up to Tommy. "Can I ride shotgun with you? I love having a front-row seat."

"That'll cost extra, Nancy."

"I don't mind."

"I was joking." He smiled. "Follow me."

Cathy watched as Nancy went up front with Tommy to the enclosed captain's quarters. Steve turned to her. "Where do you want to sit, Cat?"

Before she could answer, Mildred said, "I don't know about you two, but I'm heading for mid-ship where there'll be less motion."

"I'll come with you," Henry said, "although I'm confident I won't get sick, I won't abandon you, and we can still get a good view."

Steve said, "I'm with you guys. I don't trust the pills I took to keep the seasickness at bay, but if you'd rather sit outside, Cathy, that's fine with me."

She felt torn. She wanted an unobstructed view of the whales if they were lucky enough to see them, but she hated to leave Steve, Mildred, and Henry alone in the enclosed midship room. Suddenly, she felt a tug at her elbow. She'd forgotten about Brian. "Come with me, Cat. We can sit outside. Let those party poopers and my deserting fiancé enjoy themselves. I have some cool binoculars we can share, and it's nothing like sea air to liven the spirits."

Cathy followed Brian who took a seat on the benches that lined the outside of the boat. He patted a spot next to him as he reached into the backpack he was carrying and removed a black case. He pulled binoculars from it and hung them around his neck. Looking through them, he said, "These are great. I can see all the way to the other side of the harbor. Want to try them?"

Cathy sat next to him. "There's nothing to see right now, but I'll check them out when we start moving."

Just as she said that a voice came through a speaker. It was Raff's. She hadn't realized he'd gone to the upper deck and was talking from there. "Good afternoon, folks. Welcome to Captain Sharp's Whale-Watching Tour. I'm Raphael Wright, a naturalist, and your guide today. We'll be leaving the dock shortly on our way out to the ocean to view whales. I have some interesting facts to share about them."

Cathy heard the motor start as the boat began to move gently away from the pier. She imagined Nancy sitting with Tommy and asking a slew of questions.

Then she focused on Raff's commentary as Brian handed her his binoculars.

CHAPTER SIXTEEN

Cathy looked through Brian's binoculars. "Wow! I can see pretty far with these."

"Wait until we spot whales. You're free to borrow them whenever you want."

"Thanks!" Cathy was tempted to ask him if Nancy was right that he wasn't on board with their wedding plans, but when she started to mouth the words, Raff continued his introduction.

"Before I talk about whales, I'd like to mention that I'm an artist as well as a naturalist. I have an easel set up on the top deck and will be sketching the sea life and other sights we pass. You're free to come up and watch me work and also buy my renditions as souvenirs if you like."

"I can't believe it. That takes a lot of nerve," Brian said. "Have you seen this guy's art?"

"Actually, I have. It's nice, but I agree that he shouldn't be advertising his sketches and hawking his pieces to the customers who purchase tickets for the tours."

"Maybe we should go up and watch what he's doing," Brian

suggested. "It would be interesting to see an artist at work, and I'm sure Nancy will want to buy a souvenir for this trip."

Cathy knew her friend would definitely want a memento of the tour. She stood up. "I guess we can still have a good view of the whales from the top deck."

"Sure. If not, there's always the binoculars." Brian followed her up the stairs to where Raff was standing in front of his easel.

"Thanks for joining me," he said. "There's not much to see yet, but I'll start with a practice sketch of the ship and the bay. I'll also continue my whale talk, and you can ask me any questions afterwards."

Cathy nodded and took a seat next to Brian again. From here, they could see the enclosed mid-ship room where Mildred, Henry, and Steve were sitting at a table talking.

Raff spoke into the microphone as he drew a few strokes on the canvas. Cathy marveled at how he could multitask. His hands seemed to move in sync with his words.

"Back to my whale talk, folks. There's a lot to know about whales. If you're interested, I can recommend some books, or you can Google to your heart's content. But for the purpose of this trip, I'd like to mention a few interesting facts. The first whales appeared fifty million years ago after the dinosaurs but before humans. At that time, they were known as artiodactyl, a four-legged hoofed land mammal. Today, there are two types of whales – baleen and toothed whales. There are only fifteen baleen whale species, and most of them are larger than the seventy-seven species of toothed whales, except the sperm whale, the largest tooth whale." He paused as he shaded in an area. Cathy saw that the boat was taking shape on the canvas. Raff stepped back from the mike and whispered to them, "By the time I'm done with my talk, this sketch will be complete."

Brian gave Raff a thumbs up.

"The blue whale is the largest baleen whale," he continued. "Humpbacks and gray whales make long seasonal migrations. Baleen whales are usually found alone or in small groups and don't echolocate. For those who don't know what echolocation is, I'll define it. It's the process in which an animal assesses its surroundings by emitting sounds and listening to echoes as the sound waves reflect off different objects in the environment. Common mammals that use echolocation are bats and dolphins, as well as toothed whales."

Cathy wondered if Steve was finding this information interesting or had dozed off from a combination of his seasickness pills and boredom. She found Raff's talk engaging, as she didn't know much about whales.

"Toothed whales consist of ten families including dolphins. Yes, dolphins are considered whales."

"I never knew that," Brian said to her.

"Neither did I."

Raff continued. "As I said earlier, toothed whales use echolocation. They're also sociable and often live in groups. The sperm whale family of toothed whales have the largest-sized brains on the planet and hunt giant squid. The famous classic, *Moby Dick*, is a story about whalers hunting sperm whales." Raff took a breath.

"The Beluga whale and Narwhale family are toothed whales living in cold, arctic waters. Narwhales are famous for their unicorn-like tusks. However, the whales we may spot today will be humpbacks, fin whales, and minke whales, all baleen whales, but we might also see dolphins and porpoises, which are toothed whales."

He made some quick final strokes on his sketch and then ended his talk. "Enough about whales. If you've been watching our journey, you'll notice we've entered the ocean. Keep your eyes, binoculars, and cameras ready. Captain Mueller will notify us of any whales or other sea creatures we encounter." He took the canvas off the easel and placed it against the railing across from Cathy and Brian. "Not bad," he said, admiring his work. Cathy agreed despite her feeling that Raff was egotistical. In her experience, most artists were.

Brian said, "Nancy might like that one. How much are you asking?"

"Normally, I sell my work for a hundred to two hundred dollars, but I'm giving a ten percent discount to the people on this cruise."

Brian raised an eyebrow. "That's still a lot of money. It's just a sketch, and you aren't famous, at least I've never heard of you."

Raff smiled. "You will one day. I'm not a starving artist."

Cathy asked, "Do you sell your work on each of the whale-watching tours?"

He nodded. "Yes. I do well. People buy them as souvenirs," he glanced at Brian, "as your girlfriend might."

"She's my fiancée," Brian clarified, "and she likes to shop."

Raff laughed. "Most women do."

"Does Tina? Did Georgia?" Cathy asked.

Raff looked away. He cleared his throat and then replied in a flat tone, "Tina did for sure. I wouldn't know about Georgia. You would need to ask Dr. Shah."

It wasn't lost on Cathy that she'd ruffled Raff. She wondered why.

CHAPTER SEVENTEEN

Before Cathy could ask Raff anything else, Tommy's voice came through a speaker. "Attention, folks, look toward the starboard. There's a Humpback whale."

Brian grabbed her arm. "C'mon, Cat. Let's go down and see."

As Cathy went along with Brian, she glanced back. Raff was sketching again. "Aren't you coming? I thought you were drawing what we spot."

"I can see from here, and I've done this enough to create a rudimentary likeness." As if to satisfy her, he reached into his tote and withdrew binoculars. "Have fun, you two. It's an impressive sight, especially for first timers." He grinned.

"We should get Steve, Mildred, and Henry," Cathy told Brian when they were back on the main level of the boat.

"Leave them be. The waves are a little high now. We don't want to risk them getting sick. They should be able to see the whale through the windows."

As they passed the enclosed room, Cathy saw her fiancé and two friends' faces pressed up against the glass. She waved to them and mouthed the words, "Want to join us?" but they shook their heads in unison.

Brian laughed. "I hope you're not planning a cruise for your honeymoon."

"I haven't even thought that far. What about Nancy? Do you think she'll come out of the captain's room?"

"Why should she? She has a birds-eye view from there."

"Shouldn't she want to be with you?"

He shrugged. "I could ask the same of Steve, but you know they're good sports. They came with us. That means a lot."

Cathy wasn't so sure of that. The whale tour was Nancy's idea in the first place, and Cathy would've enjoyed having Steve at her side instead of Brian, as much as he was a good friend. She also felt Nancy took advantage of her fiancé. They could've both ridden with Tommy if she'd insisted, but then Cathy would've been alone.

As she got to the starboard side of the boat, she saw the whale. Its head was above water. "Wow!" she said. "That's quite a sight."

Brian was looking through his binoculars. "I can see its features with these. Wanna look?" He passed them to her.

"Thanks." Cathy zeroed in on the whale. "This is amazing."

"Isn't it?"

She turned to see Nancy who'd left the captain's room. "I thought I'd join you. I figure Mildred and Steve are still holding on to their cookies at mid-ship." She walked over, took Brian's hand, and gave him a kiss on the cheek. "Besides, I miss my Briany."

Briany? Cathy never knew Nancy to use nicknames. Brian's cheeks turned red. "Thanks for coming back. I was getting jealous of you in that close space with Tommy."

She laughed. "He already has a girlfriend, Angel. Besides, assistant deputies trump boat captains all the time."

Cathy, feeling like she'd turned into a third wheel, said, "I think I'll go back up on deck."

"Why would you do that, Cat?" She jumped at Steve's voice. He was right behind her.

"Steve? Aren't you afraid of getting sick out here?"

"Nah. The pills are working. I also wanted to give Mildred and Henry space."

"I feel the same way about Nancy and Brian." Cathy watched as Brian put his arm around Nancy and led her a few feet forward.

"Hey, guys. Mind if we join you, too?"

Cathy turned around and saw Mildred and Henry walking hand-in-hand toward them.

"I asked Steve for a seasickness pill," Mildred said, "I wanted to spend these special moments with my fiancé and my friends."

Nancy smiled. "Glad to have you." Cathy noticed that her smile was off.

"What's up, Nance?"

Nancy came over to her and whispered, "You don't think I was riding shotgun with Tommy for nothing. I got some good intel about Georgia's murder." She waved to Mildred. "Come over here. I want you in on this, too."

"What about the whale?" Mildred asked.

"We can watch him as I fill you both in."

Steve, Brian, and Henry left the ladies talking while they walked closer to the front of the boat, each with their binoculars. Henry said, "Despite Millie's reluctance, I think she's enjoying this."

"The whale-watching tour?" Steve asked.

"Yes, and the investigating."

"Okay, Nancy. What did you find out from Tommy?" Cathy asked.

The three of them were in a circle and, even though Nancy said they could watch the whale, they seemed more interested in her as they leaned in to hear what she had to say.

"First, you'll never guess who was also dating Georgia?"

Mildred said, "I don't like guessing games. Spit it out, Nancy."

Nancy smiled. "Very well. It was Raff."

"Raff?" Cathy was stunned. "He did seem odd when I mentioned Georgia's murder and also when I asked if she liked to shop, but I had no idea he was involved with her."

"He was and that gives him a motive for murder. It actually gives both of them motives, him and Tina."

"Don't forget Dr. Shah," Mildred pointed out. "I think he's hiding something."

Cathy considered. "Yes. I don't think Shankar was truthful to us."

"Three suspects. What about Captain Sharp and Tommy? We can't forget Angel. Do you think any of them have motives?"

"I don't know, Nancy. You're the one who interrogated Tommy."

"I did not!" Nancy turned to look over the railing as Tommy's voice over the speaker announced the sighting of a dolphin.

"What else did Tommy tell you?" Mildred asked.

"I love dolphins. I can't believe they're whales," Nancy said. "I should get my binoculars."

"Are you holding something back?"

Nancy turned around. "No, Mildred."

"But you said 'first.' What was 'second'?" Cathy pointed out.

"There doesn't have to be a "second.'"

Cathy sighed with frustration. She turned her attention to the dolphin splashing just a few feet from them, a bit of water sprayed onto the boat and hit the men.

"Whoa!" Steve said, jumping back. "Did you girls see that or are you still gossiping?"

"We weren't gossiping," Nancy said. "But because you said that, I'm glad you got splashed. I love karma."

"What about me?" Brian asked. "I got wet, too."

"Sorry about that. I was just filling my fellow detectives in on what I learned riding shotgun with Tommy."

"I'm not a detective," Mildred reminded her again.

"Yes, but you're part of our inner circle."

"Is there anything we should know, Nancy?" Steve had walked back to Cathy.

"Not yet. How long are you guys planning to stay on Long Island? When do you need to get back?"

Brian said, "It's been quiet in Buttercup Bend, so Leroy said he could do without me until next week."

"I can stay until Sunday," Steve said. "I have a friend who promised to take over my gardening appointments for a few days. He has his own landscaping company. I rescheduled some people, so he only has to see a few clients this week."

"What about you, Henry?" Mildred asked.

"I'm retired, so I have plenty of time on my hands. I'd like to spend it keeping an eye on my bride-to-be."

Mildred laughed, but Cathy saw her face redden.

They spent the rest of the whale-watching tour together, sharing binoculars and taking photos of whales, dolphins, and one another. Luckily, no one became seasick.

When the *Lucky Maiden* pulled into the harbor, Nancy rushed upstairs with Brian behind her. Cathy followed at her heels. "What are you doing, Nance? The tour's over."

"I want to see what Raff drew. I need a souvenir."

Cathy laughed. Brian said, "What did I tell you, Cat? I knew this would happen." He followed the two women up to the top deck.

Cathy called down to Steve, Henry, and Mildred at the bottom of the stairs. "I'll be right down, guys." She was interested in seeing Raff's work, too.

A bunch of canvases stood against the railing. Raff was still working at the easel. "Welcome back," he said. "If you're interested in purchasing anything, I'll let you know the price."

Nancy walked over to the canvases. "These are amazing. Aren't they, Brian?"

He shrugged. "I'm not a good judge of fine art."

Cathy followed Nancy along the railing. She didn't voice her opinion, but she found the art interesting if not remarkable. There were whales, dolphins, and the ship all created down to minute detail. The sketches had been turned into lifelike pastel renderings. She could look right into the whale's eyes, feel the motion of the ship. There was even a depiction of the six of them looking out toward the sea over the boat's railing.

"Oh, I need this," Nancy said, gazing at it. "This will make a wonderful souvenir." She turned to Raff. "How much?"

He smiled. "I knew you'd like that one. With the passenger discount, it's $100."

Brian said, "Nancy, we took photos of our group. We can frame one and use that as a souvenir."

"But this is art," Nancy insisted. She pouted, and Brian took his wallet from his pants pocket. "Do you take credit, Raff?"

The artist brought a square reader from his pocket and walked toward them. "I'll swipe it. I also provide a complimentary protective wrapping, and you can contact me for a discount on a frame."

"That's so nice of you," Brian said sarcastically as he handed Raff his card.

While Brian and Raff were dealing with the transaction, Cathy walked over to the easel to check out the unfinished drawing. She stifled a gasp when the face of Georgia Hampton looked back at her from the canvas.

CHAPTER EIGHTEEN

"Nancy, come look at this," Cathy said. "I'm in the middle of a transaction." Raff swiped Brian's credit card.

"You mean *I'm* in the middle of a transaction," Brian said.

"Thank you for buying my souvenir, sweetie."

She blew him a kiss, and he shrugged. "What are fiancés for, right?" Cathy caught the note of resignation in his words.

Raff said, "I think your friend has noticed my rendition of Georgia. It's stunning, isn't it? I'm taking it back to my studio to finish it. Unfortunately, I can't reserve a copy for you, as it's already been commissioned." He handed Brian back his VISA and covered the canvas with a protective bag.

As he handed it over to Nancy, Cathy asked, "Who commissioned it?"

"Ginny."

Cathy was surprised Georgia's sister was the one who'd asked Raff to create the drawing, but maybe she cared for her sister more than she showed. She stepped away from the canvas. "If you're all done here," she glanced at Nancy, "why don't we get going now?"

Nancy smiled. "Sure thing, Cat. It was lots of fun." She pressed the canvas to her chest. "Thanks, Raff. I'll be in touch with you about a frame."

Brian raised his eyebrows. "You heard Cathy. Let's go before you decide to buy something else. Want me to hold that?"

"No. I'll be careful with it."

They said goodbye to Raff who was packing up his supplies and headed down the stairs where they met the rest of their group.

Tommy was standing at the exit. "I hope you enjoyed the trip." He extended his hand to them. Cathy, Brian, Henry, and Mildred shook his hand and thanked him.

Steve said, "I'm glad I came and didn't get sick."

After he shook Tommy's hand, Nancy, her hands full, leaned up and gave Tommy a kiss on the cheek. "That was wonderful. I had a great time riding shotgun with you."

His face turned red. "My pleasure, Nancy."

As they deboarded the boat, Tommy called after them, "You should stop in the office before you leave and let Captain Sharp know how you enjoyed the ride."

"Will do," Nancy called back. She walked up to Cathy and whispered, "I have more questions for Sharp."

It was when they were a few yards from the office that Angel came running toward them, her blonde hair in disarray, her blue eyes wide. "Is Tommy still on the boat?"

"Yes," Cathy said. "I think he's cleaning up. Raff is still there, too. What's going on? We were coming back to let the captain know the tour was great."

"You won't be able to do that." She stopped short.

"Why not?" Nancy asked.

"Because I just found him dead."

"Oh, my God!" Mildred said. "Another one? What happened?"

"I don't know. It looks like a heart attack. I told him to stop eating all that fried fish. We need to get Tommy."

"I'm here. Angel, I just heard. The captain? Dead?" He rushed over to her and hugged her.

Raff, behind Tommy, said, "Has anyone called the police? Have you checked to see if Dan's still breathing?"

Angel began to cry and shake as Tommy held her. "I went to get Tommy. I didn't think of calling the cops, and I don't know CPR."

Brian said, "I'll find out if he's still alive. I'm trained in resuscitation." He turned to Nancy, "You dial 911. I'll see what I can do."

Everyone ran for the office. The door was wide open as Angel left it when she found the body.

Sharp was lying on the floor in front of his desk, his coffee cup shattered on the ground beside him, the brown liquid pooling at his side. Brian got down on his knees and felt for a pulse in his neck. He shook his head. "I think he's gone, but I'll try to revive him." He pumped Sharp's chest. After a few minutes, they heard sirens. Brian kept pumping as the paramedics rushed in.

Cathy, standing around with the others, felt her stomach heave. She knew it wasn't a heart attack that had felled the captain. She'd seen this type of death before when she'd found her professor dead with his parrot nearby. It wasn't natural. It was poison. It was murder.

CHAPTER NINETEEN

The police weren't happy to be called back. Cathy heard Dooley whisper to Palmer, "Looks like we have another murder on our hands." Cathy felt her suspicions were accurate when a young officer, wearing gloves, placed the broken pieces of the coffee mug and scooped up the remaining contents into an evidence bag.

Dooley turned to the group. "I need to know a few things. First, who found the body? Second, what are you all doing here?"

Angel, sobbing with Tommy holding her, said, "I found him."

Tommy said, "These people were on a whale-watching tour I gave today."

"What?" Dooley put his hands on his hips. "I spoke with Sharp earlier and told him to lock this place up. Did he disobey my orders?"

Raff, taking a step forward, said, "I'm Dan's brother-in-law and an artist and naturalist. Tommy arranged the tour and asked me to come down to narrate it. When Dan realized that, he decided to let it run."

Dooley glanced back at Angel. "When did you find him? Did you touch or move anything?"

Angel, still crying, said, "It was only a few minutes ago. I was about to leave, and I wanted to see if he needed anything before I went, maybe another cup of coffee."

The elder officer's dark eyes lit up. "Did you bring him that coffee?" He glanced at the bag Palmer was carrying.

She nodded. "When I first arrived. I picked it up in the café down on the boardwalk. Why are you asking about that? Did it cause his heart attack?"

Dooley regarded her as if she were a child. "This doesn't appear to be a heart attack, ma'am. I'll wager there was poison in that coffee mug. We need to bring you down to the station for further questioning."

Tommy let Angel go and faced the policeman. "What do you mean? Are you considering her a suspect?"

"No one is a suspect right now. We have to determine the cause of death, but I still need to speak with her."

"Can't you see how upset she is? Even if there was poison in that drink, that doesn't mean she put it there."

Angel said, "It's okay, Tommy. I'll go. I can prove I'm innocent. I didn't pour the coffee. Marci did at the coffee shop." Cathy noticed how composed the young woman now seemed. She wondered if her tears had been an act.

"I'll talk to her, too," Dooley said. "But you were the one who brought it to him. You could've laced it on the way."

"How dare you accuse her," Tommy said. Cathy noticed his face had reddened.

The officer put his hands out as if to ward off a blow from Angel's boyfriend. "Now, now. I'm not accusing anyone. I'm just stating a possibility." He looked at Angel. "Was anyone else in the coffee shop to verify your statement?"

She paused, as if remembering, and then turned around to look at Raff. "He was there with Ms. Hampton."

Cathy was shocked. When Nancy gasped, she realized that she was also.

"Yes," Raff admitted. "I was there speaking with Ginny about drawing a portrait she commissioned. It isn't finished, but I can show it to you." He gestured toward the canvases he'd brought into the office and stacked by the door.

"That's not necessary," Dooley said. "But I find it odd that you met her at a coffee shop close to where her sister was recently found murdered."

"I was here to narrate the tour, so it was convenient," Raff explained.

Dooley didn't look as if he believed him, but he waved his hand. "I don't want to hear any more excuses. We'll all talk further at the station."

Nancy said, "All? I thought you were only asking Angel to come with you."

"I need to question everyone who was here. I should've done that last time. I've learned from my mistake. I can't trust any of you."

"But we were on the whale-watching tour," Mildred pointed out.

Cathy said, "That's right. We weren't anywhere near the captain's coffee."

"And don't forget that Cathy and I are detectives," Nancy added.

"And I'm an assistant deputy, for Pete's sake," Brian said.

"That doesn't make you innocent." Dooley turned to Palmer. "There isn't enough room in our patrol cars for all of them. Let's take the girl who brought the coffee, Mr. Mueller, and that guy Raff. The others can follow us to the station in their cars."

"What about the lady who works in the café?" Palmer asked. "And we need to notify the next of kin."

"Get the café lady. She can ride with you. Make sure she closes up the shop first. You also need to track down Ms. Hampton." Dooley glanced at Raff. "You said you were the captain's brother-in-law. How can we contact his wife?"

"I'll contact Eloise. She'll be devastated when she hears what happened."

"Not until after we question you." Dooley turned back to Palmer. "Get going. I'll meet you at the station."

Palmer nodded and strode off.

A few minutes later, a medical examiner and the coroner showed up to check the body and transport it to the morgue.

"We can go now," Dooley said. "Those not coming with me should follow me in their cars, but don't think about driving off."

Cathy and Mildred got into Nancy's car. The men got into Steve's. When Dooley pulled out, they followed him.

Cathy said, "I should call Maddie and let her know why we're not back yet and probably won't be for some time."

"Yes, you should do that, but don't worry her. She reminds me of Florence who is always concerned about you."

"That's true, Nance, but she's also like Gran in that she can handle stressful situations."

Mildred agreed. "It's better she knows what's happening. I'm sure she'll notify her sister."

Cathy took out her cell and selected Maddie's contact. When her great-aunt answered, she filled her in on everything that took place including finding Captain Sharp's body.

"Oh, dear," she said. "I'm sorry about all that, but I'm sure the police will clear you right away. Keep me posted if you need anything. At least your fiancés are with you."

They arrived at the Fogport Police Station only a minute before Steve, Brian, and Henry, who parked next to them. They entered behind Dooley, Tommy, Raff, and Angel.

As they came in, the security officer at the desk looked up as if questioning the appearance of so many people escorted by Dooley.

"We need a room." Turning back to the group, he said, "I'll call you one at a time. I want to make sure your stories add up."

Angel was called in first, possibly because she found the body. Tommy wanted to accompany her, but Dooley insisted she come alone. When her questioning was over, she returned to the waiting area with tears flowing freely down her cheeks. Tommy hugged her before he was asked to see Dooley.

Raff was next and then Dooley called Nancy to be questioned. Cathy figured he wanted to speak with her as the first member of their group because she'd been outspoken and insistent about being a detective and not having to answer questions.

Nancy returned a few minutes later and walked over to her. "You're next, Cathy," she said. "I think he'll let us all go. There's no evidence to hold us."

Dooley met Cathy in the hall. "Right in here." He gestured with his hand, indicating the open door to a small, windowless room. She wondered if, like in the TV shows, people were watching from outside.

"Have a seat, please." He pointed to a metal chair on the other side of a table. He took the one across from it.

Folding his hands in front of him, after she'd sat down, he

said, "I asked Miss Meyers this same question, but I want to hear the answer from you. Can you tell me why, after finding Ms. Hampton's body the other day, you and your friends came back to the scene of the crime and took a whale-watching tour?"

Cathy wished she knew Nancy's response, but she thought it best to be honest. "Ginny hired Nancy to investigate her sister's murder. She thought taking the tour would help her learn more about the people Georgia worked with and if they had any motives."

She couldn't tell if Dooley expected this reply. His expression and voice remained neutral as he said, "And what did she learn?"

Cathy paused, but she knew she had to continue answering honestly. "She told me that she found out Raphael Wright had been dating Georgia."

"I see." Dooley gazed down at the wood table. She noticed there were scratch marks in it. She wondered if they'd been made by a knife or another sharp instrument.

When he looked back up at her, he stared at her for a few minutes. She lowered her eyes. Finally, unfolding his hands, he said, "Okay then. Call in your fiancé. I'll speak with him next."

"Is that all?" She'd expected more questions.

He stood up from the table. "I'll meet Mr. Jefferson in the hall. I can't hold any of you, but I'll let you know when you can go. I'm still waiting for Palmer to show up with the waitress from the café and Ms. Hampton."

Cathy stood up and asked, "Do we need to be here when they come?"

"Not necessarily. As soon as I finish questioning the members of your group, I'll release you all. You can go back to the waiting area for now."

. . .

Brian was the last of Cathy's friends to be questioned. As Dooley promised, they were allowed to leave but had to be reachable in case he needed to call them back.

As they left the station, Palmer pulled up in his patrol car. Ginny and a brunette Cathy assumed was the woman who worked in the coffee shop were in the back seat. A redhead crying into a handkerchief sat next to Palmer. Cathy figured she was Eloise but wondered why Raff hadn't been allowed to break the news to her.

Nancy whispered to Cathy, "I'm calling Ginny later. I want an explanation as to why she met Raff before our tour."

"This is too involved for us, Nance. Two people are dead."

"Reminds me of Maggie Broom and her sister's case."

It had been more than a year since the case of the Cat Crazy Lady in Buttercup Bend had been solved. Although that murder had made Cathy realize her interest in detective work, their boss, Howard Hunt, and the sheriff were the ones who solved it.

At their cars, Steve said, "Are you ladies interested in dinner tonight? Since Maddie treated us last night, we can take you all out this evening."

Nancy smiled. "Great idea, Steve. I'm up for that."

But Brian shook his head. "It sounds expensive. I'm pretty short on funds since Nancy bought that sketch." He glanced at the canvas Nancy was holding.

"It won't be too bad if we all chip in for the ladies and Maddie. Maybe Christine will join us, too," Henry said.

"When you get back, why don't you ask Maddie to suggest a restaurant?" Steve told Cathy. "Something nearby but not too expensive."

"I'll do that." She gave him a quick kiss on the cheek. "What are your plans now?" She looked toward the men standing by Steve's car.

"We'll head back to the hotel and then meet you ladies at Maddie's house around six. Give us a call if you need anything." Steve took out his key and unlocked his car.

Nancy and Mildred said their goodbyes to their fiancés and then got into Nancy's car. As they were driving to Maddie's house, Nancy said, "I have a theory I want to share with you two. I didn't want to say anything around the men. They're not really a part of our investigating team."

Mildred sighed. "How many times do I have to tell you that I'm not on your team."

"Admit you're curious, though? It's part of your librarian nature."

When Mildred didn't comment, Cathy said, "Okay, Nance. What's your theory?"

"I think Raff's having an affair with Ginny and that he's our killer."

"Wait!" Cathy said. "Raff is with Tina, and what motive would he have to kill Georgia and Captain Sharp?"

"It doesn't matter that he's seeing Tina. He could be cheating on her. Tommy said that he was involved with Georgia. Her breaking up with him would be his motive. As far as Captain Sharp, he's Raff's brother-in-law. Maybe they didn't get along. He certainly didn't seem too broken up when we found the body."

"It looked like Sharp got along with him."

"Maybe, but he seemed almost afraid of him."

"Nancy, that's crazy. You're reading too much into it."

"Will you two quit arguing," Mildred said. "If Raff is guilty, the police will arrest him."

"Not if we catch him first. On the other hand, it's possible he and Ginny were in it together."

"That's ridiculous, Nancy. Ginny hired you to find her sister's killer," Cathy reminded her.

"That doesn't mean anything. It would be a great cover." They pulled up in front of Maddie's house, and Nancy turned off the car. Facing Cathy, she said, "Let's all put our heads together tonight at dinner. Even though the men aren't on our team, we could get important feedback from them. Maddie and Christine are pretty sharp, too."

CHAPTER TWENTY

Maddie was happy to accept their offer of dinner at a restaurant and said she'd let Christine know. "I realize you're only here a few more days, so this will give us an opportunity to get to know you all better. It's nice of the guys to invite us."

"They felt it was only right since you hosted the barbecue and paid for the food last night," Cathy said. "Do you know any restaurants nearby that we could reserve for eight people?"

Maddie thought for a moment and then said, "There's the Fogport Diner. It's not far, or if you prefer a fancier place, there's the Minnick Inn. It's historical and features a shopping village of colonial stores."

Nancy's eyes lit up. "Sounds like my type of place."

Cathy laughed. "I think Brian would prefer the diner. He spent enough for you on that drawing."

"I think that was well worth it," Maddie said. Nancy had shown her the sketch Raff made on the ship that featured their group looking at a whale over the boat's railing.

"I think you all forgot that another murder took place today," Mildred pointed out. "We shouldn't be celebrating."

Nancy said, "We have to eat. Besides, I already mentioned to Cathy that we can discuss our theories on who killed Georgia and Captain Sharp. It'll be a great brainstorming exercise."

To Cathy's surprise, Maddie said, "I agree. I'm not in favor of talking murder over dinner, but it might be a way for everyone to come to terms with what you experienced and also compare your observations and perceptions."

After Maddie phoned and invited Christine, Cathy called Steve and gave him her great-aunt's restaurant recommendations. He said he'd reserve the Minnick Inn because it sounded nicer than eating at a diner.

A quarter to six that night, Christine picked up Maddie. Nancy followed them in her car with Cathy and Mildred. Steve had notified them that he, Brian, and Henry were on the way to meet them.

It wasn't yet dark when they arrived at the Minnick Inn, but it was lit up with white lights. The restaurant was large with weathered wooden boards. Its walkway was bordered with flower beds of brightly colored marigolds, pansies, and delphiniums. When the men showed up right behind them, they approached the entrance together, Maddie and Christine leading the way. As they entered the restaurant, soft music was playing, and a receptionist dressed in a long Victorian dress greeted them with a smile. "Welcome to the Minnick Inn."

Steve stepped forward. "We have reservations for a table of eight. It's under Jefferson."

The woman checked a list and said, "Right this way." They followed her into the restaurant. Cathy observed the brown paneled walls and chandeliers that held candles. The tables and seats were also wood, but the chairs were cushioned with embroidered pads. There was a large room with several smaller ones through arched alcoves. The receptionist led them into one that contained a rectangular table set with flowered China and gleaming silverware. Paintings of American colonists and George Washington lined the walls. There were menus at each place setting.

Steve said, "This is nice. I didn't realize we'd have our own room."

"We usually reserve them for parties on the weekends," the receptionist said, "but during the week, we allow guests with more than six members to use our private dining areas."

"Perfect," Nancy said. She turned to Brian. "Where do you want to sit?"

The receptionist said, "You may sit anywhere. A waitress will be with you shortly."

Cathy sat next to Steve. Brian and Nancy sat on his other side. Henry and Mildred sat opposite them next to Maddie and Christine.

Picking up a menu, Brian said to Steve, "These prices are high. I would've been happy at the diner."

"But the ladies wouldn't be. Besides, the three of us are splitting the tab."

"And Christine and I will leave the tip," Maddie offered.

"No," Nancy told her. "Cathy, Mildred, and I can take care of that. You've been nice enough to have us stay with you without paying rent."

"You're family and friends," Maddie said, "but we appreciate you treating us."

Nancy picked up the menu. "Everything looks good. What is everyone having?"

Cathy hoped Nancy wouldn't ask for samples, as she usually did when they ate out in Buttercup Bend.

The men said they were interested in the Old-Fashioned Pot Roast. Maddie and Christine favored the crusted salmon while Mildred wanted the chicken cordon bleu. Cathy decided on the roast turkey with stuffing and cranberries. Nancy, changing her mind twice, finally chose the veal medallions.

The waitress arrived a few minutes later bringing a basket of warm cinnamon bread and a pitcher of water for the table. She took their orders and asked what they wanted to drink and if they'd like an appetizer.

"We're ordering from the Price Fix menu," Nancy explained, eyeing Brian who suggested that. "I'll have the house salad for my appetizer with a glass of white wine please."

The waitress jotted it down and went around the table asking the others. "Mildred also wanted a salad with a glass of red wine. Cathy couldn't resist the crock of onion soup but said she'd stick to water with it. Maddie and Christine asked for zucchini sticks and glasses of white wine. The men all wanted clam chowder and soda.

After the drinks and appetizers arrived, Maddie broached the subject of Captain Sharp's murder. "I hate to bring up this topic," she said, "but I think it's important we address the elephant in the room."

Nancy laughed. "I think you're talking about the murder."

Maddie nodded. "Yes. I wasn't there and neither was Christine. Cathy filled me in about it, but I'd like to hear everyone else's take on what occurred. I know you were all brought down to the police station. Do you have any suspects or ideas about why this happened?"

Nancy said, "Cathy probably told you that they suspect the captain's coffee was poisoned. The broken mug was next to the body."

Christine asked, "Did someone bring the captain his coffee?"

"The deckhand Angel did," Cathy replied, "but she claims she didn't add anything to it after the coffee shop girl poured it."

Christine considered this information while biting a piece of her zucchini stick after dipping it into the accompanying tomato sauce. After washing it down with a sip of wine, she said, "I assume Angel could be lying. Did she have anything against the captain?"

"Not that we know," Steve said. "My money is on Raff. Nancy found out he was seeing Georgia, the wedding planner who was murdered. I think he killed her if she jilted him like she did the doctor and the captain found out about it."

"I've thought things over and am now considering that Tina killed Georgia," Nancy said. "She hurt her when she took her fiancé away. Even though she filed a stalking order against Shankar, she could've blamed the wedding planner for all the trouble she's had with him. Plus, she might've found out that Raff was seeing Georgia. That would make the second man the wedding planner took away from her."

"Whoa!" Christine said. "TMI." She gulped down more wine.

Mildred said, "Did any of you consider that Georgia and Captain Sharp might have been killed by different people?"

Nancy paused in eating her salad and looked across the table at the librarian. "That's an interesting idea. They weren't murdered with the same weapon. Georgia was shot. The captain was poisoned, or we think he was poisoned."

Maddie said, "You need to wait until the police determine the captain's cause of death. If he was poisoned, you could consider that a woman killed him, while the shooting was more a crime that would be committed by a man."

"I disagree," Henry said from the end of the table. "You can't stereotype killers. A man or a woman could've committed either or both murders."

Before anyone could agree or disagree with his comment, the waitress was back with their meals. Not all of them had finished eating their appetizers, so she only took away the plates that were empty. When she left, Mildred said, "I don't think this discussion has been too helpful. Let's enjoy our food and talk more about this after we read about it in the paper."

Nancy said, "You're right, Mildred. This might be front-page news but remember they're having Georgia's memorial service on Friday. We need to attend. I don't know what they'll do about the captain."

Brian said, "I hope you don't expect us to go with you." He looked to his left and right at Steve and Henry.

"Of course you should come, not to investigate but to support us." Nancy glanced at Brian's plate. "Also, I'd like a piece of that pot roast."

Cathy wasn't surprised. She knew Nancy would ask for some of her turkey next.

There was no more talk of murder during the rest of the dinner. As Cathy suspected, Nancy asked for samples of everyone's meals and desserts. Brian tried to stop her, but he was met with a glare.

Steve paid the bill with a credit card. Brian and Henry took out their wallets and handed him their share of the cost. Nancy left a generous tip for the waitress, while Cathy and Mildred each paid her back a third of it.

As they left the restaurant, Nancy said, "The shops are still open. Let's go see them."

Brian sighed. "I think we spent enough money tonight."

Nancy patted her stomach. "It was well worth it, but now we should walk off our meals."

"Okay, Nance. Is anyone else interested?"

"Christine and I come here when they decorate for the holidays. It's very pretty," Maddie said. "We don't mind seeing the shops again."

"We may find some unique items here," Henry pointed out.

Mildred said, "Unique is usually expensive, but we might as well check them out."

Cathy enjoyed browsing small shops, and she was happy to find a store selling baby and wedding items. She bought an educational toy for her nephew, and Nancy purchased a pair of pearl earrings. She paid for them with her own credit card but told Brian they were on sale.

"I don't think those are genuine pearls," Mildred said.

"It doesn't matter. I already have a set of real ones for the wedding, but I like to have an extra pair."

"Your money," Brian said, but he picked up a brass medal engraved with "sheriff" in a part of the store selling miscellaneous items. "Leroy will get a kick out of this."

"You're giving it to him as a gift?" Nancy asked.

"Nope. It's for me. I'll show him and ask for a promotion." He laughed. "Just a fun gag piece."

"Look who's wasting money now."

"Give me a break, Nancy. It's only five dollars."

After Cathy, Nancy, and Brian completed their purchases, they moved on to another shop. This one featured old-fashioned candy and had an ice cream parlor in the back.

"This is sweet," Mildred exclaimed. "Henry, take a look at this stuff. Remember the candy buttons, rock candy, and caramel chews? They even have packages of assorted candies from different decades." She pointed to boxes labeled from the 1950s to the present.

"What fun!" Henry took a paper bag from the counter and

began filling it up with candies from barrels. "Let me know what you want, dear. They weigh them and give us a price."

Mildred smiled. "Brings back a lot of memories from when I was a kid. I had a sweet tooth. That's why I don't have many left."

"One of the advantages of getting old. We don't worry much about cavities anymore." Henry grinned and tossed more candy into his bag.

Brian was also eyeing the sweets. He picked up a lollipop and a ring pop. "Hey, Nance. I think I'll take these. See anything you like?"

"Not in here. I want ice cream."

Cathy seconded Nancy's suggestion, and Mildred said, "I wonder if they have egg creams."

The others joined them as they walked through the arch that led into the ice cream parlor. Stools were arranged around a counter where a man wearing a pin-striped apron stood. There were also a few white tables with white steel chairs and pink-cushioned seats facing the window. A chalkboard listed the ice cream flavors. To Mildred's delight, egg creams were also available.

Henry and Mildred ordered the egg creams that were served in tall glasses with pink straws. Nancy had a double vanilla and chocolate cone with rainbow sprinkles. Brian opted for two scoops of pistachio ice cream in a cup smothered with chocolate sauce. Cathy wanted a hot fudge sundae with vanilla ice cream, dark cherries, and whipped cream. Steve asked for a scoop of butterscotch ice cream topped with caramel sauce. Maddie and Christine both had peppermint ice cream and chocolate sauce in tall ice cream glasses.

"Remember how we used to come here when you were young?" Maddie asked her daughter. "When Dad was playing golf, we'd have ice cream together and then I'd take you on the carousel."

"Of course I remember, Mom. It was so much fun. I wonder if they still have the carousel here."

Nancy, overhearing their conversation, said, "I'd love to go on a carousel."

The man who'd served them their ice cream said, "You're in luck. It's still operating and is only ten cents to ride."

"Wow! What a bargain," Brian said. "I'll join you, Nance."

"Where is it?" Cathy asked. She hadn't noticed one in the village.

"It's right through the back door," Maddie told her.

They all headed out, calling thanks back to the ice cream server and wishing him a good day.

There was a coin slot on a stand near the carousel. Nancy fished in her purse and took out a dime. "I'll pay," she offered.

Brian grinned. "Sure you will. It's only ten cents."

She nudged him with her elbow and then inserted the coin.

"Let's choose seats before it starts up," Cathy said.

Henry helped Mildred up the platform, and the two of them plopped down in the horse-drawn carriage. Maddie and Christine took the Christmas sleigh. Steve mounted a black stallion and beckoned Cathy to board the white horse next to it. Nancy, sitting on the pink pony, told Brian to take the tiger in front of her.

After everyone was seated, the music began, and the platform began to move. Cathy gripped the pole attached to her filly as it moved up and down. The ride circled around for five minutes and then stopped.

"Whoa! I'm dizzy," Brian said as he stepped off the tiger.

Nancy laughed. "Maybe you should've taken one of Steve's motion sickness pills."

Henry gave Mildred a hand off the sleigh. "That was fun," she said. "Do you want to do it again?"

"I enjoyed it," Cathy said, "but I think once is enough for me."

Nancy, standing beside her pony, said, "I would go for another round, but look who may join us."

They all followed Nancy's gaze to where a couple had exited the ice cream shop and was walking toward them hand in hand. Cathy recognized them immediately. Ginny and Raff.

CHAPTER TWENTY-ONE

Without letting Ginny's hand go, Raff waved to them with his other hand. Cathy found it strange that he didn't care that they'd caught him with Ginny. The wedding planner also showed no embarrassment.

"Fancy meeting you all here," Raff said. Ginny smiled at them.

Nancy, voicing Cathy's thoughts, said, "Fancy meeting you, too. Does Tina know you're dating Ginny?"

Raff's expression remained the same, and Ginny kept smiling. "This isn't a date. We're discussing business," the artist explained.

"What business?" Brian asked.

Ginny said, "Raff has been helping me prepare for my sister's memorial service. He painted a wonderful portrait of her that will be displayed there. I asked him to help me select a frame for it."

"I don't see any frame shops around here." Nancy looked toward the village.

Raff took his cell phone from his shirt pocket, this time

releasing Ginny's other hand. "The frames are on here. I took photos of them to show her. If you're wondering why we're doing it here, it's because Ginny is checking out this venue for an upcoming wedding."

Cathy didn't think that explanation was plausible, but Nancy nodded and said, "I see. Well, enjoy the ride. It's fun." She turned around. "Is everyone ready to go?"

The group walked around the ice cream shop and out to the parking lot as Ginny and Raff took seats on the carousel.

When they were far enough not to be heard by the pair, Nancy said, "I don't believe him. They must be seeing one another. That gives them motives in Georgia's murder."

"I don't agree," Cathy said. "Even if they are a couple now, that doesn't mean they killed Georgia. Raff must've broken up his relationship with her before he started seeing Tina."

Mildred commented, "Raff is as bad as Georgia who took guys away from their girlfriends. But I don't think he's a killer."

"We can't rule anyone out yet," Brian said. "And cheating isn't a crime."

Nancy elbowed him. "In my book it is, so don't try it, honey."

He grinned. "You'd kill me."

"See what I mean?" They all laughed at that.

Changing the subject, Steve asked, "What's the plan for tomorrow before the memorial service?"

"You're welcome to come for breakfast," Maddie said glancing at him, Brian, and Henry.

"That's a good idea," Nancy said. "We have a load of paperwork to prepare for the wedding. You guys can help."

"Wedding planning is up to the bride, or in this case, 'the brides'," Brian pointed out. "Besides, our hotel gives us free breakfast, and we don't want to impose on you, Maddie."

Cathy was relieved that Brian said that because she knew

Steve hated oatmeal. She was even happier when Maddie replied, "It's not an imposition, but it sounds like the ladies need time to themselves. You young men can discuss your part of the ceremony and then compare notes when you meet up again."

"Sounds good," Brian agreed.

Cathy said, "This has been a nice night and an interesting one." She was thinking about Raff and Ginny and what their relationship might mean.

Back at Maddie's house, after Christine left, Nancy suggested they look over the papers that Ginny asked them to complete for the wedding. "Would you mind helping?" she asked Maddie. "We could use your opinion."

Maddie looked at her across the dining room table where the four of them were seated. "I was married a long time ago, and this isn't my wedding. You three need to make your own choices. I'll put on coffee or tea if you want. I know these matters sometimes take a while to discuss."

"I don't need coffee," Nancy said. "I'm used to staying up late."

"I could use a cup of tea. Herbal, please," Mildred requested.

Cathy glanced at the thick sheets of paper Nancy had spread out. "I'd like coffee if it's not too much trouble, Maddie, but please no dessert. The ice cream was enough."

Maddie laughed. "You don't need to worry about calories, but I'm full, too. Be right back." She slipped away, and Nancy turned to the first page of the wedding document.

"The deal is we need to list how many people will be at the reception. Ginny said it can be an estimate until about a week before the wedding when we need to give her the final number. Any thoughts on this?"

"It's not easy to come up with a number, even an estimate," Cathy pointed out, "because we're inviting many of the same people, and we haven't even sent out invitations yet."

"You and Nancy may be inviting similar guests, but Henry has friends and family from Oaks Landing that he'll want me to invite."

"Sorry, Mildred." Nancy was holding her pen over the document. "The best way to figure this out is for us to make separate lists. We'll have to speak with our fiancés. Let's skip this question for now." As she moved her pen to the next question on the paper, Maddie brought in Mildred's tea and Cathy's coffee. As she placed the mugs down, she asked Nancy, "Are you sure you don't want anything? I can make decaf for you."

"I'm fine, but thanks."

Maddie nodded and left the room.

"Where were we?" Nancy glanced back at the paper, but before she could continue, her cell, which she'd kept on the table, buzzed. "What now?" She picked up the phone. "That's strange. Ginny's calling."

"Put it on speaker," Cathy said. "It might be about the wedding."

Nancy tapped the screen, and Ginny's voice came through. She sounded out of breath and upset.

"Nancy, something's happened. Can you meet me at my house? I don't want to call the police. They'll make a big deal out of it and tear my place apart."

"I don't understand, Ginny. Tell me what's going on. I thought you were with Raff."

"He took me home right after you all left. But when I went inside..." She paused. "I can't talk about it on the phone. I need to show you. Will you come?"

Nancy pushed the wedding papers aside. "Text me your address. Do you mind if Cathy and Mildred come with me?"

Cathy mouthed, 'No,' and Mildred shook her head, but Ginny said that would be helpful. After Nancy disconnected the call, Cathy said, "Why are you including us?"

"We're a detective team, remember?"

"I'm not a detective," Mildred pointed out again. "You keep forgetting that."

"Oh, stop. You have good insights into things. Let's go."

Cathy was glad she'd asked for coffee and finished it quickly as Mildred gulped down her tea. Nancy quickly explained where they were going to Maddie as they headed for the door.

"Be careful, ladies," Maddie said.

CHAPTER TWENTY-TWO

When they arrived at Ginny's house, she was standing in the doorway. Cathy was surprised to see Raff behind her.

Ginny opened the door. She held a large, manilla envelope in her hand. "Thanks for coming so quickly."

Raff nodded at them, a slight smile curving his cheek.

They entered the house. It was a modern-style ranch with white walls, hardwood floors, and geometric throw rugs with diamond accents of black and white. Ginny led them into the living room. "Have a seat, please."

Nancy said, "I'd rather stand. Tell me what happened." Cathy and Mildred also remained standing.

Instead of Ginny replying, Raff said, "I left Ginny off after we'd seen you at the carousel. I should've watched her go in, but I was in a rush to visit my sister. Eloise lives a few blocks from here. I wanted to console her about Dan. But as we were talking, Ginny called me on my cell."

Ginny picked up the story. "When I entered the house after Raff drove away, I found this slipped under the door." She waved the envelope toward them. Nancy took it. "I don't think I should touch whatever's in here, but I assume you did."

Ginny nodded. "Yes, and I showed it to Raff. It's my scarf, but Georgia borrowed it a week ago. She was wearing it when she was killed."

"What makes you say that?" Cathy asked. She recalled that Georgia didn't have any accessories on when they found her dead on the boat.

Raff answered again. "There's blood on it."

Ginny closed her eyes. "I'm afraid it's a warning. Whoever murdered my sister is after me now."

"Was there a note with the scarf?"

Ginny shook her head. "No, and there wasn't any writing on the envelope either, as you can see."

"I think this has to be brought to the police," Nancy said, surprising Cathy.

"I don't want them involved. I told you that."

"But they can offer you protection," Cathy pointed out.

"That's what I said." Raff turned his eyes toward Ginny.

"Maybe you're right," Ginny said, looking at Raff.

"Too bad we don't have gloves," Nancy said. "I'd like to see the scarf before the police examine it."

Ginny walked into another room. They heard her open a drawer and then she was back with a pair of kitchen gloves. "Here you go."

Nancy smiled. "Thanks." She opened the envelope's clasp and pulled out the scarf. Colorful parrots in shades of red, green, blue, and yellow flitted across the cream background.

Cathy thought of the parrots at the bird sanctuary she'd created after solving her parrot-loving professor's murder. "That's an original design," she commented.

"It sure is, and it's pure silk," Nancy said even though she couldn't feel it through her gloved fingers.

"Be careful of the blood splatters," Ginny said.

"I see them."

Cathy also saw them, spots of dried brown blood covering the wings and beaks of a few of the parrots. Nancy reached further inside the envelope and felt around. "You're right. There's nothing else in here."

"Did you often borrow clothes from one another?" Mildred asked.

"Once in a while. We weren't the same size, but we had the same taste in accessories, jewelry, hats, that sort of thing."

Cathy saw Nancy considering before she said, "Do you know anyone who'd have reason to want you and your sister dead?"

"Besides some of our irate customers, I can't think of anyone."

"What about the captain?" Cathy asked. "It seems that it could be connected to the whale-watching company."

"I don't agree," Mildred said. "I mentioned before that I thought Georgia and Captain Sharp's murders were perpetrated by different people. I'm also wondering if Ginny was the target instead of Georgia."

"That can't be," Ginny said. "Whoever killed Georgia knew she was on the boat that day. I had an appointment with a client to see a venue at that time."

"Which was cancelled," Cathy pointed out. She recalled that Georgia's body had been face down when it was found. From the back, especially if the scarf had been around her neck, she might've been mistaken for Ginny. Then again, that didn't quite add up. As Ginny said, an attacker wouldn't have expected Ginny to be on Georgia's boat. In addition, Ginny's hair was blonde, while Georgia was a brunette.

"Let's see what Officer Dooley thinks," Nancy said. Before she placed the scarf back in the envelope, she took a photo of it with her phone. "I want a picture of this. It might be useful."

"Aren't you still investigating my sister's murder?" Ginny asked. "I hired you and put down a deposit for your services."

"I'm still on the case and so is Cathy. Mildred is helping, too. We're also looking into Sharp's murder."

"Nance, you were hired to investigate Georgia's murder, not the captain's," Cathy told her.

"True, but they may be connected unless Mildred is right that there are two killers."

Raff took the envelope and placed it down on a nearby table. "Tina's out of town at her mother's house taking care of her while she's sick, so if you need me to stay here, Ginny, I will."

"That's okay, Raff. I'm taking you and Nancy's advice and calling the police. It might not be a good idea for them to find you here or the detectives."

"That's true," Nancy said. "I think we should go. If you need us, you can reach me again on my cell. We're at Cathy's great-aunt's house which isn't too far away."

"Thank you."

Once they were back in Nancy's car, Cathy asked, "Why did you convince Ginny to call the police?"

"Like you said, they'll protect her. I'm not too concerned that they'll solve the case. I already have another idea to pursue."

"What's that?" It was late. Cathy was tired, but she knew Nancy, a night owl, was just revving up.

"I want us to speak with Eloise."

"Raff's sister?" Mildred asked. "Why do you want to talk to her?"

"I want to know exactly what Raff's relationship is to Ginny. Tommy told me that Raff had also been seeing Georgia. That can't be a coincidence."

"I'm sure the police are checking that out."

"I'm sure they are, but that doesn't mean we can't, too."

"Okay. We can do that tomorrow." Cathy stifled a yawn.

Mildred said, "I think we've had enough for one night. I'm tired, too."

"You can both hold out a little longer. Tomorrow is Georgia's memorial. We need to act tonight. Raff said Eloise lives nearby. He might be going back to her house since he said he was interrupted from consoling her by Ginny's call." Nancy looked toward Ginny's door as Raff stepped out and gave her a hug before walking to his car.

"He'll see you follow him," Cathy said.

"I'll be discrete." Nancy waited until Raff was half a block away and then she started the car.

"I don't understand. Don't you want to speak to Eloise alone?"

"He'll leave eventually. Haven't you heard of a stakeout?"

Cathy sighed. It was going to be a long night.

As it turned out, Raff didn't stay long at his sister's house. After about fifteen minutes, he walked to his car and drove away. Cathy was relieved he didn't look down the street where they were parked.

"Okay, ladies," Nancy said, "let's go."

"I'll wait for you two here," Mildred said, sitting back in her seat.

"No, you don't. You're coming with us. We could use your insights."

There was something about Nancy's nature that persuaded

people, so Mildred got out of the car and followed her and Cathy to Eloise's door. Nancy tapped the doorknocker, and since Eloise was nearby, she answered immediately. With long auburn hair and blue eyes that were red rimmed from crying, she looked nothing like her brother but like his girlfriend, Tina, and the captain's deckhand, Angel. Besides Nancy, Cathy had never seen so many redheads.

"Hello. Who are you?" Eloise asked. "If you're selling something, it's way too late for door-to-door."

"I'm Nancy Meyers," Nancy introduced herself and turned to Cathy. "This is my partner, Cathy Carter. We're from the Hunt, Meyers, and Carter detective agency. We've been hired by Virginia Hampton to investigate her sister's murder, and we'd like to help you catch the person who killed your husband. We believe the two cases could be connected. May we come in?"

Eloise nodded. "Please do."

As they slipped into the foyer, Cathy was surprised Eloise didn't ask about Mildred, as most people did.

"Raff just left. Did you want to talk with him?" Eloise asked as she led them into the living room. Cathy immediately noticed a painting above the fireplace of Eloise and the captain. She wondered if Raff had painted it.

"No," Nancy said. "We just spoke to him at Ginny's house." She didn't mention the reason they were there, but Raff must've told his sister because she said, "I'm worried about her. My brother said someone left an envelope with a threatening message under her door."

"The police will deal with that as far as protecting her," Nancy explained. "but we want to find out who's behind everything. That's why we want to speak to you."

"Of course. Have a seat, but I'm a bit too shaken to offer you anything. I can't believe Dan is dead. He wasn't the easiest person to work for, but his employees respected him. I can't imagine anyone doing this."

"We don't want anything, except to ask you a few questions," Nancy said taking a seat on the couch. Cathy sat next to her. Mildred took the chair across from Eloise.

"Of course." Eloise folded her hands in her lap and looked at them from her spot near the fireplace.

Nancy started with a blunt question. "Is your brother seeing Ginny?"

Eloise glanced down at the embroidered throw rug. "I don't keep tabs on Raff. I'm aware he's a charmer, but, as far as I know, his relationship with Tina Farrell is solid. Ginny is just a friend of his."

"But he was seeing Georgia?"

"Who told you that?" Eloise picked up her head and gazed at Nancy.

"Does it matter?"

Eloise shook her head. "No. It's true, but that was before Tina. Ginny probably told you that her sister had a habit of taking men away from their girlfriends and then dumping them."

"We heard that. We also know Tina was engaged to a doctor and that Georgia broke them up."

Eloise looked down at her clasped hands. "So, you think they both had motives to kill Georgia? But what about Dan? What would they have against him? Raff loved him like a brother. He introduced us. And I don't think Tina ever met him."

Mildred spoke then. "We're considering there were two killers. Did you ever go on one of your husband's whale-watching tours? Did you know anyone from his business other than Raff?"

Eloise turned to her and gave her a weak smile. "Me? On a

boat? No. I get deathly seasick. I didn't know many people from Dan's business. I'd heard about Georgia from Raff but never met her. He and Tina invited me to dinner about two weeks ago with Ginny, Tommy, and Angela. I met them then."

"Was your husband at that dinner?" Cathy asked because Eloise had said that she didn't think Tina had ever met the captain.

Eloise shook her head. "No. He had other plans that night."

"Do you know why your brother invited you to dinner with those people?"

"I have no idea, Ms. Meyers. It was a nice evening. That's all."

"Please call me Nancy. What did you all talk about? How did everyone act together?"

Eloise stood up. "Sorry, but I'm very tired. I found out my husband was murdered only a few hours ago, and I really can't think of much else. You can come back or call me if you'd like. Just please give me some time."

Mildred said, "Of course. We're sorry we bothered you." But Cathy could tell that Nancy didn't feel the same way. She reluctantly rose from her chair and faced Eloise. "Thank you for speaking with us. We'll be in touch. Take care."

CHAPTER TWENTY-THREE

Cathy was surprised that Nancy was quiet on the ride back to Maddie's house. Knowing how her friend liked to voice her thoughts aloud, she found this strange. She wondered if Nancy had finally learned to ruminate in her mind.

Mildred, however, had something to say. "I still think there are two killers, and we shouldn't be pursuing Raff. Even if he is seeing Ginny, that doesn't mean he murdered her sister or his brother-in-law."

"Then who do you suspect?" Cathy asked. Nancy remained silent as she drove through the night.

"That doctor seems shady to me, and the Angel girl was too perky. She brought the captain his coffee."

Mildred's theories drew Nancy from her silence. "I doubt Shankar had anything to do with either murder, and it's too obvious if Angel killed Sharp. We need to observe the people who attend the memorial service tomorrow. You might have a point that there are two killers, but one person might be responsible for both murders. We just need to find their connection and motives."

At Maddie's house, their host offered them tea to discuss their evening, but Mildred declined saying she was too tired and went up to bed. Cathy was tired, too, but she didn't want to leave Nancy alone recounting their visit with Ginny and Eloise. She was glad she stayed because, after Maddie heard what went on, she had some interesting feedback for them.

"Mildred's thoughts about two separate killers makes sense to me," she said, "because there were two different weapons used in the murders. I realize that Georgia had enemies, but you don't know much about Daniel Sharp. Besides his wife, does he have any relatives? Who is in line to inherit his business? These are things you need to consider. If revenge is the motive for Georgia's murder, profit may be the motive to Sharp's."

After Cathy and Nancy went to their room, Nancy said, "Before you get ready for bed, Cat, I want to run something by you. It has to do with what Maddie mentioned about the motives for the murders."

"I'm listening."

"I want to get into those databases Howard has and research our top suspects. I'll ask Maddie to borrow her computer tomorrow morning. The memorial isn't until the afternoon. I also still have the list of naturalists Sharp let me copy. I know it's a long shot, but I'd like to check them out."

"I don't see how those databases will help more than Google, but who do you think are the top suspects and how many naturalists are on that list?"

Nancy put out one hand and pulled back a finger at a time as she said, "The first suspect is Raff. He was jilted by Georgia and now is cozying up to Ginny, but that could all be an act. Also, if his sister is inheriting the whale-watching business, he could convince her to sign it over to him."

Cathy shook her head. "I don't follow that, Nance. Even though he's friendly with Ginny, he seems happy with Tina. Besides, he couldn't have left that envelope with the scarf under Ginny's door. He was with her at the carousel at the time it was placed there. And as far as his wanting the captain's business, I don't think he'd kill for that."

"I still see him as a suspect, as well as Ginny."

"What?" Cathy was surprised. "You think Ginny planted that envelope to lead us and the police off the track?"

"It's possible. Raff had already driven away according to her. If she killed her sister, she'd also have access to the scarf."

"What about the captain? What motive would she have to murder him?"

Nancy shrugged. "I don't know, but Mildred seems to think there were two killers, so maybe someone else killed Sharp."

"Do you have any other suspects?"

"One more. Angel. She brought the captain his coffee. I know the police cleared her so far, but I'm not convinced of her innocence. She also knew Georgia. She cleaned her boat. We don't know anything about Angel's past."

"Those are the only suspects you have? What about Shankar? And for all we know, there might be a dozen women who have vendettas against Georgia for taking away their fiancés. The captain might also have had enemies."

Nancy got up from the bed. "We'll see who attends Georgia's memorial. They say the killer always comes to their victim's funeral. In the meantime, I want to do a deep dive on the three people I suspect and also the three naturalists on the captain's list. Even if they have alibis, they might know something that could help us catch the killer or killers. My money is still on Raff and Ginny either by themselves or together. Ginny inherited her sister's wedding planning business when she died and wasn't too broken up about her death. She was also at the coffee shop with Raff when Angel found the captain dead."

"Good luck with your research, Nance." Cathy thought Nancy was overlooking someone. She could get into Howard's database the next day, too, and do her own investigating.

CHAPTER TWENTY-FOUR

The next day, after breakfast, Maddie had no problem letting Nancy borrow her computer, which was in her den. Cathy and Mildred joined her. Nancy convinced Mildred to help her navigate the database, although she'd already been trained by Howard. "You're a librarian," she pointed out. "You're good with search terms and filters."

Mildred smiled. "I don't mind helping. I have nothing else to do before the memorial." They'd each spoken to their fiancés and agreed to meet them at the funeral home at the 3 pm service time.

Nancy recapped what she'd shared with Cathy about the three people she suspected and the list of the three naturalists. Mildred said, "I really think you should find out who the police are investigating. It's hard to rule anyone out at this point."

"The police don't have my experience and intuition," Nancy said. She turned on the PC and booted it up. Then she typed the URL for the database and logged in. "This is similar to Google, but it has private records," she explained. "I'll start with Raff." She typed in "Raphael Wright." As the program processed her request, Mildred said, "Why don't you search the victims, too? That could give us additional clues."

Us? Cathy thought Mildred didn't want any part of the investigation, but she was interested, after all.

"Good idea. I'll do that after I search the suspects and naturalists. Thank you, Mildred. I knew you could help."

There wasn't much that turned up for any of the suspects or naturalists whom Nancy searched. When she searched Georgia, Nancy found the harassment complaints she'd made against Shankar and two of the other men she'd dumped who'd lost their girlfriends. The captain was more of a surprise. He had complaints filed against him for spousal abuse.

"Wow!" Nancy said. "Our captain was a wife beater. We should include Eloise as a suspect."

Cathy was reading the screen with Sharp's info. "I notice something else, Nancy. His parents are dead, and he was an only child. I'm sure everything will be left to his wife."

"Wait a minute," Mildred said, looking through a pair of reading glasses she'd put on. "There's information about a first wife. It looks like Eloise is his second."

Nancy took another glance at the screen. "You're right. The person filing the abuse charges was a woman named Yolanda Sharp. I wonder if she'll be at the captain's funeral when they hold it."

"If he beat her, I doubt that," Cathy said. "How long were they married? Were there any children? Did Eloise also file abuse charges?"

"They were married eighteen years. That's a long time to put up with abuse. Thankfully, there were no kids. He's only been married to Eloise for two years. No report of abuse. Raff would kill him." Nancy grinned. "Maybe he did."

"Once a wife beater, always a wife beater," Mildred said. Cathy wondered if she had first-hand experience. While her husband had been dead for many years, she never talked much about him.

"That's true but look at this." Nancy pointed at the screen with her index finger. She'd typed in another search for Yolanda Sharp.

Cathy gasped. "My gosh, Nance. She's listed as being employed at the hospital where Shankar works."

Nancy jumped out of her seat. "You gals know what this means, right? We have a perfect opportunity to speak with Shankar again and also talk to the captain's ex."

"Wait a minute," Cathy said. "We have Georgia's memorial service this afternoon."

Nancy checked her watch. "We have time to go to the hospital. Before we do, I also want to create a murder board."

"I don't think Maddie would appreciate you tacking up her walls," Cathy said.

Nancy smiled. "I'm not using up any physical space. Howard installed a program that I can log into that has a murder board template. I'll list the suspects and victims with it along with their connections and also add the photo I took of the scarf Ginny received. Give me a couple of minutes to do that and then we can head to the hospital."

"What about the naturalists?" Cathy asked. "Are you planning to visit any of them?"

Nancy nodded. "All of them, but I'd rather set this up first. We can meet with the naturalists after the memorial."

When Nancy was done creating the murder board, they thanked Maddie for the use of her computer and told her they were going out but didn't say where. "The less Maddie knows, the better," Nancy said when they were in her car headed to the hospital.

The same receptionist greeted them. When Nancy asked to speak to Dr. Shah again, she shook her head. "Sorry. He's not on duty today. He called in sick this morning. We had to reschedule all his surgeries."

"What about Yolanda Sharp? Is she here?"

The receptionist looked at Nancy. "You must mean Yolanda Gerard."

Cathy assumed that Sharp's first wife had taken back her maiden name.

Nancy nodded. "Yes. May we speak with her?"

"Yolanda's in pediatrics on the third floor. She should be on the desk right now."

"Thank you." Nancy turned back to Cathy and Mildred. "Let's go see Ms. Gerard."

The three women rode up in the hospital elevator to the third floor. Nancy led them down the hall following a sign that read, "Pediatrics."

"This is a sad part of the hospital," Mildred said, looking into rooms where young patients were hooked up to monitors and IV bags. "Kids shouldn't be here."

Cathy agreed. She was already twenty-one when she was hospitalized after the car accident that ended her parents' lives. But she hated that time in the hospital and couldn't imagine how awful it was for youngsters.

An African-American woman stood at a desk looking over patient charts. "Excuse me," Nancy said. "We're looking for Yolanda Gerard."

The woman raised her head and glanced at them through dark eyes that were hooded by long lashes. Cathy thought she was pretty and younger than she expected for a woman who'd been married twenty years ago. Either she had aged well or married the captain young.

"That's me," she said. "May I help you?"

Nancy held out her hand. "I'm Nancy Meyers from the Hunt, Meyers, and Carter Detective Agency. These are my partners. We're investigating the murder of Daniel Sharp and have learned that you were his first wife."

The woman inhaled a breath and lowered her face. She thumbed through more charts and then pushed them aside. When she replied, her voice had changed. Cathy heard the anger in it. "I heard he was dead, and I can't say I'm sorry about it. I was expecting the police. You got here first. It doesn't matter. I haven't seen him in two years."

"What about Dr. Shah who also works in this hospital? Do you know him?"

Yolanda looked back at Nancy. "Of course I know him, but we're not friends. He's a colleague."

"What about Georgia Hampton?" Cathy entered the conversation.

Yolanda paused. "The wedding planner? I read that she was murdered, too. She worked for Dan. I met her once years ago when I went to the dock. I didn't go there often. I have crazy hours here at the hospital."

"Do you know if your ex was having an affair with her?" Mildred asked. The question surprised Cathy, but she knew it was a valid one.

Yolanda shook her head, her dark curls bouncing. "Not that I know of, but she had a knack for taking men away from their girlfriends and wives."

"Where did you hear that?" Nancy asked.

"Shankar, uh, Dr. Shah, told me about her."

"I thought you weren't friends."

Yolanda returned to shuffling the charts. Cathy was afraid she was putting them in the wrong order.

"I didn't ask him. He came out with the story to everyone. It was public knowledge."

Before they could ask further questions, another nurse came by wheeling a young girl in a wheelchair.

"I should go. My shift is ending," Yolanda said. "If you need anything else, you know where to find me."

"One last question." Cathy stepped to Nancy's side. "Why did you put up with abuse for eighteen years and what finally made you leave him?"

Yolanda's eyes blazed. "I'm done with questions. I have patients to attend to. Good day, ladies."

Nancy looked at Cathy and back at Mildred. "Let's go. We're done here."

Back in Nancy's car, Cathy asked, "Why didn't you pursue my question?"

"It was obvious she wasn't going to answer. We have other ways of finding out."

"How?"

"We can talk to Eloise."

"Raff may be with her. He won't like you mentioning that we spoke to his brother-in-law's ex."

"On the contrary. If he's there, I'd like to ask him more questions, like where did he introduce Eloise and Dan? Did he know Dan beat his first wife? Was Georgia ever involved with the captain? These are important questions."

Cathy agreed. It wouldn't hurt to speak with Raff and Eloise again.

CHAPTER TWENTY-FIVE

Raff wasn't at Eloise's house. She was alone when she answered the door and let them in. "Sorry to bother you," Nancy said, "but we have a few more questions we'd like to ask you if you have a few minutes."

Eloise swept a lock of her auburn hair back and invited them in with a sweep of her other hand. Cathy caught the glimmer of a diamond on her ring finger. She thought Eloise looked more composed this morning.

"Have a seat. I took off from work today to attend Georgia's memorial."

Cathy joined Nancy and Mildred on the couch, while Eloise sat in the chair opposite them.

"What do you do?" Nancy asked. Raff hadn't told them much about his sister including what type of job she had.

"I'm a secretary. It's only part-time. We were hoping..." She paused as her voice cracked, but her eyes remained dry. "We wanted to start a family soon."

"Sorry," Nancy said, but it didn't sound like an honest condolence.

"Why are you going to Georgia's memorial?" Mildred asked. "I thought you didn't know her, and when is your husband's funeral?"

Eloise took a deep breath and then said, in a steadier voice, "I'm accompanying Raff. There's no date set yet for Dan's funeral. The police are still determining the cause of death."

"Don't they think it was poison?"

"Yes, but the lab is still verifying the type of toxin that was used. It could be a clue to the killer."

Nancy changed the subject. "I think you should know that we spoke with Yolanda Gerard today."

Eloise looked toward the paintings on her wall when she replied. "I never met Yolanda, but Dan told me about her. She accused my husband of terrible things."

"He beat her," Mildred said. "How could you marry a man who did that to his first wife?"

Eloise took another long breath and turned to Mildred. "I never believed a word that woman said. She married Dan for his money. His business is worth quite a lot. He also inherited money when his parents died."

"Why would she lie about abuse?" Cathy asked.

Eloise shook her head. "I have no idea, but Dan was the gentlest, kindest man I knew. Raff would never have let me marry him if that wasn't the case."

"You and Raff are pretty close," Nancy pointed out.

Eloise smiled. "I'm his older sister, but he's always looked out for me."

"I bet you reciprocated that when Georgia broke up with him."

"I tried. He wouldn't talk about it much."

"How did he meet Tina? Have they been together long?" Cathy asked.

"She met him two years ago at an art fundraiser after Shankar left her."

"Wasn't he seeing Georgia at that time?" Nancy asked. Cathy figured she was trying to get the order of things straight.

Eloise paused. "I'm not sure. Sorry."

"What about Ginny?" Cathy asked. "Do you know anything about Raff's relationship with her?"

"I already told you that they're just friends. In my opinion, Ginny is a nicer person than her sister ever was. I felt bad that she had to clean up so many of Georgia's messes."

"Are you referring to how Georgia broke couples up?" Nancy asked.

"That's right. If it wasn't for Ginny, their wedding business would've dissolved a long time ago. In any service industry, if you get bad reviews, it's a death sentence."

"How did she avoid that?"

Eloise turned toward Cathy. "Raff said she knew how to talk to people, but I think she paid a few off. It only makes sense, and I don't blame her. I think she's better off now since Georgia's gone and so is her business."

Cathy wanted to pursue this topic, but Nancy interrupted her. "How did you meet the captain? I understand Raff introduced you."

"He didn't exactly introduce us, but he was the reason we met. Dan came to Raff's arts benefit, the same one where Tina met Raff. I wasn't planning to go that night, but Raff persuaded me. I'm shy, but Dan approached me. The two of us clicked immediately. We spent the whole evening together discussing art which I usually found boring, but Dan was as enthusiastic about it as Raff. He purchased one of Raff's paintings, the one that featured sailboats on a stormy ocean. You may have seen it hanging over his desk. After that, Dan hired him to work on the tours, and we started to date."

Cathy found that interesting. She wouldn't have pegged Sharp as an art lover. Recalling the painting in the whale-watching office that Eloise mentioned, something nagged at the edge of her memory, something else she also saw in the captain's office before he was murdered.

Her thoughts were interrupted by Nancy who stood up. "Thanks for speaking with us again, Eloise. We'll see you at the memorial."

"So, what's the plan now?" Cathy asked Nancy when they were driving back to Maddie's house.

"Plan? What plan? We're going to the memorial. I thought you knew that."

"Don't play innocent with me, Nancy. You always have a plan. What is it this time?"

"Honestly, Cathy. I don't have one. I'm just going to observe the people who attend, and I recommend that you and Mildred do that, too. We can add our notes to the murder board afterwards."

"I always observe people," Mildred said. "It's part of being a librarian."

"It's also part of being a detective," Cathy pointed out.

CHAPTER TWENTY-SIX

When it was time to leave for the memorial, Cathy checked with Steve about meeting up at the funeral parlor. Maddie invited them all back afterwards for dinner.

As they drove off, a light drizzle hit the windshield. "Rain's starting," Nancy pointed out. "It always seems to rain at funerals."

Cathy didn't agree because she clearly remembered the sun shining brightly at her parents' funeral and how she felt it was unfair for them to miss the beautiful day and how the nice weather only made her pain worse.

Mildred said, "I hate funerals. When you get to be my age, there are too many to attend."

"This is a memorial, not a funeral," Nancy said. "Although to me, there's no difference."

"I'm surprised the police released the body."

"Well, there was no doubt about the cause of death, Cathy."

"Still, Nance, you'd think they'd hold on to it a bit longer during the investigation."

"That wouldn't be good for the family. They need closure," Mildred said.

As they pulled up to the Fogport Funeral Home, Nancy exclaimed, "Look at that! The guys are already here."

Steve and Henry were dressed in dark suits, while Brian wore navy slacks and a sweater. Nancy sighed. "I'll have to adjust his wardrobe after we're married." She got out of the car. Cathy and Mildred followed. The men walked over to them.

"Maddie invited everyone back to her house to dinner after this," Cathy announced.

"That's nice of her," Steve said.

"She's probably reciprocating because we treated her and Christine to dinner last night," Brian pointed out.

"I don't think it's a matter of reciprocating. Cathy's her great-niece, but she's been nothing but hospitable to me and Mildred since we came here and even didn't mind when we extended our stay."

Mildred nudged Nancy. "Let's go inside. I want to get this over with." She took Henry's hand, and they walked toward the funeral parlor's entrance. The rest of their group followed.

The atmosphere in the funeral parlor was subdued both in tone and in lighting. A tall man greeted them. "Good afternoon, folks. The Hampton service is in Room 3."

Cathy wondered how he knew which service they were attending but then figured it might be the only one that day. As they went to the indicated room, she noticed a police officer standing outside the door. Nancy whispered to her, "I think they're also observing the attendees."

The first thing Cathy saw as she entered the room, besides the abundance of flowers and the redwood casket, was the large portrait of Georgia that Raff had painted. He was standing in front of it with Ginny and Eloise. On the other side of the room, browsing the photo boards of Georgia and chatting, were Tommy and Angel. Men and women Cathy didn't recognize sat in chairs talking in low voices. She assumed they were couples that Georgia had arranged weddings for.

Raff turned and saw them. He raised his arm and called them over. Steve, Brian, and Henry each shook hands with him and gave their condolences to Ginny and also to Eloise about the loss of her husband. Cathy noted that the casket was closed either by Ginny's request or the fact that the damage to Georgia's skull had been too severe for the morticians to cover. She wondered if that was why Ginny had commissioned Raff to paint her sister's portrait. As Cathy was pondering this and feeling ill at ease among the mourners, another officer walked through the door, and she realized it was Dooley. He surveyed the room and then focused his eyes on Raff. Walking over to them, he nodded and then, turning to the artist, said, "May I have a word with you, Mr. Wright?"

"Of course, Officer. How can I help you?"

"Outside, please."

Cathy wondered what the policeman wanted to discuss in private with Raff, and she saw Nancy raise an eyebrow in puzzlement.

Eloise asked, "May I come with my brother?"

Dooley shook his head. "No, ma'am. I need to speak with him alone, please."

Cathy watched Raff follow Dooley out the door. Nancy whispered to her, "I wonder what that's all about?"

A few minutes later, Raff returned. "My apologies," he said, "I need to go down to the station with Officer Dooley. I'll be back as soon as I can."

"I don't understand," Eloise said. "What's going on, Raff? What does he want?"

"This is my sister's funeral. He has some nerve disrupting it." Ginny's eyes glared.

"It's okay," Raff assured her, "I'm going to clear everything up."

"What are you clearing up?" Eloise asked. Cathy noticed the two women were standing on either side of Raff as if they were preparing to pull him back, but Officer Dooley stepped forward. "Let's go now, Mr. Wright."

"Answer my question before you leave," Eloise insisted.

"Yes. Please tell us what's going on."

Raff, cornered by the two women with Dooley standing behind him, said, "They found some evidence, but it's obviously a mistake. Don't worry. Either of you."

Eloise and Ginny stood there, staring at him, the unspoken question hanging in the air until Eloise voiced it, "You're being arrested, aren't you?"

Dooley replied, "I didn't want to make a scene here, but I'm afraid the gun was brought up by a diving team. It's registered to Mr. Wright."

"It may be registered to me," Raff said, "but I didn't use it to kill Georgia. Someone is framing me."

Cathy thought of Tina who Raff said had gone away for a few days. Eloise was thinking the same thing because she said, "Does Tina know where you keep your gun? Where is she? Did she run away because she killed Georgia?"

Dooley said, "I'm the one who'll be asking the questions, Mrs. Sharp. Now let me do my job and let your brother come with me."

Eloise was about to step forward when Ginny placed her hand on her arm. "Let him go, Eloise. We both know he's innocent."

As Raff turned around, his sister stood frozen to the spot, Ginny's hand still restraining her. Cathy noticed the others in the room were watching them, their eyes glued on the scene instead of the coffin or the photos of Georgia.

The rest of the memorial went as scheduled, although Cathy knew Eloise and Ginny had their minds on Raff who never returned. After the Hamptons' priest said a eulogy to Georgia, sighting her good points and not mentioning her faults, the service ended. Eloise told Ginny she was going to the police station to pay Raff's bail, and Ginny said she'd like to go with her. Walking to their cars, Ginny called to Nancy, "Please do what you can to find my sister's killer, so an innocent man isn't held responsible." She was talking about Raff, of course.

CHAPTER TWENTY-SEVEN

Back at Maddie's house, over dinner with their fiancés, Cathy filled her great-aunt in about Raff's arrest.

"It does sound pretty bad for him," Maddie said. "Besides being connected to the murder weapon, he also had a motive for killing Georgia."

"Yes," Nancy agreed. "She broke up with him and hurt Tina. He also may have had a motive for killing Sharp."

"I think he got over Georgia's rejection," Cathy pointed out. "What do you consider his motive for killing his brother-in-law?"

"Isn't it obvious?" Nancy cut into the chicken casserole on her plate. "He must've learned his sister was being abused. A lot of women hide it."

Mildred said, "It's true that once an abuser, always an abuser, but I still think there's two killers guilty of these murders."

The men each tried to voice their opinions, but Maddie waved a hand and told them to change the conversation and enjoy their meals.

Brian, saying goodbye to Nancy, asked what her next move was going to be.

"You sound like Cathy, always thinking I'm planning something. The truth is I'm waiting to see if the police release Raff. Even if Eloise offers to pay bail, if they have enough binding evidence against him, they might not let him go."

Brian nodded. "Okay, but I know you're not one to give up, and Ginny asked you to find her sister's killer. Just be careful, hon."

Nancy gave him a kiss and promised she would.

In their room at night, Nancy sat up in bed with her laptop. Cathy put down her book and turned to her. "What are you up to, Nance?"

"Just doing a little search." She tapped the keys.

"Brian was right. You're investigating something."

Nancy smiled. "Okay, Cat. You and Brian know me well. I'm trying to locate Tina."

"What? The police will take care of that."

"Not if I find her first."

Cathy sighed and closed her book. "How do you plan to do that, and wouldn't it be easier to ask Raff."

"Raff's in jail right now, and social media is an effective way to find missing people. Some users post everything they do. I'm on her Facebook page right now."

"But you're not her Facebook friend."

"Doesn't matter. Her profile is public. Her last post was asking for prayers for her mother, and she tagged her mother, 'Tonya Farell.' I followed the link, and Tonya is active on Facebook, too. She posts lots of photos. I found one of her house because she was showing off her front garden. Come here and see what important clue I found in that photo."

Cathy sighed. "Nancy, what are you talking about?"

"Come see."

Cathy got out of bed and walked over to Nancy who turned her screen toward her. "What do you notice in that picture?"

"Pretty flowers."

"What else?"

"Stop playing games, Nancy."

Nancy placed her finger on the screen and zoomed into the house. "Check out the front door."

Cathy leaned down toward the laptop. "It's white."

"What else?"

Cathy threw up her hands in frustration. "I give up."

Nancy laughed. "The number, Cat. You can see the house number."

Cathy looked again and realized her friend was right. Showing clearly on the mailbox near the front door was the number '25.'

"There's more." Nancy zoomed out and then moved her finger across the screen to view the background. In the distance, Cathy saw a street sign.

"Looks like Tonya lives on Poplar Street."

"Good work, Nance, but we still don't know the town."

Nancy grinned. "Oh, yes, we do. The 'About' section shows that Tina's mother lives right here in Minnick."

"Okay, so we know she lives at 25 Poplar Street and can check on Google to see how far that is from Maddie's house, but I don't understand if she was so close, why she didn't attend the memorial or why Raff said she was out of town. I also think that would make a weird place to escape from the police."

"Hiding in plain sight," Nancy said. "Get dressed, Cat. We have to go speak with her."

"At this hour?" Cathy glanced at the bedside clock. It was 10 p.m.

"This can't wait until morning." Nancy closed her laptop and walked to the bureau where she took out clothes. Heading to the bathroom, she said, "Meet me by the car in ten."

Tina's mother's house was only a few blocks away. She lived at the front of a cul-de-sac. The lights were off, making Cathy feel uncomfortable about disturbing the occupants. "Mrs. Farrell is sick," she told Nancy. "We should leave this until tomorrow."

"We can't." Nancy got out of the car. "We don't even know for sure that Tina's mother is ill. That could be a cover-up."

Cathy reluctantly joined her at the front door. "Don't ring the bell. Just use the knocker," she suggested, thinking it might be less jarring, but Nancy's tapping was loud.

They waited a few minutes and then, when Nancy was about to knock again, Tina appeared in the doorway. She was dressed in blue pajamas. "What are you two doing here?" she asked, recognizing them.

"We could ask the same of you," Nancy said.

"My mother's sick. I'm caring for her. It's a good thing I gave her a sedative before you arrived. You would've woken her otherwise, and you still didn't answer my question. Do I need to call the police?"

"We're detectives," Nancy pointed out. "We're here to ask you some questions and to inform you that your boyfriend has been arrested for the murder of Georgia Hampton."

Tina's face went white. "What? Why didn't Raff call me?"

"Eloise and Ginny are with him. His sister is trying to bail him out. I don't know if she was successful."

Tina opened the door. "Come in. I'll call Raff and find out what's going on."

Cathy and Nancy entered the small house. It had a musty smell and litter was strewn about. Tina said, "I apologize for the mess. My mother hasn't been able to do much housework. I come by to help, but I'm not the best housekeeper either. Raff is the one who keeps our apartment neat."

"What's wrong with your mother?" Cathy asked. She thought it was a sudden illness, but Tina said, "She has cancer. Late stage. She refused to be in the hospital. She's on home hospice."

"I'm sorry," Nancy said. "doesn't that mean she needs a nurse?"

"I'm her nurse," Tina explained showing them into the living room. "I used to work at Chester Memorial. That's where I met Shankar. I quit after we broke up and became a private nurse. I'm caring for Mom for free, of course. You can both have a seat while I call Raff."

"Wait," Nancy said, "Do you know Yolanda Gerard?"

"Is she related to the captain?"

"She was his first wife. You know he's been murdered, right?"

"Raff told me. It's horrible. Two murders so close together at the same location. Why would I know the captain's first wife?"

"She works at the hospital."

Tina looked at Nancy. "A lot of people work at the hospital. We may never have crossed paths."

Cathy said, "Eloise told us that you met Raff at an art fundraiser two years ago, the same place that Eloise met the captain. Is that right?"

"Yes. It was at the hospital. Ginny organized it. That's where Raff met her. He donated some of his work."

"Wait a minute," Nancy said, "We didn't know the fundraiser was at the hospital or that Ginny organized it. We thought she met him through Georgia, and isn't she a wedding planner, not an event planner?"

"Ginny did event planning before she partnered with Georgia to plan weddings. They're pretty close occupations," she explained. "After the arts event, Georgia invited her to go into business together, but Ginny continued to do some event planning. In fact, she organized a couple of other arts events for Raff."

As Cathy mulled over this information, Nancy said, "They found the gun that was used to shoot Georgia. It was registered to Raff." Her comment was direct and said to elicit a response.

Tina gasped. "My God. I know he kept one in the house for protection, but he was with me when Georgia was killed."

"Are you sure about that?" Nancy asked. "Or just covering for him?"

"What reason would he have to kill her?"

"She broke up with him before he started seeing you."

"Who told you that? Raff has had many girlfriends before me, but Georgia wasn't one of them."

"Tommy said she was," Nancy said. "He told me on the boat."

"Then he's lying. Give me a minute. I'm going to call Raff if the police will let me through."

"Not yet." Nancy stepped in front of her. "If Raff didn't have a motive, you certainly did and also had access to the gun."

Tina shook her head violently, tossing her red curls. "That's ridiculous. I held no grudge against Georgia. She did me a favor by taking Shankar away and then dumping him. They both got what they deserved. As far as my killing her, I've never fired a gun in my life, and Raff can confirm my alibi. He already has to the police."

"Convenient," Nancy said. "You both alibi one another, and you're both prime suspects."

"I'm done talking with you. Please leave. I have to make my phone call."

"One more minute." Nancy looked into Tina's green eyes. "Let's say you're right, and you and Raff are innocent. When did you last see his gun?"

Tina paused, thinking. "Raff keeps the gun in his bedside drawer. We don't routinely look at it."

"Is it possible that someone took it?"

"It wasn't stolen if that's what you're asking." Tina's face suddenly changed. "Hold on. I remember something. There was a night, about two weeks ago, that we had company over. Somehow the conversation got into safety and guns. Raff mentioned his."

"Did Raff show the people you invited the weapon or mention where he kept it?"

Tina gazed down at the floor. "Sorry. I don't remember. He didn't show it. I know that."

Cathy asked, "Who was at this dinner?" She recalled that Eloise, when questioned about if she'd ever met the captain, said that Raff and Tina had asked them to dinner a few weeks ago but hadn't invited Sharp.

"Eloise was there, as well as Tommy and Angela. Ginny, too."

"Ginny? Why did you invite her when you were so upset with her sister?"

Tina shrugged. "Raff was the one who invited everyone. It was fine with me because I had nothing against Ginny, and I knew she and Raff had become friends since she'd helped him sell some of his work at art fundraisers she organized."

"Did any of the guests leave the dinner table after Raff talked about his gun?" Nancy asked.

Tina shook her head. "I wasn't keeping track of who went to the bathroom or anything like that. I was busy cooking and then cleaning up. Raff helped, so he wasn't watching either. That's all I can tell you. Please let me make my call."

Nancy shrugged. "Very well. Have a nice evening, Ms. Farrell." She turned to Cathy. "Let's get out of here."

Nancy didn't start her car up right away. "What are you waiting for, Nance?" Cathy asked. Nancy was looking at her phone. I'm trying to see if Tommy and Angel have Facebook profiles I can search."

"Don't tell me you want to see them tonight. I'm exhausted, and it's almost 11 o'clock."

"I'm tired, too, Cathy. If I find where they live, we'll go there in the morning."

"Do you suspect that they killed Georgia?"

"Either one or both of them if Tina is telling the truth."

"She said Eloise and Ginny were there, too. Why aren't you including them?"

"Shoot! They both have private profiles." Nancy placed her phone back in the dashboard holder and turned to Cathy. "I'm not excluding them. However, Ginny hired us to catch her sister's killer, and I doubt Eloise would use her brother's gun to kill Georgia. She's close to him and wouldn't want him implicated if it was found."

"Maybe she thought it wouldn't be because she'd thrown it in the water," Cathy suggested.

"Hmmm." Nancy started the car. "Lots to think about. Let's get back to Maddie's and sleep on it."

CHAPTER TWENTY-EIGHT

When they walked into Maddie's house, they were surprised to find Mildred waiting for them.

"How come you're up so late?" Cathy asked.

"I heard you two go out. Why didn't you call me?"

"You were sleeping," Nancy said. "and I thought you weren't interested in being on our team."

"I'm not, but I'd like to be included in the investigation. Where did you go?"

Cathy filled Mildred in on their meeting with Tina.

"I'm not sure she was honest with you, but Raff needs to be questioned again. You'll find Tommy and Angel through him, as well."

"Good point," Nancy said. "I'm sorry we didn't ask you to join us tonight, but we definitely could use you tomorrow."

The next morning, at breakfast, Maddie said, "Today is laundry day. Do you ladies need anything washed?"

"We're still using the clothes Christine was kind enough to loan us," Cathy said. "Does she need any of them back?"

"I can wash what you've worn, but there's no rush returning them to her. I spoke to her last night. I also spoke with my sister. Florence says your cats are doing fine, so you shouldn't worry about them."

"I need to call her." Cathy speared one of the pancakes on her plate. She was relieved that Maddie wasn't serving oatmeal again. "I'm really glad I didn't enroll in any college classes this summer. This is taking longer than I thought it would."

Nancy said, "I need to talk to Brian. He might be able to help us with the investigation."

"What about Howard? Did you talk with him?" Cathy was surprised Nancy was considering consulting with Brian. His being an assistant deputy and her being a private eye sometimes caused conflict during their investigations.

"Howard's fine. I called him late the other night while you were fast asleep. He's a night owl like me, so he didn't mind. There's nothing going on in Buttercup Bend right now, so he can manage the office."

"What do you want to ask Brian?" Mildred asked.

"I'd like his feedback on what we've learned so far, and maybe he can find out if Raff has been released from custody."

"I would think you could find that out," Cathy said.

Nancy took a sip of her coffee, swallowed, and then replied, "I could, but I hate to be a pest. He'd be on better terms with Officer Dooley. Police don't usually like private detectives butting into their business."

"Aren't you ladies seeing your fellas today, anyway?" Maddie asked pouring syrup on her pancakes and passing the container to Cathy.

"At some point, I think." The men hadn't made any

arrangements with them. But just as she had that thought, Nancy's cell phone buzzed.

"Speak of the devil," she said looking at the screen. She tapped it and said, "Good morning, Brian. I was just talking about you." She placed the call on speaker, so they heard his reply.

"Good things, I hope. How are you today?"

"Always good things, Brian, and I'm great. What about you?"

"Okay but a bit bored. Leroy called and needs me back on the job soon."

"Leroy can wait." Nancy rolled her eyes, even though Brian couldn't see her expression. "You might be able to speed up our investigation, though. Can you find out if Raff has been released from jail?"

There was a pause at the other end and then Brian said, "I already have. That's actually why I called besides asking you, Cathy, and Mildred to lunch with the three of us guys."

"Is Raff a free man now?"

"He is, and he's at home. His sis bailed him out, but he can't leave town."

"I guess they didn't have enough to hold him?" Nancy glanced at the kitchen clock on Maddie's wall. Cathy knew she was planning to visit Raff before they had lunch with the men.

"Apparently not. Raff had some dinner guests over and spilled info about keeping a gun in his house."

"And you found this out how?" Nancy looked back at her phone.

"I wanted to help you, Nance. Don shared that information with me."

"Don?"

"Detective Dooley. We're on a first-name basis now. He

feels comfortable with me because I'm an assistant deputy. We're fellow officers of the law."

"Oh, gee." Nancy laughed. "but I figured that might be the case. Is noon good for us to meet today, and where?"

"The Four Pines Restaurant. It's between our hotel and Cathy's great-aunt's house. You can Google the directions. Steve suggested it. He found it online. I hope it's good. But, uh, Nancy, are you seeing Raff before we meet?"

Nancy grinned. "You know I am, honey. See you at noon."

Cathy, Nancy, and Mildred walked up to Raff's door at ten a.m. Nancy rang the bell, and he answered after a few minutes, unbolting the front door. He looked like he hadn't slept. His dark hair was mussed, and his face unshaven. "What are you doing here? I thought . . ."

"You were afraid we were the police?" Nancy smiled. "No. We're just detectives. Can we come in?"

Raff stepped away to let them enter. "How did you know I was released?"

"My fiancé is an assistant deputy. He made friends with Officer Dooley," Nancy explained.

Raff flopped down on his couch without inviting them to sit. Cathy noticed the place looked like a bomb hit it. Between Tina being away and the police searching it, it was a mess.

Nancy didn't wait for an invitation. She took the chair by the fireplace. Mildred sat in the one on the other side, while Cathy slid next to Raff on the couch.

"I'm very tired, and I'm sick of answering questions, so please keep this short."

"We will," Nancy promised. "We have luncheon dates."

"Good." He ruffled his hair and lowered his head. "I don't understand about the gun. I had a few people over and talked about it, but I can't imagine any of them taking it and using it to kill Georgia."

"Tina told us about that," Nancy said.

Raff looked over at her. "You had a lot of nerve bothering my girlfriend. She's taking care of her sick mother."

"You said Tina was out of town," Cathy pointed out, "but Nancy found that her mother lives only a few blocks away."

He turned to Cathy. "I didn't want to reveal that to the police. They would've hounded her, too."

"We didn't hound her," Nancy said. "We're just trying to get to the bottom of this. We don't have much time left until we have to give it up to the police, and who knows how long they'll take. They have two murders on their hands. Cathy and I were hired to solve Georgia's, and Ginny asked me to find her sister's killer to clear you."

Raff sighed. "I'll be cleared because I didn't do it."

Cathy asked, "Were you involved with Georgia before Tina?"

He faced her again. "Not before. At the beginning, but my heart was never in it."

"What do you mean by that?" Nancy asked. "Tina said you were never involved with Georgia."

Raff glanced down at the carpet. "It was stupid. I started seeing Tina after she told me how Georgia took Shankar away from her and had done that to others. I wanted to pay Georgia a little lesson. Tina and I weren't exclusive yet, so I didn't see the harm. I had a girlfriend before Tina. I told Tina about Claire. The woman was obsessive about me, so I shouldn't have done what I did."

Cathy wasn't following. "I don't understand."

Raff looked up. "I pretended that I was engaged to Claire but told Georgia that I was paying for the wedding. She showed me several venues and then I," he paused, "I hit on her."

"Did this girl, Claire, know you did that?" Nancy asked.

Raff sighed. "She found out and wasn't happy about it, and I didn't get my revenge for Tina because Georgia couldn't care less when I ended it with her."

"So, you never told Tina?" Mildred asked. "She didn't seem to know about Georgia."

"She didn't. It was in the early part of our relationship. After we became serious, I told her about Claire but not about Georgia."

"Why did you tell her about Claire?" Cathy asked.

"Initially for her protection. Claire was a bit unhinged. I guess you could call her obsessive. I was afraid she'd seek revenge on me through Tina, but she never did."

"You said "initially,'" Nancy pointed out. What did you mean, and where is Claire now?"

Raff paused. "If you're planning to find her, don't even try because you won't."

"You didn't answer my question, and I don't like being underestimated. Just give us her name and her last address. We're following up on everything. It might help you prove your innocence."

Raff paused again and glanced away. "Her last name is Curran, but the reason you won't find her is that she's dead. She was murdered two years ago, but I didn't do it. The police cleared me."

The silence that met his words was only broken by the ticking of his wall clock until Nancy stood up. "Thanks for that information. I'm glad you're free. Don't do anything silly. We'll keep you posted on anything we find out."

"Thank you, but please leave Tina alone. She's going through a very rough time right now."

Nancy didn't make any promises. She just said goodbye and walked out with Cathy and Mildred.

. . .

As they were driving away after their talk with Raff, Cathy asked Nancy, "What's our next step?"

Nancy took her phone off the dashboard holder and tapped it. "I still have the addresses of the three naturalists we never spoke to in my notes app. Before we meet the men, I think we should visit them."

"Aren't you pursuing Claire Curran's murder?" Mildred asked.

"Not now. I'm sure the police will look into that. I'll ask Brian about it at lunch."

Mildred took out her phone. "Well, I'd like to know more about it."

Nancy looked over at her. "What are you doing?"

"I'll search Facebook for her name on my phone. Even though she's dead, there might've been something posted on her page." After scrolling with her finger, Mildred said, "This isn't surprising. Her Facebook posts ended two years ago."

"That would've been the time that Raff pretended to be marrying Claire and started seeing Georgia," Nancy pointed out.

Mildred was still reading her phone. "Claire posted lots of photos of Raff."

"What about her Facebook friends or relatives?" Nancy asked, suddenly taking an interest in Mildred's search.

"She didn't have many friends on Facebook, and there aren't any relatives listed."

Cathy was surprised a woman of Mildred's age would be so knowledgeable about social media, but she figured it was because she was a librarian.

"Why don't you just Google her name, Mildred?" Nancy

suggested. There should be something mentioned about the murder.

"That was my next thought." Mildred swiped her phone and typed again. "Here we go. There's a news article about her murder."

Nancy leaned toward Mildred to try to read her phone and asked, "What does it say?"

"She was smothered in her bed late at night. Someone broke in. They thought it was a burglary gone wrong, but only a few of her things and a small amount of cash seemed to be missing. The case was never solved."

"I wonder if Officer Dooley knows about this," Cathy said.

"If he doesn't, he will and then he'll discover Raff's connection to Claire," Nancy said.

"It's a matter of time before he does," Cathy agreed. "It'll give him a reason to put him back in jail."

"That's for sure," Nancy agreed. "We have to beat him to it. I still think Raff is innocent, but this is too much of a coincidence. I need to talk to Brian about it at lunch. Let's check out the naturalists first." She started the car.

Cathy knew that if Nancy told Brian, he'd be obligated to share the information with Dooley, but she kept her mouth shut. They needed to prove one way or the other if Raff was a killer.

CHAPTER TWENTY-NINE

"I'm curious to see what Janice, Conor, and Max tell us." Mildred gave Nancy a blank look and asked, "Who are they?"

"The naturalists."

"What have you found out so far?" Cathy asked.

Nancy placed her phone back on the dashboard and began programming it with an address. "Janice Digby is fifty-five and has worked five years part-time for the captain. She's a fifth-grade science teacher at Fogport Elementary School. Conor Jenkins is a college student studying marine biology. He hasn't been working on the whale tours that long. I think it's a summer job for him. Max Smith is a retired police officer which is interesting. He's been working for Sharp four years."

"Good research," Mildred said. "But what if these people aren't home? Do you have their phone numbers? We could call and check."

Nancy turned the corner. "Nope. We need the element of surprise on our side. If they're out, we come back another time, maybe after we have lunch with the guys."

. . .

It turned out Janice Digby's house was the first on their way from Raff's. It was on a cul-de-sac in Fogport, a small ranch with an overgrown front yard.

"I can tell Ms. Digby isn't much of a gardener," Cathy said, thinking how Steve would comment on the weeds.

"She needs to hire a landscaper like Steve," Mildred said as if reading Cathy's mind.

"She's divorced," Nancy added, "never had kids and lives alone."

"Hmm. You sure found out a lot about her from Howard's database."

"I told you it's helpful, Cathy, but Google and social media also lent a hand."

Cathy laughed as they got out of the car and followed the path up to Janice's door. Nancy almost stumbled again over the uneven sidewalk as she had at the tour center.

"Are you sure somebody lives here?" Mildred asked. The house certainly looked neglected.

"We'll see," Nancy said using the tarnished knocker on the front door. After three taps, a woman in a housedress answered. She had short blondish-gray hair and wore glasses. "If you're selling something, I'm not interested. If you're a reporter, I have nothing to say."

Nancy took out her business card. "We're neither. We're detectives."

The woman chuckled. "Same thing as reporters, looking for information about Hampton's murder."

Cathy surmised that the police had already been there.

Nancy couldn't deny the woman's words. "It's true that we're looking for information. Would you be kind enough to answer a few questions?"

Digby hesitated, but then she opened the door. "I guess so, but I'll tell you exactly what I told them. Come in."

Entering the house, Cathy saw more signs of neglect, the peeling paint, broken tiles, trash all around. She hesitated when Digby invited them to sit on the sofa. Two cats had been there and scooted off leaving behind fur and cat litter. Cathy's grandmother was meticulous about vacuuming the furniture and floors regularly. This woman didn't seem to care. She wasn't a bit embarrassed by her house, or she didn't realize how unkempt she was keeping it."

Nancy plopped herself down on the sofa, as did Mildred. Cathy took a tentative seat avoiding the spots of fur and litter. Digby stood over them. "Make this quick. I have things to do."

Nancy asked, "Are you going to work?" Cathy recalled that Digby worked as a teacher, but it seemed like an odd hour for her to be at school.

"I quit my job. I'm sick of trying to educate bratty preteens. It's crummy having to compete with cell phones and video games. I'm looking to start my own business."

"Doing what?"

"I haven't decided yet, and it shouldn't concern you."

Nancy got to the point. "You're still doing whale-watching tours, right?"

Digby shook her head. "I'm not sure. Now that Sharp's dead, I don't know if they'll still want me. It's a boring job, anyway. Hampton's murder was the most exciting thing that's happened there, and I wasn't even around for it."

"What can you tell us about that?" Cathy asked before Nancy had the chance.

"Like I said, nothing. I was home that day."

"Were you alone?" Nancy asked.

"Yes. I told the police that. My cats were with me, but they can't give me an alibi."

"Did you know Georgia, uh, Ms. Hampton well?" Mildred asked.

"I never did a tour with her, but I didn't like her. I can understand why someone would want her dead."

"What do you mean?" Nancy prompted.

Digby looked her in the eyes. "If you're a detective, you know what I mean. She was a wedding planner and broke up relationships."

"How did you know about that?" Cathy wondered if the naturalist had heard about it through gossip at the whale center or had firsthand experience with it. She learned it was the latter when Digby glanced at the littered floor and said, "After my husband cheated on me, I met another man. We got engaged. He was everything my ex wasn't, at least I thought so. Sharp suggested I use Georgia to plan my wedding. I didn't want anything fancy since it was my second time around."

As she paused, Mildred said, "I can understand that. I'm getting married a second time myself."

Nancy glared at her to stop her interrupting the naturalist and said, "Go on, Ms. Digby, did Ms. Hampton take your fiancé away, and how long ago did this happen?"

Digby nodded. "She sure did. Two years ago. Then he tried to come back, but I'm not trusting men anymore. It'll be me and my cats from now on."

Cathy knew how soothing cats and other animals could be. After her parents died, she'd been comforted by her Siamese Oliver. She'd started her pet business because she always felt more comfortable interacting with animals than certain people.

Nancy stood up. "Thank you for your time, Ms. Digby." She handed her a business card. "If you think of anything else that might help us, please call me."

Outside, Cathy asked Nancy, "What did you think of that?"

"Another suspect," Nancy said, "but I don't think she was involved. People don't wait two years for revenge."

"Some might," Mildred said as she sat next to Nancy in the car. "Maybe she didn't have an opportunity until now, and it's weird she kept working there even after her experience with Georgia."

Nancy shrugged. "I haven't marked her off the list, but we still have two more naturalists to speak with. The college kid is next."

Conor Jenkins lived in an off-campus apartment he shared with his girlfriend, Karen Fields, a petite blonde fellow co-ed who opened the door to their knock. She was dressed in a pink striped sleeveless shorts pajama set and stifled a yawn. When they asked to speak with her boyfriend, she said, "Sorry. Conor's not here. He had an early class."

Nancy glanced at her watch. "It's after 11," she pointed out.

"I know. We stayed up late. Is there something I can help you with?"

"Maybe. Can we come in? We're detectives."

Karen kept her smile. "That's cool. The cops spoke with Conor about Ms. Hampton, an older officer, Dooley, and a younger one, Palmer. He was cute." She winked and opened the door. I'm gonna put on coffee. Want some?"

"No thanks," Nancy said, and Cathy and Mildred shook their heads.

"You can sit. I'll be right back." The girl walked into another room. Cathy figured it was the kitchen.

As they waited for her to return, Cathy couldn't help comparing the small, neat apartment to the messy house they'd just been in. Although there were piles of paper around, they were neatly stacked on a table, and the wood furniture gleamed as if it was routinely polished. It struck her as strange that a couple of college students could keep their place cleaner than a middle-aged woman who lived alone except for cats. Before Cathy could examine the room further, the girl was back holding a coffee cup that said, "Coeds are Cool," on it. She sat in a chair across from them and placed her cup on a table next to her.

"I figured you're detectives because you have that look about you, but she's different." Karen pointed to Mildred.

"You're right," Mildred said. "I'm a librarian. I help them research their cases."

"Awesome!" Karen took a sip of her coffee and then placed it back on the table. "What do you all want to know? Conor's a great guy. He knows a lot about whales and that's why he got the gig at Captain Sharp's. I hope they don't let him go. He can use the cash. He wanted me to take some classes in marine biology with him and apply there, but I have another part-time job with nice perks. It's a restaurant near campus. Free food, you know."

Nancy nodded as if in agreement with Karen's statement and then asked, "How well did Conor know Georgia Hampton?"

"Not that well. He did a tour with her once, but she usually used Mr. Smith."

"Max Smith?"

"Yeah. She thought he had more experience. Conor did most of his tours with Mr. Mueller when Mr. Wright wasn't available."

"I see. When will Conor be home?"

"He has back-to-back classes, so it won't be until after four."

"Do you know where he was when Georgia was murdered?"

"Of course. He was in class. So was I. We don't take the same ones, but they're around the same times on Mondays. We share a car and drove together to campus that day."

Nancy stood up. "Thank you for that information." She handed Karen her card. "Can you please ask Conor to call us when he gets home?"

Karen shrugged. "Sure thing." She stayed sitting and continued sipping her coffee as they left.

"You don't seriously suspect her boyfriend?" Mildred asked after they were back in Nancy's car.

"I doubt the kid's involved, but he might know something that can help us. I'm more curious about Max Smith since he's a police officer and went on a lot of Georgia's tours. I'd like to see what he has to tell us."

Cathy checked her watch. It was almost twelve. "Do we have time? We're supposed to meet the men at noon."

"Don't worry, Cat. We shouldn't be long with Smith. His house isn't far from the restaurant Steve reserved for us."

Just as Nancy started the car, Cathy's cell phone rang. She saw Maddie's name on her display. "Hold on, Nancy," she said. "I'm getting a call from Maddie." She answered the phone. "What's up, Maddie? Is everything okay?"

Her great-aunt sounded excited. "Nothing's wrong. I don't know if you're at lunch, but I need to show you something important."

"We haven't met the guys yet. We were planning to do something else, but we can drop at your house first."

"Thanks. It won't take long, and it'll be worth your time." Maddie ended the call.

"Do you mind, Nancy?" Cathy asked. "She says it's important."

Nancy shrugged and pulled away from the curb. "I'm

always late, anyway, and Maddie's house is also on the way to Smith's."

Maddie was waiting for them when they returned. She was holding a newspaper and seemed anxious. With shaking fingers, she handed it to Cathy. "You have to read what's in this morning's paper," she said.

Cathy took the page and glanced at the circled headline. Nancy and Mildred peered over each of her shoulders. The headline read, "*Police Screw Up Cause of Death. Wedding Planner Killer Still At Large.*"

Cathy read the story aloud:

> *Following the murder at Captain Sharp's Fleet and Whale-Watching Tours of Georgia Hampton, a wedding planner, and the suspected murder of Captain Daniel Sharp, forensic experts determine that Sharp's death was natural. Officer Donald Dooley had requested the leftover coffee in the captain's cup be examined for toxins. None were found, and it was determined the captain had a coronary. When asked why he assumed the captain was poisoned, Dooley said, "Because of the recent shooting of Georgia Hampton at the captain's location, I considered the possibility that Sharp had also been murdered. It was a feasible mistake, but I promise that my officers and I will continue searching for the person who killed Georgia Hampton. We have the murder weapon in custody and are questioning several suspects."*

"Wow!" Cathy said. "It looks like we only have one murder to solve instead of two."

"That's not true," Nancy said. "You're forgetting about Claire Curran."

"We don't even know that she's connected to Georgia's murder," Mildred pointed out.

"Who's Claire Curran?" Maddie asked. Nancy filled her in quickly. Just as she was done explaining, her cell phone rang.

"It's Brian," she said, glancing at it. "He's probably reminding me about lunch." But when she answered the call and put it on speaker, Brian said, "Nance, I just heard from Don, Officer Dooley. Sharp wasn't murdered. He had a heart attack."

Nancy rolled her eyes. "You're too late. We just read it in the paper."

"Word gets out quick, but I have info that hasn't been published yet."

Cathy, Mildred, and Maddie gathered around Nancy as she spoke into the phone. "What info, Brian?"

"Sharp's will was read, and it's very interesting."

"Go on," Nancy prompted. Cathy wondered if Brian had the same habit of keeping people in suspense as his fiancée.

"Okay. The bulk of the captain's estate went to Eloise. No surprise. She gets the house and enough money to live in it comfortably without working for quite a long time. What she doesn't get is the captain's business."

"Who gets that?" Nancy asked.

"I'll get to that in a minute. There were some other people who inherited. The ex-wife, Yolanda, receives some money. It's not a huge amount, but it's not too small. Sharp also left money to an anger management group. He was a member of it which might explain how he kept his temper under control with Eloise."

"It doesn't seem that she knew about it," Nancy mused. "When we spoke with her, she denied believing he'd ever been an abuser."

Cathy said, "Nancy, let Brian finish. Who inherited the captain's business?"

Brian heard her words. "It's not a big surprise, Cathy. Although you'd think he would've left it to his wife, Sharp probably thought she wouldn't be able to manage it and maybe he didn't want Raff involved. The company goes to Thomas Mueller."

"That sort of makes sense," Nancy said. "Thanks for the info, Brian. By the way, we may be a tiny bit late for lunch."

"I figured. I'll move the reservation. Let me know when you're on the way." He ended the call.

"What do you think of Tommy inheriting the whale-watching company?" Cathy asked Nancy.

"I already said it makes sense, but I'm also thinking we should go back to the dock, congratulate Tommy, and ask him a few questions."

"I thought you wanted to speak with Smith now."

"We can do both. Brian's moving the reservation, so we have time before we meet the guys at the restaurant. However, we know Tommy didn't kill the captain because Sharp wasn't murdered, and we haven't found any motive for him to kill Georgia."

"Not yet," Cathy said, "and remember Mildred's idea about there being two killers. What if Tommy and Angel worked together to murder Georgia?"

Mildred said, "The reason I had a theory about two killers was because of the two murders and the two different methods of killing, but now we know that there was only one murder and only a single weapon."

"Yes, but two people still could've been involved." Cathy looked toward the door. "Let's get going. We don't want to make the men wait that long."

"Be careful," Maddie called after them.

CHAPTER THIRTY

Max Smith lived in a nondescript ranch with a pretty garden. Cathy admired the profusion of colors and varieties of plants that bordered his walk and knew that Steve would approve. She wondered if the backyard, partially visible only through a slat in the white fence that surrounded the property, would be as attractively landscaped. She had an urge to peek, but Nancy called back to her, "What's holding you up, Cat? I thought you were in a rush to get this over with?"

Cathy caught up with her. She noticed Mildred was also eying the flowers as she stood by the door with Nancy.

Smith answered on the first knock, and Cathy wondered if he'd been watching through his window.

"Good day, ladies. How may I help you?" He greeted them with a warm smile displaying straight, white teeth. Cathy took him for a man in his late forties or early fifties. He had thick dark hair with streaks of silver and wore gray slacks and a navy-blue sweater that complimented his blue eyes. She thought he looked quite distinguished.

Nancy introduced them and explained that they were investigating Georgia Hampton's murder. His friendly expression remained the same. "Awful business. That. Come in. Let me know if you'd like anything – coffee or tea?"

Cathy followed Nancy and Mildred into the house. She noticed Max walked with a slight limp as he led them into his living room which was paneled in wood and featured an unlit fireplace. A few framed photos stood on the mantle. Cathy walked over to them and took a closer look. She held back a gasp when she saw the one of Smith and Georgia standing on the dock at Captain Sharp's, the *Lady Star* behind them.

Smith noticed her reaction and said, "Yes, that's me and Georgia. Thomas Mueller took that photo."

"Were you seeing one another?" Nancy asked.

He smiled, showing dimples on both cheeks. "I like your directness. There wasn't anything between us except on a professional level. She wasn't my type. To be as frank with you as you're being with me, I'm a homosexual."

Nancy came over to the fireplace and glanced at the photo. "I see. What did you think of Georgia?"

"I knew about her wedding business and the complaints certain people made against her. I couldn't understand them because why would she do anything to turn away customers?"

Cathy had wondered about that, too.

Smith continued. "But I also know Ginny did her best to smooth things over."

"How so?" Nancy asked. Cathy was also curious.

"She tried to make amends with some of the folks Georgia upset, but the best she could do was stop them from writing bad reviews of their business, but I doubt they recommended their wedding services to anyone else."

"How many were there?" Mildred asked.

Smith thought for a moment. "That I know of? I heard

there were others, but the ones that come to mind are Dr. Shah and Tina Farrell and Raphael Wright and Claire Curran. That was a sad case." He paused. "I used to see Claire at the dock. She came there often and went on a few of Wright's tours. I'm surprised he kept working there after, well, you know about her murder."

"We do," Nancy said, "but we didn't know that Claire used to come to the dock. Did she and Georgia know one another?"

Max shook his head. "I don't believe so. One day when I was working Tommy's tour, Georgia saw Claire leave. She asked Wright why he hadn't introduced them, and I heard him tell her that he was keeping their wedding plans secret so didn't want Claire to know he was using their services. After that, Claire stopped visiting him at the dock. Not much later, she was dead."

"Wow!" Nancy said. "What about Ginny? She and Raff seem friendly. Was there anything between them?"

"I doubt it, but that's what I meant when I said she tried to smooth things over. Georgia broke Wright and Claire up, but in a different way."

"Different how?" Nancy asked.

"Wright left Claire because he was smitten with Georgia, but he didn't get far with her. She was choosy about the men she dated."

"Did that happen around the time Claire stopped coming to the dock?"

"Yes. Wright was cleared of her murder, but now I wonder . . ." He paused and then shrugged. "Sorry. I digress. Did you have any other questions?"

"No. Please continue," Nancy urged. "What did you wonder?"

"I used to be a police officer. You probably know that since you're detectives, and it's easy to check people's backgrounds nowadays. I was injured on the job five years ago and retired on disability. I did pretty well with my pension. But I tired of staying home and always enjoyed nature, so I applied for the job of naturalist at Captain Sharp's and have been there for four years. I heard about Georgia's murder, of course. Officer Dooley and his partner questioned me. I was the one Georgia wanted to hire for her tour on Monday. I couldn't take the job because I had an appointment with my physical therapist, and she said she could handle it alone. Maybe if I'd changed my appointment, she'd still be alive, or if she'd asked somebody else." He shrugged. "Who knows? I feel bad about it, but I know Dooley and Palmer will do a competent job catching the killer, or the three of you will do it first. However, it seems to me that after Wright broke up with Claire and started dating, Terry..."

"Tina," Mildred corrected. Nancy gave her another glare to stop interrupting.

"That was her name, Tina. Well, that was when Claire was murdered. It seems odd that Georgia is dead now, too."

"What are you saying?" Nancy asked. Cathy also needed clarification.

"I think you can figure it out. Wright didn't talk much about Claire, but when I'd seen her at the dock with him once, he mentioned to me afterwards that she was possessive of him I think he got sick of it, especially after he started seeing Tina. He was even afraid of what she might do to his new girlfriend."

Cathy recalled how Raff mentioned his fear of that.

"That doesn't explain why he'd kill Georgia, if that's where you're going," Nancy said.

"It does if she was doing the same thing."

"Wait a minute," Mildred said, "I thought you said Raff was the one who pursued Georgia."

"And I thought that was over after Claire was murdered," Nancy added.

Max laughed. "The thing about Georgia was that, the harder it was to get something or someone, the more that thing or person appealed to her. And once she wanted it, she didn't give up. Tommy told me they hooked up again recently. What I'm saying is that Raff didn't like possessive women. I don't think he was serious about Georgia in the first place but was trying to use her to get away from Claire. I met Tina once, and she struck me as a lady who a man like Wright could manage more easily."

"I don't think that's true," Cathy said, "that Raff would run from dominating women. Most men are flattered when women pursue them. I'm not saying Raff was turned on by Claire stalking him, but I don't think he would've killed her for that. The same with Georgia. Dr. Shah had more reason."

Max turned toward the door. "You'll need to make your own observations. It's your case. Good luck!"

He was dismissing them.

Back in her car, Nancy said to Cathy, "Now we know that Raff and Georgia were seeing one another again it will help with our investigation."

"What do you mean? Are you more confident now that Raff killed Georgia?"

"No. I'm thinking Tina is a better suspect at this point and that's why we're going to check something at the wedding planning office." She started the car and pulled away.

Cathy was confused. "What are we checking there?"

"You'll see."

"It would be nice if you filled us in," Mildred said.

Nancy grinned. "Look who's talking, the librarian detective? I'm checking out the file on Claire Curran and Raff's faux wedding. I'm assuming Georgia kept it."

"I don't know about that," Cathy said, "but I guess it's worth a try. I'm not sure you'll learn anything from it, though."

"You never know."

When they entered the wedding planning office, the office manager, Stephanie, was at the desk. She smiled at them, but the expression wasn't welcoming. "Good morning, ladies. If you're looking for Virginia, she's not in today."

"We don't need her," Nancy said. "You can help us. We'd like to see a file on one of Georgia's clients. It's about two years old."

Stephanie shook her head. "The police went through Georgia's files. They're in a mess, and I don't know if we kept any files from that far back, but you can look if you'd like." She took a key from her desk and stood up.

They followed her down the hall where she unlocked Georgia's office. She was right that the police had made a mess of the files. Dozens of them were strewn around, a bunch on the floor, and a few spread out on the desk.

Cathy walked over to a tall metal file cabinet and read the label. "This goes back to the time we need, Nancy." She pulled the drawer open and flipped through it. "Looks like it's intact."

Nancy and Mildred joined her at the file. Stephanie stood in the doorway watching them. The files were arranged alphabetically, but the one on Claire Curran was missing. "It's not here," Cathy said.

Nancy turned to Stephanie. "Were any of these files kept elsewhere?"

Stephanie sighed. "I told you the police were here. They went through them and may have taken some."

Cathy asked, "Did they ask about a Claire Curran?"

The secretary's face suddenly paled, but the color returned quickly. "They didn't. How do you know that name?"

"That's not important," Nancy said. "Did Ginny take any of Georgia's files in her office?"

"It's possible. Virginia had her own clients, but there were times that she and Georgia worked together on a wedding."

"Can you open her office?" Cathy asked.

"You might want to wait until she comes in, but I'm not sure when that will be. I don't like invading her privacy."

"Didn't the police ask to see her files?"

Stephanie shook her head at Nancy. "No. They were only interested in Georgia's files."

"We can get a warrant," Nancy told her. Cathy knew she was bluffing. Although they were detectives, it would take time for them to get a warrant.

Stephanie glanced at the key ring in her hand. "That won't be necessary. I'll open it."

Ginny's office was the opposite of Georgia's. It was neat as a pin. What surprised Cathy were the paintings on the walls. As Nancy went through the files, she browsed them. They were all signed with the initials "RW." One was a portrait of Ginny herself, similar to the one Raff had painted on the boat of Georgia. The other two were of the dock, one a twilight scene; one at night with the moon reflecting the water. She wondered why Georgia didn't have these paintings in her office when she was the one who worked at Captain Sharp's.

"It's here," Nancy said, pulling out a manila folder from a hanging file. Stephanie looked on from the door.

Nancy brought the file to Ginny's desk. Cathy and Mildred stood around her as she went through it. She pointed a finger at the dates at the top of the application. The end date was listed a month after the application was filed with a red stamp next to it that read CANCELLED. "That date's a few weeks after Claire was murdered," Nancy said.

"You remember the date?" Mildred looked at Nancy. "What do you think it means?"

Before Nancy could reply, Cathy said, "I find it odd and not a little creepy that the wedding was cancelled after her murder."

"I agree." Nancy glanced at the clock above the desk. "We're running out of time, ladies. This hasn't helped us learn much."

Stephanie stepped quietly into the room. "If you're done with that, please put it back." Cathy had forgotten the office manager had been watching them as they browsed the file.

Nancy went back to the cabinet and refiled it. "Thank you for letting us into Ginny's office," she said.

Stephanie nodded. She jangled the office keys in what Cathy thought was a nervous reaction and paused a moment before asking them to leave. "I see you're looking into Ms. Curran's murder. There's something that happened that you should know. I told the police about it at the time, but no one asked me about her when they came to question Ginny after Georgia was murdered."

"We'd be interested in anything you might know about Claire's murder," Nancy said joining Stephanie in the hall. Cathy and Mildred followed her from the room.

Stephanie, still holding the room keys but no longer jangling them, said, "The day before Ms. Curran's murder, she came here looking for Mr. Wright. She stormed past me into Georgia's office. I heard their loud voices as they argued."

Nancy asked, "Who was arguing, and what did they say?"

"I don't usually listen into client's conversations, but Ms. Curran was yelling, and she hadn't closed the door behind her.

She accused Georgia and Mr. Wright of having an affair. She said some other things I found odd."

"What things?" Nancy prompted.

Stephanie locked up the office and then turned back to them. "She said that she'd been following Mr. Wright for a while and that he'd been spending time at our office with Ms. Hampton. She accused him of cheating on her."

Before Nancy could ask another question, Cathy said, "Did you hear Georgia's reply? Was anyone else around that day, another client or Ginny?"

"Virginia was here. She broke up the argument. She told Ms. Curran that there'd been a misunderstanding and that Mr. Wright was going to propose to her and was planning their wedding as a surprise."

Cathy recalled how Max said Ginny smoothed things over when Georgia upset customers, but in this case, it was Raff who'd lied about his engagement to Claire. She could see the wheels turning in Nancy's head as she asked Stephanie, "How did Georgia react to what Ginny told Claire?"

"I think she was relieved. Ms. Curran apologized, and she had a wide smile on her face when she left the office with Mr. Wright."

"A happy customer," Nancy said. "She thought she'd be getting a ring soon, but she was dead the next day."

Stephanie nodded. "Yes. It was a shock."

"What did the police say when you told them what you heard?"

She shrugged. "Well, they'd already cleared Mr. Wright by that time, so I think they just felt it was a terrible coincidence."

"He had an alibi then, I take it?" Cathy was thinking of what Max told them Raff had said to Georgia when she'd seen Claire at the dock.

"I believe he was with his current girlfriend, Tina Farrell, at the time."

"What did the police think of that?" Cathy found it strange that Tina had been Raff's alibi for two murders.

"I'd like to know that also," Nancy said. "Didn't they question him about why he'd spent the night with another woman when he was about to propose to someone else?"

Stephanie smiled. "I'm sure they did, but there was nothing to tie Mr. Wright to Ms. Curran's murder. They considered that the unknown person who broke into her home and stole some of her clothing and the cash she had in her purse was her killer."

"I assume Dooley and Palmer weren't the officers overseeing that case?"

"No, Ms. Meyers, I don't believe they were, but I'm sure they'll be consulted of it soon."

Cathy had already come to that conclusion, and she knew it wouldn't be good news for Raff.

CHAPTER THIRTY-ONE

"Are you planning to see Ginny about what Stephanie just told us?" Cathy asked when they were back in Nancy's car.

"Not just yet. Let's go to the dock as planned and speak to Tommy and Angel."

The sun shone brightly over the dock when they arrived. Nancy got out of the car and signaled for Cathy and Mildred to join her. As they made their way to the office, Cathy saw that the front door was propped open. She had a sudden feeling of déjà vu when she recalled the captain lying dead on the floor. But when they entered, Tommy was alive and sitting at Sharp's desk, a huge pile of papers in front of him. Angel was seated in the chair next to him. They looked up when the women entered.

Tommy smiled, but Cathy noticed it was strained. "Hi, there. What's up, guys?"

"I think congratulations are in order," Nancy said. "We heard you're the new owner of Captain Sharp's Whale-Watching Tours."

Angel beamed. "Yes. Isn't it great? I'm so proud of Tommy."

A red blush bloomed on Tommy's cheeks. "Angel's been a great help sorting out all the paperwork involved in my taking over. The captain wasn't the best organizer. He should've had a secretary, but he wanted to save money on staff."

Cathy said, "Did you know you were in his will?"

Tommy shook his head. "Nope. No clue. To tell the truth, I'm overwhelmed. I need to hire more people. Someone has to check the books because I'm no accountant. Also, the police keep coming here, and we haven't had many tour bookings after the newspaper stories. I may have inherited a sinking ship, excuse the pun."

"You'll do fine, Tommy," Angel said. "I have faith in you, and don't worry about the cops or the reporters. It'll all be old news soon. I'm not happy the captain died, although it's a great break for you, but I'm glad he wasn't murdered." She paused and looked at them. "You know about that, right?"

"Yes," Nancy said. "We read the article, and my fiancé called right afterwards to inform me. He's made friends with Officer Dooley who also told him about the contents of Georgia's will."

"Cool!" Angel stood up. "Would any of you like drinks or snacks? I'm running over to the coffee shop."

Cathy thought about how they'd suspected Angel of poisoning the captain's coffee. Even though that was no longer a possibility, she still didn't feel comfortable about asking her to get her a drink. She was relieved when Nancy said, "Thank you, but we'll stop there on our way out."

Tommy said, "Grab me a coke, please, Angel."

She smiled. "Will do. Be right back."

After she'd jogged away, Nancy turned to Tommy. "What

are your plans for this place? Will Raff still be working for you?"

"He quit."

Cathy gasped. "When was this?" Raff hadn't mentioned quitting to them when they'd last seen him, but that was before Tommy had inherited the business.

"He called this morning. I tried to talk him into staying, but he said he wants to devote his time to his art now." Tommy stood up from the desk. "I hate to cut you ladies short, but I have a ton of things to do. If I can help you in any way, you can always call me."

"Thanks," Nancy said. "We have to run, too. Take care, and congratulations again!"

Tommy flashed her a wry grin and shrugged.

Back on the dock, Cathy noticed that Nancy was passing her car. "Aren't we meeting the men at the restaurant now?" she asked.

"Soon, but I was serious about dropping into the coffee shop." Cathy knew Nancy had an addiction to coffee, so she said, "Grabbing a latte to go?"

"That and a talk with the girl who works there."

"That's a great idea," Mildred said. "The shop is directly across from Georgia's boat. The coffee shop girl may have seen something that day."

"If she did, she would've told the police," Cathy said, "but I don't think we have anything to lose speaking with her now."

As they entered the shop, Cathy almost collided with Angel who was carrying Tommy's coke and a large smoothie. "Whoops!" she said. "Sorry."

"No harm. At least you didn't spill your drink."

She giggled. "True. See you around," and jogged back down the dock.

Cathy joined Nancy and Mildred at the bar where a tall blonde was mixing drinks for a few patrons. Nancy hoisted herself onto a stool. Cathy sat next to her. Mildred sat at the end.

The coffee shop bartender finished serving her customers and walked over to them. "Good day, ladies. How may I help you?"

Nancy withdrew her card from her purse and flashed it like a badge at the woman. "I'm Nancy Meyers from the Hunt, Meyers, and Carter Detective Agency. I'd like to ask you a few questions about Georgia Hampton's murder."

The woman raised a light eyebrow and lowered her voice, so the people at the other end of the bar couldn't hear. Cathy noticed that they were too absorbed in their drinks and their own conversations.

"I'm Marci Tanner. I've already spoken to Officer Dooley about Captain Sharp. It's a relief that he wasn't murdered."

Cathy said, "I'm sure the police also spoke to you about Georgia Hampton."

Marci shook her head. "I didn't have much to tell them."

"But you were here the day she was killed," Nancy pointed out.

"I was at work that day, yes. I mentioned to them the one odd thing I noticed."

"What's that?" Mildred asked entering the conversation.

Marci moved in closer to them. "I get in early every day. The shop opens at 6 a.m. When I got here, I noticed someone was on Georgia's boat. I figured it was the deckhand, Angel, who was just in now picking up soda and a smoothie. She was in charge of cleaning the boats before tours."

Cathy recalled being told that Georgia preferred to clean

her own boat, but she didn't want to interrupt Marci. Nancy, however, cut her off before she could continue. "What made you think it was Angel on the boat?"

"It might not have been her. I only saw the back of a head. Whoever was there had red hair."

Cathy mentally went through her list of redheads involved in this case. Besides Angel, there was Tina and also Eloise.

"How long was this redhead on the boat?" Nancy asked. "What time did Georgia show up?"

"I'm not sure how long she was there or when Georgia arrived. I got busy with customers. The morning rush, you know."

Mildred asked, "Did you hear the gunshot?"

Marci shook her head. "No. The police said the gun had a silencer."

"What did they think of the redhead you mentioned seeing aboard the boat?" Nancy stared ahead at the blackboard drink menu.

"They took down the information. I'm sure they're checking it out."

Cathy, knowing the gun had been licensed to Raff, thought that there was a good chance Georgia's killer was Tina or Eloise. But the fact that they had met Angel coming out of the coffee shop before finding Georgia's body, also could implicate her.

Again, Nancy spoke Cathy's thoughts. "The day Georgia was killed, we met Angel on the boardwalk. She said she'd been in the coffee shop earlier. Do you recall that?"

Marci tapped long red nails on the counter. "I do. It was busy when she came in. It was around 11:30. If she was on the boat earlier and shot Georgia, I doubt she would've hung around. That's what I told the police, anyway."

Mildred nodded. "I agree, but there are times killers hang around the scene of the crime afterwards."

"It's called hiding in plain sight," Nancy said. She looked back at the menu. "I'll have the Rock the Boat mocha latte, by the way."

Marci smiled. "And your friends?"

Cathy knew the murder talk was over. "I'd like a Ship's Ahoy pink lemonade." Even though she knew they'd be going to lunch eventually, she was starting to get hungry and thought the drink would tide her over until she ate.

"Make a Sailor's Rum Smoothie for me, please." Cathy and Nancy looked at Mildred and laughed.

CHAPTER THIRTY-TWO

Holding their drinks in go cups, Cathy, Mildred, and Nancy headed back down the dock. Nancy jangled her car key.

"I guess we go to the restaurant now," Cathy said. She looked at her watch and realized that they would be a few minutes late from the time Steve moved their original reservation.

Nancy took a sip of the latte from her straw. "We're not going to the restaurant."

Cathy stopped short. "But we have luncheon reservations with the men. They've already changed them once."

"This is more important. We're close to cracking this case. That clue about the redhead could help us solve it."

Mildred said, "It could also end our engagements."

"Don't be silly." Nancy clicked her keychain to unlock her car and strode ahead of them.

. . .

In the car, Cathy asked, "Mind if you tell us where you're taking us?"

Nancy smiled as she placed her phone in its holder. She was enjoying the intrigue. "I had a brainstorm about our next move. Since there are three redheaded suspects and three of us, we can each speak to one of them to save time."

"And how are we getting to them if you're the only one with a car?"

"Taxi Nancy." She pointed to herself.

"Angela's right here," Mildred said.

Nancy turned to her. "That's right. I'm letting you out at the office. I'll come back to pick you up. If you run into any trouble, just call me on my cell."

"What about me?" Cathy asked. "And aren't you even going to tell the guys we're cancelling?"

Nancy tapped her phone. "I'm texting Brian now. I told him something came up. He doesn't need to know the details, or he might blab to Dooley."

Nancy pulled up at the office, and Mildred got out of the car. "I really don't like this, Nancy. We already spoke to Angela."

"Not about Georgia's murder and the fact that a redhead was on the boat before she was killed. You're good at asking questions and figuring out stuff. Take your rum drink with you. It might help."

Mildred turned around and walked toward the office.

Cathy opened her door, stepped out, and moved up front next to Nancy. "Who am I speaking with?"

"Tina's closest."

"I was afraid of that. Raff told us not to bother her again. She might slam the door in my face."

"We'll chance that." Nancy pulled away from the dock.

"I'll drop you off and then see Eloise. I'm thinking Raff might be with her. Two birds with one stone. They could've worked together. Raff quitting like that is suspicious."

"He probably was disappointed that his brother-in-law didn't leave him the business." Cathy stared out the window at a seagull circling the water. It was a lovely sight, but thinking about Georgia's murder, made her stomach turn.

When they arrived at Mrs. Farrell's house, they saw police cars outside. "Oh, no!" Cathy said. "It looks like Tina's mother may have taken a turn for the worse."

"I don't think so. There's no ambulance there. Let's find out what's happening." Nancy jumped out of the car and headed toward Officer Dooley who Cathy saw standing by the front door with Tina.

Cathy, following, also noticed that Dooley was holding an envelope in his hand. She and Nancy strode up to him.

"Ms. Meyers. Ms. Carter," Dooley addressed them. "Fancy meeting you here."

"We were passing by and noticed all the police cars," Nancy lied. "Is everything okay?" She glanced at Tina.

"Mom and I are all right," Tina said, "but we called the police because, when I collected the mail this morning, I found an unaddressed envelope in the box."

Cathy recalled the envelope Ginny found that contained the scarf her dead sister was wearing the day she was murdered. "What was in it?" she asked.

Before Tina could reply, Dooley said, "That's not for public information. We're considering this a threat. We'll post a man here to watch the house for a few days. We're still giving Ms. Hampton protection after the envelope she received."

Nancy stepped closer to him. "Let me remind you that Ms.

Carter and I are detectives assigned to Ms. Hampton's murder by her sister. We should be privy to any evidence you're keeping."

"I don't know why Ms. Hampton hired you, but this needs to be kept confidential even to amateur detectives."

Nancy's face reddened. Cathy knew her temper was about to flare. "It's okay, Nance. Let's go."

"No." Nancy wasn't about to back down. She moved even closer to Dooley. "You know that Brian Fitzcullins is my fiancé, right? I don't think he'll appreciate you not cooperating with us."

Dooley's expression changed. "My apologies." He opened the envelope with his gloved hand. "Come over here, and I'll show you what Ms. Farrell received."

Cathy and Nancy followed the officer away from the house and the onlookers who'd gathered near the police cars. Tina accompanied them. "I don't understand why someone would leave that by my door," she said when Dooley removed a photo from the envelope and held it up for them to see. There were two people in the photo. Cathy recognized the man as Raff, but she'd never seen the woman who she noticed was also a redhead.

"This was taken at a distance," Nancy commented. "The couple aren't even looking at the camera. It reminds me of those photos Howard takes for people trying to catch cheating spouses."

"They don't appear in a romantic pose," Cathy pointed out. "It's as if someone snapped this just to show them together. But why? And who's the woman?"

Nancy said, "May I take a photo of the picture, so I can examine it more closely?" Cathy knew she wanted a copy of the photo to add to her digital murder board on Maddie's computer.

Dooley nodded as she used her phone to take a picture of the photo and then handed it back to him in its envelope. "I agree it's not a great shot, but I know who the woman is, or should I say 'was.' I recognize her from a crime scene photo taken about two years ago. It's a cold case Palmer and I didn't cover, but we're looking into it now. If we confirm this, it's Claire Curran, Raphael Wright's old girlfriend."

CHAPTER THIRTY-THREE

"That crazy woman Raff used to date?" Tina said. "Why would someone send a photo of her and Raff to me? A burglar killed her." She turned to Dooley. "Raff had nothing to do with her murder. He was with me that night and was cleared by the police at that time."

"We don't think a burglar killed, Claire," Nancy said. "And it's very odd that Georgia is dead now, too, and Ginny is also receiving threats."

"We also find that strange," Dooley said. He looked at Nancy. "How did you know about Ms. Curran?"

"We're detectives, like I told you." Cathy noted the smugness in her reply. She was proud to have found a piece of the puzzle ahead of Dooley. Cathy wondered if she was also going to share the information they'd learned from Marci at the coffee shop, but instead, Nancy said, "I'll put money on it that the person who sent this killed Claire and is also the one responsible for Georgia's murder."

"This doesn't look too good for your boyfriend," Dooley told Tina. "But, according to the crime file, another officer questioned him back then and cleared him of Curran's murder as you said. I also don't know why he'd leave this for you if he's our killer."

Nancy said, "I agree." She turned to Cathy. "Let's go. Officer Dooley can handle the rest of this."

Dooley smiled. "If you see your fiancé, please fill him in on what's going on. I'd like his input when he gets the time."

"My pleasure." Nancy's smile was broad as she walked away with Cathy.

As they got to the car, before Cathy could ask Nancy what she was planning next, Nancy's cell phone buzzed. She looked down at it. "That's Brian." She tapped the screen. "Yes, dear. Did you get my text?"

He didn't sound happy when he replied, "I sure did. What are you girls up to? Steve and Henry are upset that you cancelled on us."

"Sorry, but I have important information to share with you. Can you reschedule our reservations again? We can meet you and the other guys at the restaurant in a half hour."

"I'll see what I can do." The line went dead.

Nancy smiled. "He'll be in a better mood when he hears about all the clues we uncovered."

"What about Mildred?" Cathy asked. They'd left her back at the dock, and she hadn't yet called them to pick her up.

"Don't worry about Mildred. I'm sure she's fine. I'll drive by there, and we can grab her."

It turned out that Mildred was waiting for them on a bench outside the office. She was still sipping her rum drink.

"Why didn't you call?" Nancy asked.

"I didn't want to disturb you two, and my phone is very low on charge."

"You could've asked Tommy to borrow the office phone," Cathy said.

"It's okay. It's a lovely day. I needed some fresh air to think things over. I knew you'd be back for me eventually."

Cathy glanced at Nancy. "Are you going to tell her what happened?"

"Not now. Let's save it for when I give the guys the news when we meet them at the restaurant."

"Did Angel tell you anything important?" Cathy asked Mildred as they walked to Nancy's car.

"I'll save that for the restaurant, too."

The Four Pines Restaurant was aptly named because it sat between four large pine trees. However, Cathy hadn't realized from its moniker that it was a burger place. She should've suspected it because Steve loved his hamburgers.

The men were already seated at a table when they arrived. Each stood up and kissed their respective fiancée. They saved seats for the ladies next to them at a round table that sat six.

"I know it's nothing fancy," Steve said, "but it's costing us a bit to stay at the hotel."

Brian said, "Tell me about it. I hope you girls are close to solving this murder because if I lose my job, I won't be able to pay the bill or the rent on my apartment."

"Don't worry," Nancy said, picking up the menu that featured burgers of all types along with salads. "What we have to tell you will ease your mind about our investigation. Let's order first."

Cathy didn't eat a lot of meat, but she chose the Four Pines Cheeseburger platter. The others ordered burgers, too, except

Henry who was a vegetarian. He ordered a house salad along with Mildred who Cathy noticed eyed the burgers when they arrived at the table. She thought that Mildred only ordered the salad because of Henry and wondered how they'd manage meals after they were married.

After Nancy had finished most of her burger, she started the conversation about what they'd done that day. She began with their talk at the coffee shop that revealed a red-headed stranger aboard Georgia's boat before she was found dead. Pointing to Cathy, she said, "Tell them about the file in Ginny's office and Claire Curran." Cathy proceeded to do that to a rapt audience. When she was done, Nancy swiped her phone and passed it to Brian. "Tina found this in an envelope in her mailbox. It's a photo of Raff and Claire." She watched Brian as he glanced at it. "They just look like they're walking together, and it's taken at a distance."

"That's what I thought, but Dooley is considering it a threat against Tina and is putting police outside her mother's house. He wanted me to share what happened with you, but we wouldn't have even seen the photo if I hadn't reminded him I was your fiancée."

Brian smiled and handed her back her phone. "I'm glad I gave you a perk. He's a nice guy actually. He has a tough job. I know what it's like. I admire Leroy. I wouldn't want to be sheriff."

"What do you make of what we found?" Cathy asked. She knew Nancy wanted Brian's feedback.

"It's obvious Raff is at the root of this. I'm not sure he's your killer or collaborating with the killer, but there's a connection."

"I agree," Henry said, pushing his empty salad bowl aside. "I'm wondering if Eloise is the guilty party. She's a redhead and Raff's sister."

"Did she have an alibi for the time of Georgia's murder?" Steve asked.

"I don't know," Cathy said. "She wasn't at the dock that day that we know of, so the police may not have questioned her."

"Well, I didn't tell Dooley about what Marci saw," Nancy said, "so we can still talk with Eloise."

"What do you guys make of the fact that Raff quit his job at Sharp's?" Mildred asked.

"It's understandable," Brian said, "but it might also be an indication of his guilt."

Nancy turned to Mildred. "Did you find out anything from Angel?"

Mildred shook her head. "Not much. She admitted being at the coffee shop that day, of course, because we saw her. But she said she'd only been on the dock a short time. There's no way to prove or disprove that without a reliable witness. Tommy would support her no matter what, and Marci said she only saw the back of the woman's head."

Brian was fiddling his thumbs and then stopped and grabbed a French fry from his plate when Nancy looked at him. Cathy could tell he was frustrated because, while Nancy promised they were close to finding Georgia's killer, the clues weren't clear yet.

"I think we need a break from this," Nancy said after the bill was paid. That surprised Cathy because Nancy had previously been gung-ho about trudging forward on the case.

Brian said, "I'm cool with that. Sharp's wake is tomorrow, and I'm sure you'll all want to attend. We can wait until then to see what clues we pick up from the people who come."

"Tomorrow?" Cathy hadn't expected it to be so soon but

then realized that, since they'd ruled out murder, there was no reason to delay the service.

"Same place, same time," Brian said. "Dooley tells me that Eloise is eager to get it over with. I wonder what that means."

Nancy didn't pursue that comment. Instead, she said, "I'm still completing our wedding application for Ginny. I need to get it to her by tomorrow. I could use some help from you guys."

Steve shook his head. "We don't want anything to do with that except meeting you at the church or the gazebo or wherever. The brides are responsible for all the planning."

Cathy sighed. "That's crazy. The grooms should have input. It's a joint event."

"I agree," Mildred said. "We need an idea of how many we're inviting." She looked at Henry. "You want your friends from Oaks Landing, but I don't think I met all of them."

"Why don't we go somewhere and help you ladies fill in the blanks," Henry suggested.

"You can come back with us to Maddie's," Cathy said.

"Good idea." Nancy stood up and pushed in her chair. "It'll help us clear our minds which may give us more focus into our next move to solve this murder."

Cathy wasn't sure that would help, but she joined Nancy and the others as they left the restaurant.

CHAPTER THIRTY-FOUR

At Maddie's house, after Nancy had uploaded the copy of the photo Tina received to the murder board on Maddie's computer, she joined the others in going through the paperwork for the wedding. They all sat around the dining room table with snacks that Maddie served. As time dragged on, Cathy proposed they order Chinese takeout, as not to inconvenience Maddie with cooking. They agreed on that and over their paper containers of chicken chow mein, General Tsao's chicken, brown rice, and won ton soups, they continued to discuss their plans.

"I think we're almost done," Nancy said finally. "I know the guest list took the longest, but we're in the home stretch now."

Brian sighed. "Thank God!"

"Luckily, we'll never have to do this again," Steve pointed out.

Henry smiled. "My first wedding was a simple affair. This is too complicated, but we need to please the ladies."

"If it was up to me, dear, we would've eloped," Mildred reminded him.

Nancy gave her a glare. "Don't even think that. This is going to be a beautiful wedding." She turned to the final page of the application. "There are a few optional items here. The wedding planning service offers discounts for add-on services."

"What type of services?" Cathy asked. "Are you talking about wedding gowns, jewelry, that sort of thing?"

"Yes, and also a few salons for hair, nails, and makeup." Nancy skimmed the page. "Oh, this is funny. One of them even rents out hair pieces, extensions, and wigs for men as well as women."

Brian, who was conscious of the fact that his hair had started to thin, said, "That's no surprise. People want to look their best at their weddings."

"Can you see a guy renting a toupee and having it fly off during the ceremony?" Steve, with his full head of blond hair, joked.

"I won't check off the box," Nancy said, "but I'll take down the name of the place. Whether you guys want your locks enhanced, I think all us brides need our hair done before the big day."

"Not me. I'm happy with my gray," Mildred said. "I can do my hair myself. I like to keep it natural."

"What Nancy means is that we all want to look nice for the wedding. It doesn't mean we have to make major changes, but a little spiffing up won't hurt."

"I agree, Cathy," Maddie said, entering the room. She'd eaten her food in the kitchen to give them privacy for their discussion. "Have you finished your application?"

Nancy placed down her pen and let out a long breath. "All done."

Cathy gave Maddie a hand clearing away the trash as the men stood up and stretched their legs. "I guess we'll meet up before the wake tomorrow afternoon," Steve said. "This has been an interesting experience." He walked over to Cathy and kissed her gently on the lips. "Call you in the morning, honey."

After the men had gone, Nancy placed the completed application in its manila envelope. As she did, her cell phone buzzed.

"Is that Dooley?" Cathy asked, thinking the officer had new information for them, but Nancy shook her head as she answered the call.

"I don't recognize the number."

"Hello." She spoke into the phone. As usual, she put it on speaker for Cathy and Mildred to hear.

"Hi. It's Conor Jenkins. My girlfriend said you were at my house today. I got home from school, and she gave me your number. She said you were asking about Ms. Hampton."

"Yes," Nancy said. "Thanks for calling me. Is there anything you can tell us about her that might help us figure out who killed her? We're detectives investigating her murder."

There was a pause on the line. "Karen told me. I, uh, didn't know Ms. Hampton well. I went on one or two of her tours. That was when I first started two years ago. I only worked summers for Captain Sharp."

"I see. Did you know Mr. Wright?" Nancy glanced at Cathy and Mildred who were quietly listening as she spoke to the young man.

"Sure. He worked there, too. He was nice to me. He gave me a painting once. He used to do them on the tours."

"Did you recall a redhead who used to visit him at the dock around that time?"

Conor paused again. Cathy assumed he was trying to remember. When he continued, he said, "Yes. That was Ms. Curran. I felt horrible when I heard she got killed."

"I'm sure you did," Nancy said. "Did anything unusual happen during the time that she visited the dock to see Mr. Wright?"

The young man was suddenly defensive. "Why are you asking me that? Are you trying to blame Ms. Curran's death on Mr. Wright? A burglar broke in and killed her. It had nothing to do with him and neither does Ms. Hampton's murder."

"I'm not saying it does," Nancy told him. "I'm just asking if you noticed anything odd before Ms. Curran stopped coming to the dock."

A longer pause, until he said, "Actually, I told the police at that time that there was another man who came to the dock. He argued with Ms. Curran. Mr. Wright and Captain Sharp made him leave."

Nancy's eyes lit up. Cathy recognized it as a sign of interest. "What did they argue about, and do you know the man's name or recall what he looked like? Was Ms. Hampton around?"

"I gave a description to the police. He had light hair and was tall. He asked Ms. Curran to stop bothering him. Ms. Hampton wasn't there that day. I think she was planning a wedding."

"And his name? Do you remember that?" Nancy asked again.

"Sorry, Ms. Meyers. I don't, but I know it began with an 'S.' It was strange."

"Strange in what way?" Cathy could literally see the wheels turning in Nancy's head.

"Even though he had blond hair and all, his name sounded like he came from India."

CHAPTER THIRTY-FIVE

After Nancy ended the call with Conor, Cathy said, "Are you thinking what I'm thinking?" She smiled. "If you're thinking the man who argued with Claire before she was murdered was our friend, Dr. Shah, you're right."

"We should talk to him again," Mildred said.

"I agree. It's really strange that Tina had a restraining order against Shankar for stalking her and Raff seems to have accused Claire of the same thing."

"I know what you mean," Nancy pointed out. "Tina also told us that Georgia made a complaint against the doctor. We have to follow up on this, but we also still need to talk to Ginny."

Just as she said that her cell phone rang.

"Speak of the devil," she said picking it up again and glancing at the screen. She put the call on speaker. "Hello, Ginny."

"Hi, Nancy. I've been going crazy at home with the police outside my door. I know they're just being cautious, but I can't stand it much longer. I told Officer Dooley that I needed a break. I'm heading over to the office. I have to catch up on work, and I was wondering if you have your wedding application done yet and could drop it off?"

"We actually finished it a few minutes ago. I was planning to bring it to your house tomorrow, but I could meet you at your office now if you prefer."

"That would be great. I need to get my mind off things. I heard about Tina receiving a threat. Raff is upset. He went over there, but the police wouldn't allow him in. I'm afraid they still suspect him of killing my sister. I know you're doing your best, but I wish you would find the killer soon."

"We're trying, Ginny. Thank you for trusting us with the case. I'll see you in a few minutes." She disconnected the call and looked at Cathy and Mildred. "You two can stay here with Maddie. This won't take long. While I'm gone, you can think of questions to ask Dr. Shah when we get a chance to speak with him again. You can also plan a strategy we can use at the wake tomorrow to find our red-headed killer."

After Nancy left, Cathy and Mildred went into the living room. Maddie was there knitting in the rocker by the fireplace. Cathy thought of Gran and missed seeing her craft her own creations.

"What are you making?" Mildred asked Maddie.

Maddie looked up from the yellow material, her hands in mid-stitch. "It's a baby blanket for Christine, but if you see her, don't let her know I told you she was expecting. She hasn't even broken the news to her parents. I'm going to be a great-grand-mother again."

"That's wonderful!" Cathy said. "Congratulations!"

"Why don't you two join me while Nancy's out? I can

come back to this later." She placed the knitting on the table beside her chair.

"We don't want to take you away from your work," Mildred said.

Maddie laughed. "I have plenty of time, more than seven months, to complete that."

"What does Christine and her husband want?" Cathy asked, taking the seat next to her great-aunt. "They already have a daughter and a son."

"She doesn't care as long as it's healthy, but I think Christine would love another daughter."

Cathy thought of her brother and his wife. She was sure Becky would want a daughter when she had another child, and she wondered how long she and Doug would wait before giving Doug, Jr. a sibling.

Mildred plopped down on the couch. "Changing the subject, Maddie, do you think Eloise, Tina, or Angela killed Georgia?"

Maddie turned to her. "Are those your only suspects?"

"They're the only redheads," Cathy pointed out.

"And why do you think the killer has red hair?" Maddie leaned forward on her chair as she addressed Cathy.

After Cathy filled her in on what Marci at the coffee shop saw, Maddie said, "I believe you should be looking into other possibilities."

"Like what?" Mildred asked. "We're interested in any suggestions you have. Time is running out because we all have to get back to Buttercup Bend soon."

Maddie began to count off on her fingers. "First, you don't know if the woman at the coffee shop was telling the truth. Second, just because she said she saw someone with red hair on the boat, doesn't mean that was the killer. Third, even if that person is the killer, they may have adopted a disguise."

Cathy's heart began to race as a thought entered her mind. "What do you mean, a disguise?"

"The killer could've been wearing a wig."

"Wait a minute!" Cathy jumped up. "Maddie, may I use your computer a moment?"

"Of course. You know where it is."

Cathy turned to Mildred. "Come with me. I want to check something on Nancy's murder board." She hurried down the hall, Mildred behind her.

Booting up the computer, Cathy entered the password Nancy had created for the notes and photos she'd uploaded to the folder. She took a few minutes browsing them. When she came to the latest photo uploaded, the one of Raff and Claire, she zoomed in on it. "Take a look at this, Mildred," she said. "Do you see what I see?"

The librarian peered over her shoulder. "Are you talking about the scarf?"

Cathy's heart raced faster. She could feel it pounding against her chest and hear the beat in her ears. When she'd first viewed the photo with Nancy, it hadn't been too obvious, but up close she noticed the colorful cloth Claire was wearing around her neck. The pattern featured parrots. It was the same as the one in the envelope that had been mailed to Ginny.

"Oh, my God, Mildred! I think I know who murdered Georgia. Follow me." She closed the PC's window and raced back down the hall to where her great-aunt had resumed knitting.

"Maddie, may I borrow your car?"

"Where are you going?" Maddie put aside the baby blanket again.

"Sorry, but I can't say. I could be wrong, but if I'm right, I don't want you involved."

"What about me?" Mildred asked. "I'm already involved. I'm coming with you."

Cathy paused, considering. "Okay. I might need some help."

"I can help, too," Maddie offered.

Cathy shook her head. "No. You stay here."

Maddie followed them to the door and handed Cathy her car keys. "Be careful, ladies."

"We'll try. C'mon, Mildred. We have to hurry."

CHAPTER THIRTY-SIX

As Cathy started Maddie's car, Mildred asked, "Are you going to tell me who you suspect and what the rush is all about?"

Cathy pulled away from the curb. The car made a screech as she stepped on the gas. "I think Nancy's in danger, Mildred."

"You suspect Ginny? But she's a blonde, and she received a threat, the bloody scarf her sister wore the day she was killed." Mildred paused, suddenly connecting everything. "The scarf. It was Claire's."

"Yes. I'm sure she planted it. No one saw her retrieve the envelope. As far as her hair color is concerned, she could've worn a wig. In fact, the wedding application we completed included a hair salon that sold them."

"And what was her motive?"

Cathy took a turn a little too sharp, and Mildred grabbed onto her seat. "Whoa. Take it easy. Answer my question."

Cathy eased slightly up on the gas. She didn't want them killed before they saved Nancy. "Ginny was envious of her sister who took boyfriends away from their fiancées and even a man she was involved with years ago."

"You think she would've killed Georgia for revenge, but why now after all this time?"

"Ginny's motive wasn't only revenge. She killed her sister because Georgia found out that she'd murdered Claire Curran."

"What?" Mildred's exclamation was high-pitched. "Raff's old girlfriend? Why would she have killed her?"

"Mildred, do I have to spell it out for you? Weren't you there when Ginny was holding Raff's hands at the restaurant carousel? Don't you see how she looks at him? Didn't you find it strange that she asked him to paint a portrait of her sister for the memorial service, and didn't you see Raff's portrait of her in her office? Also, wasn't it odd that she had Raff and Claire's wedding file there, too?"

"That does sound suspicious, but how can you prove it?"

Cathy took another turn, this one much slower. "I can't. That's why I need her to confess."

"Like you had Doris Grady's killer?"

Cathy recalled how she'd gotten a confession from the murderer of Mildred's friend at the llama farm. "Exactly. But if we catch her harming Nancy, I won't need to do that."

"Do you really think she'll hurt Nancy?"

"She's already killed two people, so it's possible she'll try to get Nancy off the case before she digs much further." Cathy thought of the files they'd gone through in Ginny's office. Maybe she'd found them. Even though Ginny said Dooley had allowed her to leave the house, she could've called from the office. Cathy didn't want to think that they might be too late.

"Don't worry about Nancy," Mildred said from beside her. "If you're right about Ginny, she's planned her murders carefully. She won't rush into killing Nancy."

"As much as I agree with that, Mildred, I can't help worrying."

"If you're right, I'm worried, too, but I know that Nancy can handle herself."

That was true, but Cathy didn't want to take any chances that could mean her friend's death.

As they arrived at the darkened parking lot of the wedding planning office, Cathy saw Nancy's car parked next to Ginny's. There was only a dim light on in the office.

"I don't like this," Mildred said. "You should call Dooley or Brian. We shouldn't go in there alone."

Cathy understood Mildred's concern, but there were two of them against Ginny and, if Nancy was okay, there would be three.

"We can handle it, Mildred. We'll surprise her. There must be a rear entrance. Let's use that." Cathy opened the car door and got out.

Mildred followed her toward the back of the building. The night wind blew behind them, but Cathy didn't feel cold despite her light top. Adrenaline was pumping through her body. Her friend could be in danger. She found the door, gripped the handle, and turned. "It's open," she whispered to Mildred.

They stepped into the hall. The front light hadn't reached back that far, so they walked into blackness. Cathy's heart beat faster. She heard Mildred's quick breaths behind her. They made their way forward into the hall. The light they'd seen from outside was shining faintly from Ginny's office.

Mildred stopped. "Are you sure about this, Cathy?"

"We've come this far. C'mon." But Cathy wasn't sure at all.

The building was silent except for their ragged breathing. Then she heard Nancy's voice and sighed with relief.

"I hope we answered everything you needed. If not, please call me."

The creak of a chair sounded as if someone had stood up from sitting and then Ginny's voice. "Just one minute."

"What's going on?" Mildred whispered to Cathy.

Cathy placed a finger against her lips. "Be quiet. Listen."

"Ginny, what are you doing with that gun?"

Cathy's heart thundered. She was right. Ginny had asked Nancy here to kill her.

Mildred took her phone from her pocket. "Let's call the police now."

"They won't get here in time. She doesn't know we're here."

"But we don't have any weapons."

"She won't kill all of us. Let's go." Cathy thought surprise would be on their side, but as she rushed through the door with Mildred following reluctantly behind her, Ginny grabbed Nancy and held the gun to her head. "Isn't this sweet? Your detective buddies are here to save you."

"Drop the gun," Cathy said. She was surprised that Ginny had acted so quickly.

"And why should I do that? The three of you should've gone back to your small town with your boyfriends when you had the chance." She laughed. "I have to give you credit for solving my sister's murder, but I'm afraid you're too late."

Nancy struggled against her. "You won't get away with this. I'm sure they've called Dooley and Brian."

Cathy didn't have the heart to deny Nancy's words. Instead, she said, "That's right. Officer Dooley and Assistant Deputy Fitzcullins are on their way."

"They won't get here in time. I can kill all of you in a matter of minutes. I'm a good shot."

"Then what will you do?" Mildred asked. "They know we're here." She picked up Cathy's lie.

"I have an escape plan." Cathy noticed Ginny was wearing gloves that she must've put on when taking out the gun.

"What's that?" Nancy asked. Cathy knew she was stalling for time thinking that Brian and Dooley were coming.

"This gun isn't mine. It's Eloise's. Raff made sure she had one when she married the captain just in case his anger therapy didn't work too well. Sharp made him promise not to tell his sis about his temper and agreed to private therapy sessions. That was the only way Raff would give their marriage his blessing because he's so protective of Eloise. I called at her house before I phoned you to check up on her and take the gun from her bedroom when I pretended to use the bathroom. It was in my purse when I left. She told me Raff was at an art show tonight. I already knew that because I'd spoken to him earlier. That means she's at home without an alibi. The police were too busy guarding my house to put any men on patrol at hers yet. That's too bad. When they find your bodies and the gun, I'll have shot myself. Nothing big. A small wound. Enough to make them think I was a victim, too. I'll tell them she was trying to frame me and Raff for the murder of my sister."

"That plan won't work," Cathy said. "They won't believe it because I shared my suspicions about you with them."

Ginny laughed. "Suspicions aren't facts." She pulled Nancy tighter. "I think I'll get this over with."

"Aren't you going to tell us why you killed Claire Curran and Georgia, threatened Tina, and now are seeking to frame Eloise?" Cathy knew the answer, but she wanted to delay Ginny to think of how to stop her.

Before Ginny could reply, Mildred added, "I'd also like to know how your sister found out that you murdered Claire."

Ginny smiled. "You're the detectives. You tell me."

"It's because of Raff," Cathy said. "You've had an obsession about him since the time you met him at the art fundraiser you organized before you became a wedding planner. As for Claire, we learned that she came to the office shortly before her death when you and Georgia were there. I put two and two together and figured out that she was wearing the parrot scarf that you stole when you killed her. You must've worn it recently, and Georgia recognized it. Even though I'm sure you had an explanation for her, you couldn't trust her to keep it from the police. You had the scarf with you, probably in your purse, when you boarded Georgia's boat with Raff's gun wearing a red-headed wig. You made sure to get some blood on it, so you could use it as a false threat against you. I figured that out when I saw it on her neck in the photo you left for Tina. Am I right?"

Ginny squeezed the gun barrel harder against Nancy's head. "You're smart, Ms. Carter, but not smart enough."

Cathy said, "Do you really think once Eloise is behind bars, Raff will turn to you? He'll be with Tina."

Although Ginny shook her head, Cathy saw she'd planted a seed of doubt in her mind. "She's taking care of her sick mother. By the time she returns, I'll have him."

"Are you sure about that?" Cathy prodded. "You can't make someone love you. Besides, it's possible they won't arrest Eloise. They might think Raff used the gun. It'll confirm their suspicions about him."

"I told you. He's at an art show. He has an alibi. Eloise doesn't." Ginny was mad now. She cocked the gun trigger. "I'm sick of playing games. Say goodbye to your friend."

Before she could squeeze the trigger, Cathy leaped

forward, knocking Ginny to the ground. The gun flew out of her hand. Nancy grabbed it as it rolled toward her.

Cathy screamed back to Mildred, "What are you waiting for? Call the police."

CHAPTER THIRTY-SEVEN

Brian and Dooley arrived with several officers behind them along with Steve and Henry. Nancy was still training the gun on Ginny as Cathy held her back. The men rushed in.

"I'll take it from here," Dooley said, handcuffing Ginny while Brian relieved Nancy of the gun. "You okay, hon?" he asked.

"I'm alive," she replied, "thanks to Cathy and Mildred."

Ginny glared at them as Dooley read her rights. "You'll be sorry. Raff will get me out of this. He'll get me a lawyer. These women are framing me."

Cathy laughed. "You're lucky if Raff will even look at you after he learns you killed his previous girlfriend, threatened his current one, and planned to blame the murders on his sister."

Brian handed Dooley the gun as the police officer pushed Ginny forward. "No more talking out of you. Let's go."

"Will you need to speak with the ladies at the station?" Brian asked.

"Yes, but there's no rush. I'll be dealing with Ms. Hampton for quite some time."

When Dooley and Ginny were gone, Brian said, "I can't believe you took that risk. What were you all thinking?"

Nancy said, "In Cathy and Mildred's defense, I was the one who stupidly agreed to meet Ginny at this hour. Because we were hired by her and she received that threatening envelope, I doubted she was the killer."

"I was fooled, too," Cathy said, "until Maddie pointed out that the person we were trying to find wasn't necessarily a redhead and then I looked at the murder board Nancy made on the computer and saw the scarf Claire was wearing in the photo of her and Raff."

"There were other clues," Mildred said. "We just didn't put them all together in time to stop Nancy from meeting Ginny."

"There's one thing I still don't understand. Was Raff ever serious about Georgia? Was he seeing her?"

"No, Nance. I believe Ginny started rumors that Georgia was seeing him again so that it might get back to Tina. It was all part of her plan to take him away from those he loved including Eloise."

"Well, you prevented that. You and Mildred got here in time to save me." Nancy looked at Brian. "But there's going to be a problem."

"What's that, honey?"

"We no longer have a wedding planner."

"Maybe that's for the best," Mildred said. "We can all do our own thing. Henry and I can elope."

Cathy knew Nancy wanted the three of them to get married together. She took the manila envelope with their wedding application from Ginny's desk. "There's no reason to change our plans. We all agreed on everything in this packet. We can divvy up the work and arrange it ourselves."

"That should be cheaper," Brian, always looking for ways to save, said.

Henry put in his two cents. "Millie, I think sharing our special day with your friends is nicer than running away to elope."

"I agree," Steve said. "The six of us can create a memorable wedding."

"Before we do that, we need to let Maddie know what went on here tonight," Cathy pointed out, "and then we need to speak with Dooley."

"He said it can wait." Brian stood by the door. "Go back to your great-aunt's house, and we'll meet for breakfast tomorrow morning before you go to the station."

"What about Raff?" Cathy asked. "He should be informed."

"Ginny said he was at an art show. I think we can wait until tomorrow to contact him, too."

Cathy was relieved they only had to tell Maddie. She suddenly felt exhausted even though it was only 8 p.m. She knew it was from the adrenaline jolt that was now leaving her body. She was sure Mildred and Nancy were tired from their ordeal, as well.

The men followed them in Steve's car to Maddie's house before heading back to their hotel. Nancy drove her own car while Cathy and Mildred rode together again in Maddie's.

"You can all come in," Cathy told Steve speaking to him through his window after she'd parked and gotten out.

"Thanks, but you ladies are better prepared to tell your story. We only came in after it was all over."

"You're right. See you in the morning then."

Steve leaned over and kissed her. "I'm proud of you and glad you're okay."

Maddie was at the door waiting for them. "I see my car's in one piece and so are the three of you."

"We nearly weren't," Nancy said.

"Come in and tell me all about it."

They joined Maddie in the living room.

"You were right," Cathy began. "The killer wasn't a redhead."

"Oh?" Maddie raised an eyebrow. "I gather you caught him or her."

"We did," Nancy said. "Georgia's killer was her sister."

"My gosh! That's awful. She hired you and received a threat on her life."

"She hired us to confuse us, and the threat against her was false," Mildred said. "She also killed Claire Curran. It was all because of her long-standing infatuation with Raff and her envy of her sister."

"Incredible! I'd say neither sister was very nice."

"That's being modest," Cathy said. "Georgia stole boyfriends away from their fiancées and Ginny was a murderess."

"She's at the station now," Nancy added. "We have to go down there in the morning to be questioned, but Brian assured us it wouldn't be anything major."

Maddie sighed. "What about your wedding?"

"We're going to do it ourselves," Cathy told her.

"No, you're not." Maddie looked serious. "I'll help and so will Christine."

"Thank you," Nancy said. "That'll be a relief to the men. They prefer the brides do all the work."

Maddie laughed. "Typical guys." She turned to Cathy. "You owe Florence a call. She phoned earlier and misses you. She kept asking when you'd be home."

"I miss her, also, and my cats. I'll call her and let her know we should be able to leave here in a few days."

"What about the captain's wake?" Mildred asked.

Cathy had completely forgotten that it was being held the next day. "I don't think it matters anymore, but we can attend to pay our respects if you'd all like to do that."

"I think we should," Nancy said. "I also think we need to see Raff. He'll feel awful when he learns about Ginny."

"From what you've told me, I guess it won't hit him that hard," Maddie said. "He has Tina. Ginny was only a friend to him. It was her view of their relationship that was distorted."

"You're very wise," Cathy said.

"Just like my sister." Maddie winked.

CHAPTER THIRTY-EIGHT

Before going to bed, Cathy called her grandmother. She hoped it wasn't too late because Florence was an early riser, but she answered on the first ring as if she'd been waiting for the call.

"So happy to hear from you, Catherine."

"Sorry I haven't been in touch. It's been crazy here, Gran, but I have good news. We solved the case, and Ginny's been arrested for her sister's murder and also that of another woman's."

"Goodness! Wasn't she the one who hired you and Nancy?"

"Yes, but that was part of her strategy to confuse us."

"Well, I'm glad it all worked out. I was worried about you. You should be home soon, then, right?"

"I expect it'll take a few days. We have to go to the station tomorrow for routine questioning and the wake for Captain Sharp who had a heart attack. Georgia's murder may have precipitated it. We'll definitely be back by next week."

Florence was silent a moment, and Cathy wondered if she

was disappointed that they weren't returning sooner. But then she said, "What about your wedding plans?"

"We'll work on that ourselves. Maddie and Christine offered to help us."

"I'll help, too."

"Thanks. How are Harry and Hermione?"

"I'm spoiling them, but they miss you. They're still sleeping on your bed every night."

"Awww." Cathy thought of her two cats. "I miss them, too." Nancy was signaling to her from the next bed, so she ended the call. "Bye now, Gran. Love you. Be back soon."

Cathy put her phone on the charger and turned to Nancy. "What do you want, Nance? Was I keeping you up?"

"Of course not. I had a call from Raff. My phone's on silent, so you didn't hear it. I want to call him back. I'll put it on speaker."

"He must've heard about Ginny." Cathy walked over to Nancy and sat next to her while she redialed. Raff hadn't left a voicemail.

"Nancy," he answered after two rings. "I thought you'd gone to bed early."

"Me? Are you kidding?"

He let out a strained laugh. "No, but I heard what happened to you tonight." He sighed. "I can't believe it. I've known Ginny for two years. We were becoming closer friends. I never suspected…"

"She fooled all of us, Raff."

"Did she kill Claire Curran?"

"Yes. She admitted that. She was obsessed with you. Luckily, she only threatened Tina."

"Thank God. I've spoken to her. She's relieved. It's such a difficult time for her now with her mother so sick."

"I understand. I'm glad we were able to help."

"You and Cathy were great. Mildred, too. I'll see you at the station tomorrow. Dooley wants me there for questioning, as well. He said he needs more information about Claire Curran."

"I assume you're also going to the captain's wake?"

"Yes."

Then Nancy asked Raff a question that surprised Cathy, but knowing her friend, she should've expected it.

"I bet you were shocked and disappointed about Sharp's will."

There was a long pause before Raff replied. "Actually, I was neither. When Dan turned sixty last month, he told me he'd changed his will. He did it because Eloise said she didn't want the business. He considered leaving it to me, but he knew I couldn't devote much time to it because of my art. Tommy was the logical choice. He'd been Dan's second-hand for several years."

"Is that why you quit?"

Cathy didn't think Nancy would ask that and was surprised at Raff's reply. "It's true I wanted more time to devote to my painting, but to be honest, I don't get along with Tommy too well. He disliked the fact that Dan and I were related and once mentioned that there should've been a nepotism policy. He also may have known that I was being paid more than him, although it was on a per-job basis."

Nancy seemed to have run out of questions because she said, "Well, I guess we'll see you at the wake then tomorrow unless we run into you at the station."

"Either or both places. Goodnight, Nancy." He ended the call.

"He doesn't sound too upset about Ginny, but I didn't realize his feelings toward Tommy."

"Neither did I, Nancy, but I can understand them. As for his not caring that much about Ginny, I'm sure it's because he's relieved it's over, as are we. Maddie was right that he viewed his relationship with her differently than how she viewed her relationship with him."

The questioning at the station the following day was simple and quick, and they didn't run into Raff. Dooley informed them that Ginny was being held without bail on two murder charges. "Thank you for your assistance, ladies," he said.

"We were only doing our job," Nancy replied.

"About that, I think Ms. Hampton hired you to keep us out of the loop."

Cathy agreed with Dooley. She'd wondered why Ginny had been so against the police investigating her sister's murder.

As they left the station, Nancy said, "Luckily, I got a retainer from Ginny because there's no way we'll receive the balance of our fees from her now."

"It isn't always about the money, Nancy. We solved the case. Howard can add it to our tallies."

Nancy laughed. "Actually, you solved the case. I'm happy you did, or I would've been Ginny's next victim."

They walked together to Nancy's car. As she opened the door, she turned to Cathy. "Let's go meet the guys. They promised us breakfast, although we had a nibble with Maddie."

"Before we meet them, can we stop at the dock?" Cathy asked. "Tommy and Angel need to be told about Ginny's arrest."

"They may have been notified already, but it's on our way, so let's visit them just in case."

CHAPTER THIRTY-NINE

Cathy was surprised when they knocked on the office door and Tommy let them in. The place was different than it had been the day before. The desk no longer contained a disarrayed pile of papers and the previously dirty floor had been swept clean. She also noticed that Raff's sailboat painting of a rough sea that had hung over the captain's desk had been removed and replaced with a shelf displaying nautical books including Moby Dick.

"Wow!" Nancy said as they entered. "This looks great."

Tommy smiled. "Angel helped me straighten things out. She told me she'd gone to business school and is very adept with figures, so it cut back a lot of my paperwork. She also couldn't stand how messy the office was, so she cleaned it."

"Nice," Cathy said. "We come with good news. Well, it's not good for Ginny. She's been arrested for her sister's murder. You and Angel are in the clear."

"Ginny killed Georgia? Wow! That's a surprise, but I'm glad to hear Angel and I have been cleared. Oh, and here's Angel now with my coffee from the café."

Angel walked through the door holding a to-go cup. When she saw them, she smiled, but Cathy thought it was strained. "Hello," she said, handing the cup to Tommy.

"Hi, Angel. We're not here to question you further," Nancy explained. "In fact, we were just telling Tommy that Georgia's killer has been caught." Cathy expected the young woman to be relieved, but her expression didn't change. She didn't even ask who'd been arrested.

"You've done a nice job here," Cathy pointed out, to end the silence when Angel didn't respond to Nancy's comment.

"Thank you," she said, her eyes lowered. Cathy wondered why she was acting this way.

Tommy cleared his throat. "It's nice of you ladies to come by with such great news, but Angel and I need to prepare for the wake. We're both saying a few words about the captain during the service."

"We'll leave you then and see you there," Nancy said.

Outside, Cathy asked, "Did you find it odd how Angel was acting?"

"What do you mean?"

"She didn't even want to know who killed Georgia."

"I'm sure it's just a reaction to the stress she's been under, Cathy. After all, she was one of the red-headed suspects, even though we ruled her out pretty early."

"True. She'd also been accused of poisoning Sharp until they discovered his death was natural, and she may be mourning him. He was her boss."

They got into Nancy's car, and she started it. "Let's meet the guys before Brian complains we're late."

As they headed for the hotel where their fiancés were staying, Cathy couldn't help thinking about Angel's strange behavior. She felt that stress couldn't totally explain it.

. . .

The men were in the lobby waiting for them. Brian said, "I take it Don was easy on you with the questions."

Nancy smiled. "He said it was only routine. Ginny is locked up until her trial."

"Good. That means we can be on our way back to Buttercup Bend. Leroy will be pleased, and I'll still have a job."

"Leroy would never let you go," Steve said, "but my clients might drop me."

"I don't have to worry about rushing back to a boss or customers. That's a benefit of being retired," Henry pointed out.

"I'm not retired yet," Mildred reminded him, "but I'm using up my vacation leave."

Cathy said, "We all need to get back for some reason. My grandmother and cats miss me."

"There's no reason we can't leave after the captain's wake," Nancy told them.

When it was time to head to the funeral parlor, Nancy drove Cathy and Mildred in her car. Brian and Henry rode in Steve's car ahead of them. They arrived together and noted that the parking lot was already full.

Getting out of Nancy's car, Mildred said, "It looks like Captain Sharp was well-liked. There seems to be more people here than attended Georgia's memorial."

"That's interesting," Henry said, "but I notice there's no police presence."

"It's not necessary," Brian pointed out. "Unlike Ginny, Sharp died of natural causes."

As they walked into the familiar darkness of the building, the funeral parlor director pointed them toward the same room where Ginny's service had been held. It was packed indeed, mostly with people Cathy didn't recognize but who'd probably been on some of the captain's whale-watching tours. She also saw Eloise and Raff standing by the casket. Eloise, dressed in a black pant set was sniffing into a handkerchief, while Raff had his arm on her. A bunch of other people from Sharp's business and the dock, including Marci from the coffee shop, gathered around the room.

Nancy whispered to her, "Where's Tommy and Angel?"

"They should be here soon. They said they were saying some words about the captain."

"How come Raphael didn't paint a portrait of Daniel Sharp?" Mildred asked.

"He probably hasn't had time," Henry said, "and I guess it's no surprise Sharp's ex-wife, Yolanda, isn't present."

"Let's give Eloise our regards," Cathy said, walking toward the widow and her brother.

After each of them had spoken to Eloise and Raff, a man in a dark suit sporting a clerical collar stepped forward and cleared his throat.

"Can everyone please have a seat? I'm Pastor Gordon, and I'd like to begin the service for Daniel Sharp."

Cathy and her group took the row behind Eloise and Raff.

The pastor cleared his throat again and then said, "We're here today to honor the memory of a man who built up a business and was fair and loyal to his friends, family, customers, and employees."

He looked out over the gathering. "He wasn't a perfect man, none of us are. But in God's eyes, we are his children, and Daniel was his son."

The door that the funeral attendant had closed during the service creaked open as Tommy, followed by Angel, entered. They stood in the back of the room.

"I'll end my part of this service with a prayer and then open it to those who want to add their words about the captain."

After the Pastor's prayer, Raff was the first to speak. "I'm Raphael Wright. I was the brother-in-law of Dan Sharp. I also helped out on his boat tours. I was shocked and saddened by his death. He had a temper, but he learned how to control it after seeking help. That takes a lot of willpower. I was proud of him and respected him. I will miss him."

When Raff stepped down, Eloise, dabbing her eyes with her handkerchief, walked to the front of the room. Sniffing, she said, "I loved Danny. We were hoping to start a family." She choked on her words. "But all I have left now are my sweet memories of our short time together." Bowing her head, she walked back to her brother.

Tommy was next. Walking up from the back of the room, he faced everyone. "I'm Thomas Mueller, the new owner of Captain Sharp's Fleet and Whale-Watching Tour company. I'm honored that he left the business to me, and I don't have much to say about him except that I thought of him like a father rather than a boss and will miss him greatly." He looked toward Angel. "I believe Miss Price also has a few words to say about the captain."

Passing him on the way up, Cathy noticed that Angel didn't meet Tommy's eyes. "Something's wrong," she whispered to Nancy. "Angel isn't even looking at Tommy."

At the front of the room, Angel paused. It seemed like she was having trouble forming the words she wanted to say and wasn't glancing at the paper she held. The pastor placed a hand on her shoulder. "It's okay, Ms. Price. Take your time."

"I, uh," Angel looked down at the floor.

Cathy heard Tommy say, under his breath, "What's wrong with her? I told her what to say. All she has to do is read the sheet I gave her."

Suddenly, as if she heard him, Angel looked toward Tommy. With a swift motion, she tore up the paper in her hand and watched the pieces fall around her. The pastor gasped. She turned to him. "Tommy gave me that paper to read, but I have something different to say." Her voice was strong as if she'd held something back so long and was finally releasing it.

"Go ahead, please," the pastor urged.

"Captain Sharp didn't have a heart attack."

The room filled with murmurings, but she spoke above them. "He was murdered, and his killer is right there." She pointed a finger across the room at Tommy. He rushed up to her. "She doesn't know what she's saying. She's overcome with grief." He grabbed her arm as if to lead her away, but she broke his grip. "Take your hands off me. You thought I'd keep your secret because I loved you, but I can't be involved with a killer."

Brian, as if anticipating an altercation, stood up. The pastor moved closer to the arguing couple.

"She's crazy," Tommy said turning to face everyone. "Why would I hurt the captain?"

"For the business," Angel said. "When you put me in charge of the accounts, I saw how much money was there. You convinced him to put you in his will ahead of his sister and then you planned to kill him because you didn't want to wait for him to kick the bucket. They didn't find anything in the captain's coffee because it was in the food you gave him instead. You explained it all to me, how you ground up the peanuts he was allergic to and added them to his sandwich, and now you deny it. Your plan would've worked if you hadn't told me."

At Angel's words, Cathy had a flashback of the half-eaten sandwich that Sharp threw away the day they went to the dock for the whale-watching tour.

"Is this true?" Eloise asked. "Mr. Mueller, did you kill my husband?"

Raff, holding her back, looked over at Brian. "Someone should call the police."

Brian took out his cell. "Good idea. I'll get Officer Donnolly over here right now."

"You'll do no such thing," Tommy said, reaching under his jacket and removing a pistol. "Unlike Ginny, I have my own gun. I'm glad I thought of bringing it today."

As people scurried for the door, the pastor, visibly shaken, tried to control the situation. "Now, now. There's no need for violence. We can resolve this matter amicably."

Tommy laughed and waved the gun at him. "Oh, yeah. I'm not going to jail for this. My old man was in there for shooting my mama's boyfriend, and he told me how awful it is in there."

As Angel and the pastor inched backwards toward the captain's coffin, Cathy saw Brian inch forward. Nancy whispered to him, "No, Brian. Don't try it."

"I have to, Nance. I can't let him get away."

Tommy heard them and turned around. "Don't worry. I'm not going anywhere except to a better place." He raised his gun to his head and fired.

CHAPTER FORTY

When Cathy, Nancy, and Mildred were back at Maddie's house relaying what happened at the wake, Maddie said, "Oh, you poor girls. What a shock." They were sitting at her dining room table with teacups in front of them. Brian had accompanied Dooley to the station after he arrived in answer to his call. Even though Sharp's killer was dead, there was still paperwork to be filed. Steve and Henry had seen the women home but hadn't joined them. Steve said they were going back to the hotel to start packing. Now that it was all over, there was no reason to stay in Fogport.

Nancy said, "I wonder why Tommy told Angel. It caused his downfall."

"He was proud," Cathy said. "Not remorseful."

"Everything he mentioned about Sharp at the wake was a lie," Mildred added. "He didn't see him as a father. He was planning to kill him from the time he was hired and then Georgia's murder gave him a great cover."

"I'm not sure that's true." Cathy took a sip of her tea and then said, "He may have seen Sharp as a father, but his view of fathers was distorted. I don't think it was just for the money or the business. It was personal. In killing Sharp, he was killing the father who ruined his life."

"I agree," Maddie said. "And Millie had it right that there were two killers. She's a sharp lady. But now that you're leaving, I'm going to miss you all."

"We'll be back for the wedding," Nancy told her. "We'll have to get started planning that as soon as we're home."

"Oh!" Maddie suddenly got up. "I almost forgot. A man came here while you were gone. He was disappointed he missed you. He left an envelope. Let me get it."

When she returned with the envelope, Maddie handed it to Nancy. Cathy, next to her, saw it had her name on it. She watched as Nancy opened it and withdrew a piece of paper. The writing was small and dark. It wasn't easy to read, so she was glad Nancy read it aloud.

Dear Ms. Meyers,

I heard about Virginia's arrest, so I know that you and your friends no longer have a wedding planner. It just so happens that I've become engaged and am planning a September wedding aboard my yacht. It would be my pleasure to host you and your friends' nuptials. All you would need to supply are the guests and any extras you'd like. Please let me know before you head home.

Best Regards,
Dr. Shankar Shah

"My goodness!" Mildred exclaimed. "He's offering to pay for our reception!"

"Sounds like it. Brian will be happy." Nancy looked up

from Shankar's letter.

"That's quite generous," Cathy said. "And we suspected him of Georgia's murder at one point."

"I think it'll be wonderful," Maddie said.

When Cathy called her grandmother later that day to update her and let her know she would be home soon, Florence said, "A wedding aboard a yacht. How lovely. I don't know if you remember, but William used to love boating."

Cathy recalled how her grandfather used to take her and Doug fishing aboard his boat. It was one of the happiest times she'd had with him. "I remember, Gran. I wish he could attend."

"So do I, but I'm sure he'll be there in spirit. I can't wait for you to come home, and neither can Harry and Hermione." In the background, Cathy heard meowing. Did her cats realize she was on the phone, or did they just want her grandmother's attention?

Right after Cathy hung up with Florence, Nancy called Shankar and thanked him for his kind offer. "Before we leave, can we see the yacht?"

She nodded at his reply, so Cathy figured he'd agreed.

When she ended the call, Nancy said, "Shankar texted me directions to his yacht. He wants us to meet him there in an hour. I'm calling Brian and asking him to bring the guys with him to join us."

Brian was back from the police station and answered the first ring. Cathy heard Nancy ask him to have Steve drive him and Henry to meet them at Maddie's house in an hour.

"I thought the case was solved," Brian said through Nancy's

cell phone's speaker.

"It was, but Shankar dropped by while we were at the captain's wake and brought an invitation for us to have our wedding with him aboard his yacht. We're going to see it at four o'clock. And here's the best part," Nancy winked at Cathy, "he's picking up the whole tab."

The line was silent for a moment and then Brian said, "Gee, that's kind of him. I'll round up the guys and meet you at Maddie's at 4 p.m. sharp."

When they arrived at the marina where Shankar's yacht was docked, Brian let out a low whistle. "That's some boat," he said.

Cathy was also impressed. With three levels and spanning a huge area, Shankar's yacht was double the size of all the boats in Captain Sharp's fleet.

"That's no boat," Steve said. "It's a yacht."

Nancy smiled. "I can't wait to look around inside. C'mon. I see Shankar waiting for us."

Cathy glanced over to where Nancy was pointing. Shankar was there waving to them. A woman stood next to him. From a distance, Cathy couldn't make her out well, but she reminded her of someone. As they grew closer, she realized who it was. The woman hugging Shankar was none other than Yolanda Gerard, the captain's ex-wife.

"That's the nurse we spoke to at the hospital," Mildred said. "She was married to Captain Sharp."

"It's a small world," Cathy said.

They joined Shankar and Yolanda aboard the boat. The men shook hands with him. He gave each of the ladies a hug.

"Thank you so much for your kind invitation," Nancy told him. "And congratulations on your engagement. We met your fiancée previously."

THE CASE OF THE WHALE WATCHING WEDDING PLANNER

Yolanda said, "That wasn't under the best circumstances, but I hope we can all be friends now."

"That would be wonderful," Cathy said.

Yolanda added, "You might be wondering why I denied knowing Shankar well when we first met. I didn't want gossip spread around the hospital about our relationship, and I didn't feel it was appropriate to mention it to detectives."

"No worries," Nancy said. "We can certainly understand that."

"Let us show you around," Shankar offered. He led them through all the levels of the boat, pointing out where the food would be served, the band would play, and the guests would dance.

"This is amazing," Steve said. "Cathy, do you see those hanging bulbs? I bet this place will be even more incredible at night."

"I'm sure it will be. We're very thankful, Shankar."

Nancy, taking everything in as she leaned against a rail, said, "May I ask why you're doing this for us? It's so generous of you, but you hardly know us."

Shankar smiled. "I know you lost your wedding planner and solved a murder. That's enough for me. While Raphael isn't my favorite person, I'm glad to know that you absolved him by catching Georgia's killer."

Cathy, remembering what Conor had told her about Shankar visiting the dock when Claire came to see Raff, said, "There's one thing that you might be able to clear up for us."

"What's that?" Shankar turned to her.

"We learned that you were involved with Claire Curran, Raff's old girlfriend who Ginny also killed. Is that true?"

Shankar glanced out toward the sea. "It was a brief affair. You also heard that Ms. Curran was obsessive about the men she dated. That's why I'm sorry I pursued Georgia and Tina after they broke it off with me. I should've known how uncomfortable it made them."

"We also discovered that Captain Sharp was murdered," Nancy pointed out. "You'll read about it in the paper soon."

"That's interesting," Yolanda said. "During our marriage, he gave me plenty of motive to kill him, but I never had the nerve."

"He sought help to control his anger," Cathy said. "He left money to an organization that he joined, so he could change."

"A leopard doesn't change its spots." Yolanda hadn't forgiven Sharp. Cathy couldn't blame her.

"According to Eloise, he became gentle and a good husband," Nancy said.

"I'm glad. I wouldn't have wanted anyone else to go through what I did." Yolanda looked out toward the sea. "So, who killed him?"

"Thomas Mueller," Brian told her. "The man he'd left his business to in his will. It'll go to his wife now, the person who should've gotten it to begin with. Her brother will help her run it, I'm sure."

"A happy ending," Shankar said. "Yolanda, please bring out the champagne. We need to toast."

Shankar's fiancée went to the cooler next to Cathy and withdrew two bottles and glasses she set on a tray. Shankar pushed a button in the wall, and a table lowered. The couple set everything up, and Shankar poured champagne for all of them. When he was done, he raised his glass. "To solving murders, upcoming weddings, and friendship."

They took their glasses and clinked them around. Cathy felt a bubbling rise in her as bubbly as the champagne. It was indeed a happy ending for all of them except Tommy and Ginny.

EPILOGUE

THREE MONTHS LATER

Cathy, Mildred, and Nancy sat together in their wedding gowns upstairs in the room Maddie provided for them to prepare for the ceremony aboard Shankar's yacht. Florence and her sister were downstairs.

"I can't believe this is happening," Nancy said. "I've waited all my life for this, but it feels like a dream."

"I know what you mean," Cathy said, checking herself in the full-length mirror. Her hair had been styled by Christine who used to work at a salon. She'd created ringlets that framed Cathy's face. She'd also styled Nancy and Mildred's hair. She piled Nancy's red locks atop her head with a pearl clip. It made Nancy look older and very distinguished. Mildred hadn't wanted Christine to dye her hair, but she'd convinced her to add touches of silver amid the gray and curl her short hair in loose waves. The result was natural and appealing.

Mildred, in a simple ivory skirt set that just topped her knees, said, "You both look lovely. I'm glad you and Henry talked me into this. I feel like a girl again. While my first wedding was a big affair, the marriage didn't turn out to be a happy one. I don't talk much about it, but Henry is much different than my first husband. I'm glad I can share this event with him."

"You're beautiful, too," Nancy said, glancing at the blue and white cameo broach pinned to Mildred's skirt top. Maddie had given it to her. She'd let each of them borrow a piece of blue jewelry to help complete their outfits and comply with the "something old, something new, something borrowed, something blue" saying. Nancy received a blue pearl bracelet. Cathy got a necklace with a sapphire stone that she suspected was genuine. It went well with her low, lace neckline. Christine gave them each bridal garters. Florence gifted them handkerchiefs she'd embroidered with flowers when she was a young girl. She'd added their initials to them. "Consider these something old but also new," she'd said with a wink when she handed them out.

Nancy said, "While this promises to be a wonderful day, I thought you all should know that Brian informed me that Ginny was sentenced yesterday to life in prison. I can't say I'm sorry about that. I don't know how she could've taken her own sister's life."

"I don't have a sister," Cathy said, "but I agree that it was awful."

"Talking about sisters," Mildred added, "It was nice meeting yours at the rehearsal dinner, Nancy."

Nancy smiled. "Thank you. I also enjoyed meeting Henry's sister and her husband."

Cathy knew that Mildred had been the youngest child in her family, and her siblings were all gone. The only remaining ones were on her husband's side, and she didn't keep in touch with them. However, she was happy that her daughter and son-in-law were able to attend the wedding.

"About Tommy," Nancy continued, "he had a will where he left everything to Angel and requested that his ashes be scattered at sea. Brian said there was a brief, private ceremony. The only people attending were the pastor, Angel, and Marci from the coffee shop. It was done off Tommy's boat."

"What a shame," Cathy said. "He was so young."

"How is Raff doing, and Eloise?" Mildred asked.

Cathy knew the answer to that because Raff, although he wasn't attending the wedding, had sent flowers to her with a note. "Eloise got the captain's business. She'll have help from her brother who has also gone back to work there and the employees who are still on staff. Tina's mother sadly passed away last month. Raff proposed to her and is planning a wedding and honeymoon in Paris."

"How romantic!" Nancy said. "You definitely were right, Cathy, that this turned out well for everyone except Ginny and Tommy."

The women were interrupted by a tapping at their door. Cathy answered it to find Florence and Maddie standing outside. "Are you beautiful girls ready?" Florence asked. "Your handsome husbands-to-be are on the boat, and the limo is waiting outside."

Cathy felt a flutter in her stomach. This was really happening. She took a deep breath and followed her grandmother and great-aunt downstairs, Nancy and Mildred at her heels.

"Be careful with your gowns," Maddie told them as they descended. She'd shown them how to lift the hems. Only Mildred, in her shorter dress, was able to keep both hands free to hold on to the bannister.

Christine and her husband were sitting in the car. Christine's slightly rounded stomach showed under her peach gown. Cathy, Nancy, and Mildred had unanimously chosen her to be their maid-of-honor. A babysitter was watching her children while she and her husband were at the wedding. Because of the number of brides, they hadn't selected bridesmaids. Cathy had worried that her sister-in-law, Becky, would feel excluded, but she'd told her she preferred to be a guest and was happy that Doug would be walking Cathy down the aisle which was a red carpet on the yacht. Nancy's parents had flown in for the wedding with her sister, so her father would be giving her away. Mildred would be on her son-in-law Mark's arm as the three made their way toward Pastor Green, who'd arrived that morning from Buttercup Bend.

As the limo pulled up to the dock, Cathy was amazed at the number of people standing there awaiting their arrival. Not only did Shankar's guests include those from India, but also many of his and Yolanda's co-workers from the hospital. And while the brides had invited many of the same people from Buttercup Bend, relatives and friends from other areas were also there. The only ones missing were the grooms who were on board the yacht. Cathy figured that was because they weren't supposed to see their brides before the wedding.

The first people to greet them as they stepped out of the car were Danielle, Dylan, and their daughter, Sherri from Oaks Landing Farm. Sherri looked adorable in her peach dress carrying a basket of fall-colored flower petals as she ran up to Cathy and hugged her. "Cathy, Mama and Lulu had baby girls. I have a sister named Doris. We call her Dori. She's at home with Aunt Mavis. She's sorry she couldn't come, but she's sending you a gift."

Cathy smiled. She was happy they'd all agreed to have Sheri as their flower girl. She already knew about her new baby sister from her phone calls with Danielle but hadn't heard about Lulu.

"Congratulations!" she said. "What did you call Lulu's

baby?" She was curious as to what they'd named the llama's offspring.

"I named her Luna. That means moon. She was born at night, and there was a full moon."

"I like that," Cathy said. "It also goes well with her mother's name." She turned to Danielle. "Speaking of mothers, I'm so glad you were able to come, and congratulations again on the birth of your daughter."

"Thank you. I wouldn't miss this for the world. I was hoping you'd visit the farm first, but I've never attended a wedding on a yacht, no less three weddings."

"Four," Nancy said walking over to them. "Our host, Dr. Shankar Shah, was kind enough to invite all of us to join him on his yacht for his wedding and ours."

Dylan, next to his wife, said, "That's incredible. This promises to be quite an event."

Before they boarded the ship, Yolanda, in a knee-length ivory dress because, like Mildred, this was her second wedding, greeted them. She held three bouquets and handed each one to Cathy, Nancy, and Mildred. They contained late-blooming roses, mums, and other autumn flowers that matched the petals in Sheri's basket.

"These are beautiful," Cathy said, "but where is your bouquet?"

"I left it inside. It's the same as yours. My mother chose the flowers." She glanced toward a woman in a cranberry suit who was standing in Shankar's guest group speaking with a blonde woman who looked to be about her age.

"She did a great job," Nancy said.

Yolanda smiled. "I agree. Shankar's mother, the lady next to her, decorated the boat. She also did a terrific job. You'll see when you come aboard but wait until the guests board first.

The grooms will be waiting for us by the red carpet. You'll hear the music start to play."

Cathy began to feel jitters in her stomach again. She was glad the boat wouldn't be moving during the ceremony. She imagined Steve was relieved, too.

Pastor Green and another man with a long beard moved to the front of the queue where they faced the people on the dock. Pastor Green cleared his throat and said, above the chattering of the crowd, "Can everyone be quiet a moment, please. The ceremony will begin shortly. I need everyone except the brides to board the boat. The ushers will guide you to your seats." He nodded his head toward two men, Brody and Michael from Buttercup Bend. Cathy was touched that her ex-boyfriend but still friend, Michael, had agreed to be an usher at her wedding. She was happy to see his new girlfriend Stacy behind him smiling in a beautiful burnt orange gown, her long blonde hair swept back.

After everyone had boarded the boat except the brides and the men giving them away, the opening bars of "Here Comes the Bride" began to play. Yolanda said, "That's our cue. C'mon, ladies. It's time to get hitched."

Cathy swallowed a lump in her throat. "We're all doing it at the same time?"

"No, silly," Yolanda laughed. "I'm first since Pastor Charles is marrying me and Shankar. Then it's Nancy and Brian followed by you and Steve. Mildred and Henry will be wed last."

"Who decided that order?" Cathy was glad she wasn't going first, although she did want to get it over with as quickly as possible before she fainted.

"We couldn't toss a coin between the three of you, so

Shankar just randomly made the decision. Do you have your vows handy?"

"I've memorized mine," Nancy told Yolanda.

Cathy was surprised that Nancy seemed composed. She had her vows tucked into the top of her gown. There was no way, being so nervous, she'd be able to remember them if they weren't written down.

Mildred, like Nancy, said she knew hers. "The vows I'm saying to Henry are short and sweet," she announced.

Yolanda nodded. "Very well. Let's get in line and join our grooms." Her father came up by her side and took her hand. Nancy's father took hers. When Doug reached for Cathy's hand, she was so afraid it was sweating that she whispered to him to take her by the arm instead. "Nervous, Cat?" he grinned.

"A little bit."

Mildred, behind her holding her son-in-law's hand, said, "Don't worry, Cathy. It'll be over before you know it. Trust me."

Even though she was shaking, Cathy realized that she didn't want it to be over quickly. She wanted to savor her wedding day and remember all the precious moments to share with her and Steve's future children.

Despite Cathy's intention of paying attention to the ceremony, she found it difficult to concentrate. She was vaguely aware of the multi-colored hearts that were strung around the rails of the ship, the banners with the couples' names that hung above the red silk carpet stretching across the yacht's top floor, the notes of the wedding march, and the guests gathered in chairs, eyes on the six of them as each bride entered. She hardly registered the grooms standing beyond the carpet, all except Steve smiling at her.

As Yolanda and Shankar and then Nancy and Brian were wed, Cathy could focus on nothing but Steve's face and her thundering heart. When it was time for her to walk down the aisle, Doug had to whisper to her. "Now, Cathy. It's your turn."

On shaky legs, Cathy walked down the red carpet toward Steve. Pastor Green smiled at them. "I've known Steve since he was a baby and Cathy since she visited her grandmother as a young girl. I'm honored to wed them today." He turned to Steve. "Do you have any words for your bride?"

Steve took a piece of paper from inside his tuxedo. "I do." He grinned. "Sorry, that's too early." He cleared his throat and looked at Cathy. Her heart hammered as he read them. "My beloved Cathy. I was so happy when you moved to Buttercup Bend and Florence chose me as the gardener for your home and pet cemetery. It was hard for me to approach you and ask for a date at first. I'm shy with women, so it wasn't easy. I'm glad I took the plunge and that you accepted my marriage proposal. I promise I'll make you a good husband and father to your children. I love you very much."

Tears sprang to Cathy's eyes. She let them roll down her face. The photographer and videographer Shankar had hired for the event stood by and captured the moment.

The pastor turned to Cathy. "And you, Cathy?"

Cathy took out her paper, but her eyes were so blurred from her tears that she could hardly see it. She inhaled a breath and then improvised by saying what was in her heart. "Oh, Steve. You make me so happy. I love your gentle nature, your way with animals, how you make me laugh." She paused as her voice choked. "I want to spend my life with you and our children. I love you."

Pastor Green's smile widened. He looked toward the

assembled guests. Although Cathy still couldn't concentrate on anyone but Steve and her thumping heart, she knew her grandmother and Maddie were crying in their seats.

"Those vows were beautiful. Now it's time for you two to tie the knot." The Pastor turned to Steve. "Stephen Joseph Jefferson, do you take this woman to be your bride, to love and to cherish, in sickness and in health, until death do you part?"

Steve took Cathy's hand and looked into her eyes. "I do forever."

Pastor Green repeated his question to Cathy, "Catherine Lynn Carter. Do you take this man to be your husband, to love and to cherish, in sickness and in health, until death do you part?"

Choking back her tears, she replied, "I do... forever."

The crowd cheered, and Cathy could finally breathe.

"I now pronounce you man and wife." The pastor turned to Steve again to let him know he could kiss the bride, but he was already doing that.

Sheri ran up and scattered the autumn flowers in their path as they proceeded down the aisle where Mildred and Henry were waiting their turn. Cathy smiled at them. Her heart was exploding with happiness.

After Mildred and Henry were wed, everyone gathered to congratulate the couples. There were hugs, kisses, and tears. Florence and Maddie dabbed at their eyes with handkerchiefs. They gave Steve and Cathy big hugs and then Christine, her husband, Howard, and Doug stepped in and did the same. "I'm so happy, Gran," Cathy said, "and I want to thank you, Maddie, for all you did to make this possible."

Maddie smiled. "It's Shankar you need to thank. I was just thrilled to get to know you and your friends better."

. . .

The celebration moved to the upper deck that had also been decorated and where the buffet tables and musicians were set up for the cocktail hour and reception. The party lasted into the night as the lights strung across the ship came on and the candles on the tables were lit. Cathy enjoyed dancing with her brother and then her first dance with Steve as his wife. The cake cutting was fun, and Cathy admired again the custom toppings Nancy had ordered. Shankar had provided his and Yolanda's own cake, while Maddie and Christine had insisted on supplying the cake for the three brides. It was an appropriate three-tiered sheet cake with white, fluffy whipped cream frosting. The first layer, Nancy and Brian's layer, was filled with chocolate. The second layer, Cathy and Steve's, was filled with custard. The bottom layer, Mildred and Henry's, had strawberries inside. Cathy wanted to taste a slice from each, but she was too nervous to eat more than half of hers.

The finale of the evening was the tossing of the bouquets. Yolanda's friend who also worked at the hospital caught her bouquet. A fellow doctor that Shankar had introduced her to seemed happy about that. Sandra caught Nancy's bouquet and made eyes at Brody who turned beet red at the sight of the innkeeper's catch. Cathy secretly hoped they would get married. Sandra's ex had been an abusive man, and Cathy couldn't imagine her finding a gentler husband in Brody.

When Nancy's bouquet landed in Florence's arms, Howard smiled. Cathy hoped he would propose to her grandmother soon.

Pauline caught Mildred's flowers. When she did, Brian patted the sheriff on the back. "Hey, Leroy," he said, "looks like you have marriage in the future." Leroy's cheeks suddenly turned as red as his curly hair.

Next, came the tossing of the garters. Each of the men connected with the women who'd caught the bouquets caught a garter. Cathy hadn't aimed for Brody, but she thought the other women had directed their throws at certain targets.

As they all said goodnight, Cathy felt exhausted. She couldn't wait to take the Just Married limo back to the hotel that had been booked for them. Each couple would have their own honeymoon suite until they departed on their honeymoons. Yolanda and Shankar would be heading to India, the first time Shankar had been back there in many years and the first visit for Yolanda. Although Brian had made a fuss when Nancy suggested a honeymoon in Paris where Raff and Tina would be spending theirs, he agreed to a long weekend in the City of Light. Leroy had presented him with a wedding check that made his eyes bulge, so Cathy was sure it would help with the expense. Mildred and Henry weren't going anywhere special, but they'd spend their first week as husband and wife in Oaks Landing. Cathy was jealous that they'd be seeing Danielle and Dylan's baby daughter and Luna, the baby llama, but she knew she could visit them another time. As for her and Steve, she still didn't know where they were going. Steve had taken it upon himself to plan the perfect place for their honeymoon. She knew it would have a garden nearby. Otherwise, she had no idea but knew it promised to be another adventure.

ACKNOWLEDGMENTS

I'd like to thank the staff at Next Chapter Publishing, especially Miika Hannila, whose vision for marketing, distributing, and promoting books worldwide in various formats has allowed several of my other titles to find their places on both virtual and real bookshelves. I also want to acknowledge my fellow Next Chapter authors. I'm honored to be a part of this talented team of writers. Thanks also to my author friends, my husband, daughter, and all those who have encouraged my writing, especially my readers who make the hard work worthwhile.

While the Long Island towns in this book were fictional, Fogport is based on Freeport; Minnick on Merrick. Captain Sharp's Fleet and Whale-Watching Tours is based on Captain Lou's Fleet and the Long Island Seal and Whale-Watching Tours in Freeport where I participated on a whale-watching cruise for research. I also gathered information about whales from the Whaling Museum at Cold Spring Harbor and online resources.

If you enjoy this book and any of my others, I'd be grateful for a brief review on any book sites you prefer and/or your blog.

ABOUT THE AUTHOR

Debbie De Louise is an award-winning author and a reference librarian. She is a member of Sisters-in-Crime, International Thriller Writers, and the Cat Writers' Association. She writes two cozy mystery series, the Cobble Cove Mysteries and Buttercup Bend Mysteries. She's also written a paranormal romance, three standalone mysteries, a time-travel novel, and a collection of cat poems. Her stories and poetry appear in over a dozen anthologies. Debbie also writes articles for cat magazines. She lives in South Carolina with her husband, daughter, and two cats. Learn more about Debbie and her books by visiting her website at https://debbiedelouise.com.

~

To learn more about Debbie De Louise and discover more Next Chapter authors, visit our website at www.nextchapter.pub.

Printed in Great Britain
by Amazon

43095082R00152